Love
Me
Blind

By

Nandra Hoffman

Nandra Publishing, LLC
Catering to all your publishing needs

E-book
ISBN-13: 978-1950697-04-5
ISBN-10: 1-950697-04-5

Paperback
ISBN-13: 978-1-950697-03-8
ISBN-10: 1-950697-03-7

Nandra Publishing, LLC
Orlando, FL
www.nandrapublishing.com

Front and cover design by Nandra Publishing, LLC.
Photo credit: Michael Cresset obtained from nicepik.com (royalty free)

CONTENTS

DEDICATION

"Dedicated to the former me, the new me, and the me who wouldn't quit."

Thank you to all who saw the potential in my writing and gave me a chance. I started something years ago and vowed to finish it through trials and tribulations. You saw a talented person when I could only see lost potential. I was a kid with big dreams. I am now an adult who intends to act on them.

PROLOGUE

Mona

TWO MONTHS.

That's how long she questioned how everything fell apart.

Three days.

That's how long she continued picking up the phone to call him before chickening out at the last minute.

Seven hours.

That's how long ago she got the tip that he was leaving town for good.

Ten minutes.

That's how long it's been since she was left on read.

MONA: *Were you going to leave without saying bye?*

Read at 2:35 pm.

They hadn't spoken since their fight. Since he'd left her alone with Calvin Elkins. Since she was almost killed at the palm of Calvin's hands to which she wasn't even sure Andrew knew. Her scars were still fresh on her body. As much as she wanted to blame him, though, in her heart, she knew she couldn't. She was the one who pushed him away. She was the one who told him she didn't need him. She was the one who tore his heart open.

Blinded by Calvin's sweet talk.

Blinded by his seemly caring nature.

Blinded by the monster that lay within.

Blinded by love.

The same love he used to beat her whenever she looked another way. The same passion he used to manipulate and tear her away from her family and friends. The same love he was very much capable of killing her with.

And now she was a mess.

The underlying anger continued to linger, however. If he wanted to leave, it was fine by her. Maybe she didn't need him after all. Perhaps she was better off without him.

So, why did it feel like there was hole in her heart?

Maybe because Andrew saw it from day one. He had warned her, and all she could think to do was take Calvin's side.

Looking around the bustling café shop, memories flooded her brain. No matter where she went, he was there. Now, they were like strangers.

Close and yet, so far away.

What would happen to their friendship? Could she even classify it that way anymore?

Her eyes welled, but she quickly blinked them away. She couldn't continue to like this. And yet, the lump in her throat became harder and harder to swallow.

"Don't call me when he finally succeeds. I won't be

around."

Those words stung now as they did two months prior, but worse considering he really meant it.

Staring at the message again, she had a sudden motivation to type.

MONA: *I'm sorry. About everything. Please don't go...*

Her fingers hovered over the send button briefly before erasing the entire thing. She couldn't do it. What did it matter now? Things had changed.

Putting down the phone, she decided to watch him instead.

For the last half-hour, he and Adam were catching up inside the café in which she sat. She happened upon them by accident as she was heading there to pick up an iced coffee for her father, who worked across the street.

He hadn't looked up when she entered, nor when she chose a booth near their table out of sight.

His smile was bright like he hadn't a care in the world. It only made her feel worse. Though, nothing hurt like watching him unlock his phone and read her message only to frown before putting it back in his pocket.

Finally, he and Adam stood to leave. Adam walked ahead of him outside while Andrew flagged a waiter over. Mona did her best to obstruct her face with a menu from her table, making her unable to see their exchange.

Peeking over the top, she saw Andrew get up to leave and follow Adam to his car before taking off down the street. Blowing out a breath she wasn't aware she was holding, she put down the menu and leaned against her chair.

She picked up her dad's order and prepared to leave but was stopped by the same waiter that was at Andrew's table.

"Ma'am?" the lanky waiter addressed her. He couldn't have been any older than seventeen.

Eyeing him curiously, she answered, "Yes?"

He took a folded napkin from his apron and handed it to her. "I believe the gentleman at table two wanted me to hand this to you." He swiftly left before she could ask any questions.

Opening the napkin, she recognized the handwriting. It was from Andrew. He had seen her after all.

It was never forever.

She read it over-and-over again, trying to figure out what he meant. Was he not planning to stay away forever, or was he suggesting that their friendship was not meant to last forever?

Either way, she couldn't stop the tears from falling from her eyes, blurring the words on the napkin.

Maybe it was time to let go, after all.

Chapter One

Mona

"WE SHALL CONTINUE to keep him in our prayers. Amen."

A collective "Amen" resonated throughout the packed church. Movement stirred, and the people began to leave, the funeral service now ended. Mona Louise couldn't bring herself to move, though. Her eyes fixated on the mahogany coffin that held the man she once considered her world—still did. For a man with such legal power in the state, he was untouchable—at least, that's what he'd always joked about to Mona after winning a long case.

She thought about his laughter, the times they shared around the table as she helped him with paperwork, the goodnight kiss to the forehead, and the ice cream he'd bought her after a few too many breakups. Her father was her best friend. And now he was gone.

Too soon.

Too fast.

Too unexpected.

He always told her to expect the unexpected. She should've

listened.

Sympathetic hands from the attendees collectively rested on her shoulders as they walked by. She felt nothing but the beat of her heart catching in her throat. Condolences repeated until it became a deaf motto on replay. Not a tear had fallen. The shock was still clearly elevated.

Too zoned out, she didn't notice Adam Breaill, her good friend from high school, sit beside her on the now-empty bench. He didn't say anything for a moment, just followed her gaze to the coffin and reveled in the fond memories of her father, whom he once shared a loving relationship with. Her father had had a profound impact on Adam's life.

Hey," he spoke softly.

Mona turned to him but said nothing. Her eyes averted back to her father's coffin. What was she expecting? For her father to rise and say, "Gotcha, honey!"—maybe. Or was it the reality of the situation? When would the out of body experience end? It was a silly thought, but her pain was something she wasn't sure she could ever be rid of.

"I remember back in high school when we decided to do that senior prank," Adam laughed slightly to himself. "Putting frogs in the principal's office—what were we thinking? And then, we ended up getting caught sneaking out of the school. My first and last time being arrested."

Adam shook his head with a smile. Fiddling with the ring on his pinky, he continued, "Boy, was I happy to see your father that night. I expected the worst. Obviously, he knew you had been with us. He never even said anything. He wasn't even angry, I remember. He just smiled and asked what the prank was and took Andrew and I home after a good laugh."

Mona shifted uncomfortably at the mention of Andrew Sumpter. Adam took notice but said nothing about it. "Your dad was cool. Not just because he got the charges dropped, of course."

Mona smiled meekly at the memory. She had indeed been with them when they broke into the school that night. Dressed entirely in black on the night before their last day of high school, they had successfully planted the frogs inside the principal's office. It ultimately set off a silent alarm in the school. The cops had arrived shortly after, but Andrew and Adam had forced her to run. Instead, they took sole responsibility for the incident, evidently getting legal help from her father. Their record was still clean to this day.

"Yeah, he was, wasn't he?" It was the first time she had spoken all day. Her voice, scratchy yet somehow still steady and strong, was a blessing to hear.

Chancing a glance around the church, she realized that everyone had gone, apart from Nina Watson, who was watching them from afar with sad eyes. Her best friend smiled weakly at her when their eyes locked. Unconsciously, she scoured the church for a pair of familiar green eyes that she had managed to avoid the entire service. She sighed, whether out of relief or sadness, she wasn't sure.

"We should probably go. I don't think sitting here all day is going to bring him back. No matter how much we want him to." Brutal but honest. As straightforward as it was, Mona needed to hear that. With one last look at the coffin, she got up. Her gaze, however, stood frozen on her father's face.

Adam turned to her with confliction. Very softly, he called her name. She ignored him and tenderly headed toward the coffin. Her father had such a peaceful look on his face. It looked as if he was having a pleasant dream, not an eternal sleep. Before she could stop it, a flood of tears broke the shield she fought so hard to uphold the entire service. Her fingers ran through his peppered hair sliding down to his cheeks. They were so cold and stiff.

This was real, she thought. Reality had hit her like a ton of bricks, and finally, since hearing the news of her father's passing, Mona grieved.

The tears could never bring back her father.

The tears could never make life the same.

The tears couldn't fill the gaping hole that now and forever would reside in her.

But she cried as her heart bled for the only man in her life she had left to hold on to. She kissed him gently on his cold cheek. She wanted that moment. Needed it.

So caught up in the moment, she barely even registered the arms that embraced her until she had settled into the comfort of them. The familiar scent of cologne filled her nose, and she bore her face into it. Despite the drift, she could not have been more comfortable right then in his arms. Those green eyes she could not mistake. Those green eyes she longed to gaze upon for so long. Eyes that made her feel safe and secure. *Those* green orbs now boring into her grief-ridden face.

"It's going to be okay. I'm here."

For how long? She wanted to ask, but her quiet sobs wouldn't allow her to say her piece. The distance that had grown between them in the past two years was still deeply embedded in the back of her mind. Forget that they hadn't spoken since their demise. Forget that they hadn't seen each other since.

Right there in his arms, she was safe. Wanted. Protected. He gave her the one thing that she had secretly longed for in the days that followed the falling out and the days since her father's passing.

A friend.

A shoulder to lean on.

She could always count on the people she was surrounded by every day, but they would never be him. His place in her heart was strictly reserved, no matter how much she tried renting it out.

Time flew by once the funeral was cleared. He had let her be after her quiet sobs ultimately died. A part of her wanted to thank him. A part of her wanted to tell him she was sorry. But looking around the empty parking lot she realized she may never get her chance.

He was gone.

Or maybe, it was simply not meant to be.

Chapter Two

Andrew

WHEN HE GOT that phone call that night from Adam, he wasn't sure how to take it. The news about Mona's father passing had nearly knocked him off course. Mr. Louise was a prolific figure and even greater father figure to not just him, but to anyone he knew. Whenever he was in a bind, calling Mr. Louise for help was never out of the question.

Mr. Louise would truly be missed.

But he couldn't help but wonder how Mona was doing. Obviously, she wouldn't have been doing fine or even remotely close to it. With her mother's well-known distant nature, he could only imagine the pain and stress Mona was going through in isolation. She would surely feel alone having lost the closest family she had. He felt for her. He wanted to be there for her, but he was miles away. His help could only extend to phone calls until the funeral.

Before getting off the phone with Adam, he had asked to send his regards to his former friend. Despite their sour history, he couldn't find himself wishing anything bad for her. He couldn't. He wouldn't. Their lives had intertwined so much in the past, he too was hurt as Mr. Louise had been like a second father for most of his life.

There was nothing more he wanted than to hold her close. To tell her everything would be okay. To reassure her that he was there to ease her pain, though he knew that fantasy was a fluke. He had moved away just for that reason. He needed that space because he couldn't think clearly when she was around.

Never could.

Instead, he lay in his bed, staring at the ceiling, imagining the what-ifs. What if he called her? What if he threw caution to the wind and drove the long distance to her place unannounced?

He didn't have to think too long about it because within the week, he had gotten an invitation to the funeral. He stared at the invite with Mr. Louise's smiling photo staring back at him. It seemed to have been a recent photo because his hair seemed more peppered, and his smile was littered with a few more wrinkles. It was a photo taken in the back of his house, probably from one of his many cookouts as Andrew remembered he enjoyed. He was always ready to jump in front of a grill, something Andrew credited for his interest in being a chef.

Andrew smiled fondly at the photo. No matter the case, no matter the stress, Andrew always remembered Mr. Louise to be a vibrant and happy man. Even in death, he was sure of it. Mr. Louise was quite a leader in the city and was well-known and loved by most.

Although he desperately wanted to, a small part of Andrew wasn't sure if he should attend. Despite the invitation from Mona, they still held their differences, and it had been a solid two years since he had last seen or spoken to her. He wanted to support, but would he honestly be welcomed? For all he knew, she got help with the invitations. Was she even aware he got one?

He threw the invitation down on his dining table and sighed. Even with their animosity, he wanted to go. Not only for himself but for Mr. Louise and deep down, for the woman he once considered a best friend. If he was honest with himself, he still did.

The funeral was scheduled for that Sunday. He took two days off to pack and get his truck ready for the long drive. Leaving everything behind, he drove out of the apartment complex he called home for two years by sheer will.

Andrew laid in his hotel room, contemplating what he would say or how he'd react to both seeing Mr. Louise's casket and seeing Mona again. Albeit, it wouldn't be the time to talk about anything, but he wasn't sure how to approach the situation. A simple greeting wouldn't suffice.

It turns out he wouldn't know what to say on the day of the funeral, either. He watched her throughout the service. Her eyes seldom left the casket. Seeing her in a state of hollowness almost broke his heart. Many times, he had to refrain from moving closer to her to comfort her.

She didn't bother to do a eulogy; instead, she let Father Paul read her notes. She wasn't strong enough to handle that, though it was understandable. Many of Mr. Louise's past colleagues took the podium as well. Some offered laughs, some were a tear-jerker. Nonetheless, all positive words.

When the church finally cleared, he waited out of sight while she sat staring at the coffin. He watched as Adam approached her and sat next to her. Seeing her smile at something Adam said lifted a heaviness in his chest he hadn't known was there.

Mona looked back at Nina, who was patiently waiting near the exit. For a minute, he thought she had spotted him. The only person who was aware of his presence was Adam, as he had seen him enter the church when the service first began.

Mona and Adam had gotten up at the same time, but something about the look on her face worried him. Adam had called out to her in concern, but she ignored him.

She was ready to break; Andrew could sense it.

As she grieved heavily for her father, Andrew found himself walking to her. All the problems they had together took a back seat, and it wasn't until he grabbed her in an embrace that he realized how much he missed the feeling of her.

"It's going to be okay. I'm here," Andrew found himself saying.

Thank you, Mr. Louise, he couldn't help but think. For bringing them together again for at least a moment in time. Though, under the worse circumstances, he couldn't have been more grateful because she needed him. She needed a friend and he wanted desperately to be that for her again.

While he held her, he drank her in.

Her scent.

Her tears.

Her skin.

Her arms around him.

Andrew memorized it as best as he could because as much as he wanted to stay, he knew this wasn't the way.

He'd never leave if he stayed any longer.

As quickly as he came, he slipped out her arms and left when she finally settled. Nodding to Adam and Nina, who noted his presence when he approached Mona, he exited the church feeling like he was leaving another piece of himself behind.

CHAPTER THREE

Mona

"COME ON, MONA. You need a break. You've been holed up in here every day since—"

"Don't say it. Please," Mona said with her head still buried in her paperwork.

Nina stood over her desk with her arms folded and clearly irked by her friend's lack of acknowledgement. It had been six months since Mona's dad had passed due to an unexpected heart attack. Her father's untimely death had hit Mona hard in the first few months as well as the law offices that were well acquainted with her father's line of work as a State Prosecutor.

Nina had yet to see any improvement in her friend's mental state. Although she stopped crying as often, the stoic face and the unwillingness to interact with the rest of the world, even to her dear friends, said it all.

Nina sat on the edge of Mona's desk and leaned over to place a hand on hers. Mona looked up at Nina expressionless. With a defeated sigh, she put down her pen.

"It's time you eat something, Mona. When is the last time

you took a day to yourself? It's okay to rest, too," Nina spoke softly.

"I guess I should, huh?" Mona looked at the hour-glass-shaped clock on her wall. It was nearly five in the evening. She had been in her office all day doing paperwork, having not paid any attention to the time.

"Did you at least have a snack?"

As if on cue, Mona's stomach began growling. She blushed when Nina started laughing.

"I'm going to take that as a no. Come on, let's pick up some Chipotle." Nina grabbed Mona's hand and pulled her from her chair.

"But wait, what about the store?"

"The store will be fine, Mona. That's why Lemay is out there. Now, come on."

Lemay was the manager of Mona's store, *Mo-tique*, a small clothing store she opened with the help of her father a year ago. A hard worker and a dedicated one at that, Lemay took pride in her work at *Mo-tique* and often took over on days they were low on staff. Mona had no doubt that Lemay was fully capable of running the store while she was gone. After all, she had done it on the days she was home after her father's funeral.

They walked through the store where a few shoppers were rummaging through the racks of clothes in search of summer wear. Lemay was by the cash register cleaning the countertop.

"We're heading out, Lemay! Be right back!" Nina exclaimed across the store. Several shoppers looked at them in annoyance as they made it through the door.

"Alright!"

Thankfully, Chipotle was down the street, so the drive wasn't long. They both ordered chicken tacos and sat quietly in Nina's Toyota Corolla to eat.

"Thank you," Mona said as she cleaned sauce off her shirt with a napkin.

"What are friends for?"

"For buying food?" Mona joked. It was the first time in a while she had even attempted to joke around.

Progress, she thought.

Nina pinched her arm playfully. "Ow! I was kidding! You're the best."

"And don't forget it."

A burst of music began to sound before Mona could reply. She recognized Nina's wizardly ringtone.

"This is Nina," she answered without looking at the caller ID.

"Where are you guys?" Mona could hear Adam ask.

"Well, hello to you too, Adam. I'm great, by the way."

Mona snickered as Nina rolled her eyes. Nina put the phone between them before pressing the speaker icon.

"If I cared, I would've asked."

Adam and Nina, although friends, had a love/hate relationship since high school. After Nina had rejected his advances when she had first joined their group, Adam had made it his mission to bug Nina whenever he could, much to Nina's dismay.

"Asshole—"

"Where are you guys?" he repeated, cutting off Nina. His voice had taken a serious undertone. "I need to talk to guys about something important."

"Is everything okay?" Mona asked worriedly.

"Yes. No need to worry. Actually, it's about that cabin— you know the one we used to spend our summers back in high school?" Both girls nodded their heads but forgot that he couldn't see them.

"The one in Hunter's Creek?" Mona questioned.

"The one and only," Adam said proudly. "Well, there's been some new development, and I wanted to know if you guys were willing to help me out. I don't want to do this over the phone, though. Can we meet somewhere?"

Mona checked the time. It was forty-five minutes past five. She had to go back to the store to close soon.

"Actually—"

"We're on lunch right now. We have to head back to the store in a few," Nina interrupted. Mona frowned but said nothing.

"Lunch this late? Aren't you supposed to take lunch at noon?"

"Well, Mona here won't eat when she's supposed to; I had to drag her to Chipotle." With Mona's mouth agape, she turned to her friend with a look of betrayal on her face. Nina challenged her with a hard look and shrugged.

Adam sighed on the other end of the phone. "Mona, what did we talk about?"

"I know! I know. It was a mistake. I got caught up in work. Won't happen again. I promise." Mona did her best to reassure Adam. Once he went into an overprotective mode, she had no control over his actions. Most of the time, it was endearing to know someone cared so effortlessly about her, but other times, it was downright annoying. She was an adult, and she'd like to be treated as such.

"Good. So how about we meet at Nina's apartment tonight?"

"Why my apartment? I'd rather come to you."

"Oh, I like a girl who takes control," Adam growled playfully at Nina.

"Adam!" Nina shrieked.

"Kidding! Your apartment. I'll let you guys know when I'm on my way. And Mona?"

With a sigh, Mona answered, "Yes?"

"Please take care of yourself. I don't want any more reports like the one I just got. I worry. Take care." Adam and Nina both hang up the phone simultaneously. Nina started the car and turned to her friend with an apologetic smile.

"I'm sorry."

Mona smiled back, not able to stay mad at her. She knew they had good intentions. It was just frustrating that they made a big deal out of it. Adam was like the big brother she never had and Nina the same but a sister. They've been looking after her since they stepped into her life. The least she could do was compromise.

"You're both right. I need to take better care of myself. I

don't like you guys worrying over me. It's just that sometimes I don't want to think. I get so caught up in trying not to think, and I forget to do simple things like eat."

Nina nodded with understanding. "Well, in any case, as long as you try to at least think about yourself during the day, I'm happy."

Nina pulled out of the parking lot and back to the store. Mona watched as trees and streetlights zipped past her vision.

Another day and more of the same, she thought.

***

SINCE ADAM HAD decided later was better, Mona headed home to freshen up before heading to Nina's apartment. As soon as the front door closed, she threw off her clothes and headed straight to the shower. She washed her shoulder-length dark brown curls and lavished in her spring-scented Dove soap before stepping out to get dressed.

Fumbling through her outdated wardrobe, she pulled out her favorite pair of skinny jeans and a plain black shirt. Throwing on her black and white sneakers, she was out the door as fast as she came.

Nina lived about fifteen minutes away in an apartment with her older half-brother, Spencer, near the heart of the city. She used to spend her free time there during her college days. Lately, she was spending her days in front of her flat-screen TV eating ice cream and watching reruns of *The Office*.

So much for the adventure she'd promised to partake in as an adult.

She pulled into a parking space in the garage of the high-rise and took the elevator to the seventh floor. She knocked three times before Spencer answered the door, inducing an eye roll from her. Sporting a light blue t-shirt and black sweatpants with his hair slightly wet, he looked like he had just completed a shower.

He smirked at her suggestively. "Well, hello there, Button."

"Button" was a name he had conveniently given her when she was in high school and had been going through her "I-don't-wear-cotton" phase. Every day at school, she would wear a different button-up polyester or nylon shirt in a variety of colors until she had realized how ridiculous she was. He always made it a point to tease her about it.

"Hi, Spencer. Are you going to let me in?" Mona asked dreadfully. He moved aside slightly but just enough so she'd have to brush him to completely slide through. It was typical of him to try and make her as uncomfortable as possible. She entered the living room, where she greeted Adam who was munching on Cheetos in front of the TV.

"Mona! Finally, you're here. What did you do? Drive to Mexico?" Mona whacked him on the top of his head before taking the seat next to him on the plush black sofa.

Mona grabbed a capped bottle of water from the coffee table and took a sip before answering, "I wanted to get out of my work clothes. Sue me."

Looking around the living room, she noticed the absence of Nina. "Where is Nina anyway?"

Spencer answered, "She's in her room changing. I highly doubt she can get rid of all that ugly, though."

"Hey! I leave for a minute, and already you're bashing me. Some brother you are." Nina came into the living room with a white t-shirt and Yogi Bear pajama pants. Her usual naturally curly 'fro was resting in a top knot.

Adam laughed as Nina glared at him, her hands resting on her hips. Spencer simply shrugged and sat on the loveseat close by Mona. Nina grabbed the remote from Adam and began flipping through the channels.

"What did you want to talk about that was so important that you had to invade my space?" Nina asked.

Adam teasingly smiled at her. "Well, Miss 'I-don't-like-to-share,' I came here to tell you guys that the cabin may or may not be going on the market."

The cabin was in Hunter's Creek, a couple hours west of Savannah, Georgia. During the summers in high school, the group would stay in the cabin with Adam's parents until a month before school started. They would spend that time walking the trail, swimming, and lazing around. Some of their fondest memories were stationed there. Adam's parents had bought the cabin several years before as a vacation spot. It was unbelievable to hear that they may be giving it up.

"Your parents are selling it? Why?" Nina asked.

Adam shrugged. "Can't afford to keep it if no one is staying in it. We haven't been there since high school."

It was true. Nobody had gone back to the cabin in almost five years besides his parents. After college ended, everyone jumped into the working field. No one had time to spend vacations over there anymore.

Mona shook her head in disbelief. "But you said, 'may or may not be.' That means they haven't fully decided."

"No, but they are feeling pretty strongly about letting it go."

"Where do we come in? We don't have that kind of money for a cabin to upkeep it if that's what this is about," Nina chimed in.

Adam reached into his jeans pocket and pulled out a bundle of cash folded neatly. Spencer's eyes widened. "Where the hell did you get all that?"

"Overtime at the office. Being senior accountant has its perks. This is enough for one month's payment in the cabin, which I promised my parents I'd take care of while we stay there. Since my parents already have someone in mind to buy the place, we really don't have much time left until the place gets taken. Let's face it; it's not going to stay on the market for long. The cabin is a catch."

Both Nina and Mona nodded in agreement.

"I wanted all of us to spend a month at the cabin one last time before they lock the doors for good. What do you guys think?" Adam glanced between Nina and Mona to gouge their reaction. Both girls turned to each other for an answer.

"I don't know," Mona drawled.

"Come on, please? When's the last time you've taken a vacation? When's the last time we've even been together on vacation? Don't let all this money go to waste," Adam whined as he wadded the cash in their face.

Mona contemplated Adam's plea. There was still the store to run, and she couldn't just drop everything for a month to spend at the cabin. But when was the last time she had taken a break and just enjoyed herself? Too long, obviously. She fiddled with her nails as Adam waited for an answer.

"We can't just leave for a whole month, Adam. We have jobs, a place to upkeep. Plus, my boss just gave me a new project to work on. Don't get me wrong, I'd love to go, but I don't think this is going to work," Nina said carefully.

Adam's shoulders noticeably sagged. "What's one last rendezvous? We can make it happen."

Mona placed her hand on his shoulder reassuringly. "How soon would we go?"

"The last Saturday of this month."

"I think we need time to think. How about we let you know by next Thursday? I would honestly like to go, but like Nina said, we can't just leave everything at the drop of a dime. I have a business to run. I do miss hanging out with you guys as a group, though. It is long overdue."

Adam threw her a wink, exposing his perfect white teeth. "I knew you were my favorite for a reason."

"Hey!" Nina whined.

"What? It's the truth," Adam exclaimed. Spencer high-fived Adam, laughing at Nina's pouting face.

"Hardy-har-har guys. That was so funny I forgot to laugh," Nina grumbled as she threw a pillow at the laughing duo.

Mona sat and watched her friends in amusement as they

bickered over the "favorite" title. She missed this more than she realized. She traced the infinity symbol inked on her left wrist, the feeling of loneliness overcoming her. She loved her friends dearly, and they would always hold a special place in her heart, but it was times like these that felt bittersweet. The sense of absence began to overtake her mind.

Things could never be the same, no matter how much she desired it deeply.

She shook her head to rid the thoughts. The sudden pitter-patter of rain struck against the sliding door by the balcony signaling yet another dreary evening. She got up and stretched.

"I think I'm going to head home," Mona said.

"So soon? You just got here!" Adam whined. Mona ruffled his recently dyed blond locks, earning a hand slap from him. She snickered at his familiar unease of others playing with his hair. His fear had stemmed from a former girlfriend who had attempted to shave his head back in high school as an attempt of revenge for their disastrous breakup. He was still mentally scarred to this day.

"Do you need me at the store tomorrow?" Nina quipped as she also stood to lightly stretch.

Mona shook her head. "I might not go in until eleven, anyway. I need to sleep as I've been advised." Mona looked pointedly at Adam.

Holding up his hands in mock surrender. "Don't kill the messenger."

Mona frowned. "Messenger?"

"My lips are sealed. Well, would you look at the time! Big day tomorrow. I should get going as well. Let me know your decision. Bye guys!" Adam rushed through the front door so fast they could almost see the trail left behind him.

Nina shook her head at her eccentric friend's behavior. "I swear that man is strange."

Mona decided to head out moments after. Nina hugged Mona tightly before bidding her goodnight and a friendly reminder to eat something before bed. She headed out of the living room, and Mona could hear the soft click of her door closing.

Spencer looked at her expectantly as she headed to the door. "I don't get a 'goodnight?'"

Mona rolled her eyes and turned to him. "Goodnight, Spencer," she murmured.

She pulled the door open but was stopped by him putting pressure on it. His hot breath was near her ear. Irritation crawled through her skin and fixated on her face as she reluctantly turned to him again. Spencer had always made it a point to invade her personal space and try to get under skin in the worse possible way. For the most part, she handled ignoring him and tolerating him when needed, but they were far from friends.

"What do you want, Spencer? I don't have time for this." Mona dragged the door open a little more as his weight loosened from it.

"Go out on a date with me," he simply stated. Never a question. Always an unwarranted demand.

"No."

"Why not?"

"Because I'm not attracted to you, Spencer. You and I both know that. We established that years ago."

"But feelings can change…"

"Mine never did," Mona snapped. She knew it was harsh, but the guy just couldn't take a hint. It was borderline creepy in how he always found a way to corner her. He was part of the reason she didn't visit as often anymore, though she dared not tell Nina. She'd probably kick his teeth in, and Mona didn't want to cause any sibling drama, especially if he hadn't done anything unbearably physical.

He released his hold on the door entirely and Mona took no time yanking it open and walking right out. But as usual, he always had to have the last word.

"You'll come around one day, and I'll be waiting!" Spencer yelled as she power-walked down the hall.

She didn't bother responding but continued to walk to the elevator like it was a newfound mission. She drove home with fatigue beginning to weigh heavy. Thankfully, she made it with no troubles despite the slick road. She discarded her clothes for nighties and switched on the TV in her common area with a bowl of corn flakes in front of her. It may not be a five-star dinner, but it was something to ease her into relaxation.

Since she lived alone, she had but one sofa in front of her fireplace that faced the TV on the wall. Her apartment was barely furnished due to the lack of commitment to the place. This had been her fourth time moving in the past two years because of the area and careless apartment repairmen.

"Good, *The Office* is on," she mumbled to herself as she snuggled into the blanket taken from her room. The only light penetrating the area was from the TV. She sighed and leaned her head back on the sofa, briefly closing her eyes. She felt taxed as her overstay at the store had finally taken its toll on her. She began to drift slightly but was soundly awoken by her cell phone ringing.

Mona grumbled as she answered without looking at the caller ID. "Hello?"

Silence. She looked at the phone to make sure the call had gone through. It was a number she didn't recognize.

"Hello?" she tried again.

She could hear a bit of shuffling in the background but still no response. The caller hung up, not a second later. Staring at her phone as if it were foreign, she couldn't help but be curious about who was on the phone. But instead of calling it back, she shrugged off the strange call and placed her phone on the armrest. It could've been a butt dial for all she knew. Within the hour, she was fast asleep.

Chapter Four

Andrew

CONSTANT CHATTER AND the clatter of utensils and plates reverberated throughout the restaurant. Waiters and waitresses dressed in their usual grey and red uniform passed each other in speed, tending to the typical customers. Andrew stood in the busy kitchen staring off into space and chewing his thumbnail. As owner of the restaurant, he didn't have to wear the usual uniform; however, he chose to as a symbol of equality for his workers.

A hand waved in front of his face getting him out his stupor. Andrew turned to the source to find his friend and assistant manager, Dave Sutton, standing beside him, a peculiar look on his soft features.

"What are you doing?"

"I was trying to remember where I put my notepad."

It had been an hour since he last saw the thing and he really needed it. It was where he kept his schedule on a day-to-day basis.

Dave reached into his pants pocket and pulled out a four-inched tattered notepad and waved it in front of Andrew. "You mean this old thing? I found it on the bar table earlier by some customers. You should really keep your stuff organized."

Andrew narrowed his eyes at Dave for a split second. Dave was right as usual, but he wasn't about to admit that. He muttered a "thanks" as he reached for his notepad from Dave, but he quickly pulled away with a knowing smirk.

"Nah-uh. I want to know whose face you drew on the back. She's rather pretty."

The question caught Andrew off guard, but when he realized what Dave was talking about, he blanched. Dave noticed this and chuckled.

"It sure doesn't look like Cassidy." Andrew was finally able to snatch it away from Dave's prying fingers.

"It's no one, and it's none of your business," Andrew grumbled. He flipped through the small notepad to make sure all his important notes were still in their rightful places. He dared not turn it over with Dave's prying eyes and inquisitive mind.

"You sure about that?" Dave pressed, but the shrill of Andrew's iPhone saved him from answering his invasive question.

Andrew stepped into a corner away from the noise, leaving Dave to jump straight back to work to Andrew's enlightenment. "Hello?"

"Hey! Long-time, no hear!" Adam exclaimed.

Pocketing his notepad, he maneuvered into the smoking

area outside in the back of the restaurant. He took a cigarette from the front pocket of his uniform and lit it up. "What's up?"

"Haven't heard from you in, oh, I don't know... forever? Is your life too perfect for checking in?" He could hear the laughter in Adam's voice although there was an underlying seriousness.

It had been about two months since he had last spoken to Adam. It was unusual, considering they used to talk at least once a week to check in on each other. They practically considered each other as close as brothers, and he knew it bothered Adam that Andrew had been so reserved as of late. Adam was never one to hold back his thoughts and feelings.

Andrew sighed. "No, of course not, Adam. It's just... I've been busy."

There was a pregnant pause before Adam added, "Well, I hope all is well. Anyway, I called because I wanted to know if you can take some time off in the next couple of weeks."

Andrew frowned as he took in another draw. "Depends. What's the occasion?"

"Well, the cabin is being sold, and I wanted to gather some friends for one last stay. It wouldn't be a party without you."

Andrew mulled this over before answering. As the owner of the restaurant, he could take off as much time as he wanted. The question was, did he want to? He would be lying if he said he didn't miss hanging out with his friends and family back home, but he couldn't bring himself to face them.

"I don't know... "

"Before you say no, it's only for about a month. Everyone

would like you to come. Please? It would mean a lot to us," Adam pleaded.

After outing and tossing his cigarette, Andrew dragged his hand through his short dark curls and down his face. Everyone? He highly doubted, but if there was a chance see her, maybe it would be worth it.

Drawing a deep breath, Andrew gathered his resolve. "I'll think about it, Adam. Plus, Cassidy—"

"—Bring her! The more, the merrier," Adam interrupted.

Andrew tipped his head back against the brick of the building. Adam was persistent when he wanted to be. "When?"

"The last Saturday of this month. I'm trying to give everyone enough space and time to figure out their plans. By then, we should be leaving for Hunter's Creek."

"Who exactly are you inviting?"

"Hmm... Nina, my girlfriend Symoné, maybe Spencer, Mona—"

Andrew stopped listening as all he could see were cloudy gray eyes. They haunted him at times, more often than he'd like to admit. The last time he had set eyes on them, they were filled with tears. And just like that, he had made up his mind.

"Just text me the details. I'll let you know when I make up my mind," Andrew rushed Adam off the phone before he could fully finish his statement.

Ending the call, Andrew made his way back into the kitchen, where Dave was speaking to one of the waitresses. Dave saw him approaching and dismissed the employee.

"Can you do me a favor?" Andrew asked before Dave

could open his mouth.

Dave narrowed his eyes skeptically. "Yeah, sure. Just so long it doesn't involve me naked, drunk, or otherwise in bed with a stranger."

Andrew stared at him with disbelief before shaking his head and continuing, "You're weird. Anyway, I need you to run the restaurant while I'm gone in the next couple of weeks."

"For how long?"

"I don't know yet. Probably for a while, though."

"Where are you going?"

Andrew opened his mouth to tell him his plans but thought better of it at the last minute. It wasn't that he didn't trust Dave. Andrew just wanted to be sure he was one hundred percent on board before he opened his mouth.

"I got some, uh... business to take care of back at home, and I don't want to leave the restaurant in just anyone's hands."

"But why me? I'm just the assistant manager. Wouldn't Eddie be a better fit? He has more management experience than me."

Andrew grabbed his shoulders and looked him straight in the eye. "I trust you, Dave. I've known you since I moved here two years ago, and you know how I like to run my business. You keep things in order more than Eddie and I combined."

"Don't I know it," Dave muttered.

Andrew playfully punched him in the arm. "Don't let it go to your head. I'll have Eddie take care of my paperwork, but I want you to handle the floor. You work best with the employees, and they trust you."

Although it seemed like a small and simple task, Andrew trusted that Dave was a great leader. He worked hard for his title and depending on how well he was able to handle the floor in his absence, Andrew may make use of the surplus in budget he had calculated not too long ago.

Dave smiled brightly, wrinkles forming at the side of his eyes. "You really want me to oversee the floor?"

"I think I just said that."

Dave held out his hand, and Andrew gave it a firm shake, sealing the deal. "Alright. I won't let you down."

"I know you won't. But I want updates at least three times a week."

Dave nodded in understanding. "So, would this business have anything to do with that picture you drew on the back of the notepad?" Dave asked, wiggling his eyebrows.

Andrew rolled his eyes and walked away, leaving a laughing Dave in the corner.

"I'll find out one day!"

***

ANDREW KISSED HER bare shoulder before pulling the sheet away from his naked body and standing. He shivered slightly as the air conditioning slammed into him. Brown eyes followed his movements to the bathroom appreciating the view as the sound of the shower invaded the rather quiet room. Andrew walked back out with a towel around his waist.

"Why so serious?" his girlfriend of two years, Cassidy Ramadi, commented on his unusual mute behavior. She laid on her side, her hand propping her head, and the covers barely covering her chest. A lazy smile graced her lips as she watched Andrew look for clothes.

"Me? Serious? I'm just thinking," he muttered as he fiddled with the clothes in the dresser with his back to her.

"About?" The slam of the dresser drawer made her jump slightly.

"It's nothing you need to worry about."

Andrew entered the bathroom and closed the door before she could initiate further conversation. Within minutes, she had thrown on a t-shirt and joined him as he stepped into the foggy mist awaiting him.

"Obviously, it's something. You seem distracted. Even earlier, you felt distant. What is it?"

"How do you feel about taking a vacation?" He shifted the curtain so she could see him as he lathered his body in soap.

Confused, Cassidy scrunched her nose. "A vacation?"

"In a couple weeks," he elaborated.

He watched her frown. "As fun as that sounds, can we afford to take off any time? You got the restaurant to run, and I just started my internship with Baker's Law Firm. Why the sudden need for one?"

"An old friend of mine called and asked if I wanted to join him and some friends to stay at a cabin we used to visit every summer throughout high school. I'd feel bad to turn him down. He seems adamant to have me—us there."

He waited for an answer as he turned off the shower and

stepped out. Grabbing the towel from counter, he wrapped it around his torso before giving her his undivided attention.

Cassidy shook her head with a frown still etched on her features. "I really don't see the point in going if I'm honest. We're supposed to just pick up and leave because he begs you to come?"

Andrew threw on his last article of clothing before turning to her in the mirror. "He didn't so much beg me, per se... but I'd be lying if I said I didn't want to go."

It was the disapproving look on her face that made him wait to tell her about the plans in the first place. Cassidy was as by-the-book as they came. Surprises and non-planned events were like asking her to compromise. It wasn't going to happen.

However, unexpectedly, her eyes twinkled. Taking her into his arms, Andrew nuzzled her neck tenderly, doing his best to persuade her.

"So... what do say?" he asked. Staring into his deep green eyes, a smile slowly traced her lips. He needed her to say yes. He couldn't do this alone.

"I don't know. Maybe I need a little convincing," Cassidy teased.

Andrew leaned in and brushed her lips with his tenderly. His slightly wet fingers traced her bare thighs as they wrapped around his waist. He nibbled her bottom lip as he sat her on the counter before pulling away with a smirk.

"I think you and I both know who's the boss at this game. Better to give up now."

She playfully shoved him and got down from the counter, putting some space between them. "I'm going to get started on dinner. I suggest you get dressed before neither of us has time to eat."

As she exited the bathroom, the smirk that had graced his lips had slowly slipped away. He had gotten her to agree.

Deciding to stay in the room while she handled dinner meant he could busy himself in bed with his laptop. He checked his email and went through his usual bookmarks before landing on his old Facebook account. Since Instagram had picked up several years ago, he found himself less inclined to use his account though he never had the heart to the delete it. Scrolling down his timeline, he stopped at a photo that Adam had tagged him in not too long ago. It seemed Adam still used his account frequently.

It's was a throwback photo they had taken with the girls in front of the cabin back in the summer of Grade 12. Under the picture the caption read, "Vacation here we come, baby!" Andrew zeroed in on the line of people in the image and stopped at those cloudy gray eyes that seemed to penetrate even through the screen.

He took a deep breath and traced her features in his mind. Her lips were parted slightly in a pleasant smile. Her fair delicate hands raised in the air. Her brown curls fanned around her in a way that he had loved to secretly admire back then. He remembered how he used to love when there was wind. The scent of her hair would catch him off guard every time.

Vanilla coconut. That smell was something he'd always

associate with her and never forget.

His eyes trailed down to the bikini she used to love to wear. The black and white material hugged her figure perfectly. He remembered how mad he had gotten at her when she had first worn it. It left too much to the imagination, and that bothered him back then for reasons he couldn't explain. His eyes would never leave her sight whenever she had it on, much like in the photo. She flourished with the sun. He couldn't help but admire how blindly perfect she seemed.

Not wanting to get lost in memories, Andrew quickly scrolled down further to see if her username was a part of the people Adam had tagged and sure enough it was.

He couldn't help it. He knew he shouldn't, but impulse gave way. He clicked on her name but was startled when Cassidy entered the room.

"Food is almost ready," she said as she walked over to him. He had already clicked onto another tab, the word "Google" staring blankly at him.

"What were you doing?" She eyes him suspiciously.

"Nothing. Let's eat."

She had caught him switching to a different screen, he was almost sure. If she had, she didn't comment any further on it.

He turned the computer off and followed her out of the room. She didn't say anything else for the rest of the night. Instead, she opted to go straight to sleep right after. The suspicion in her eyes said it all. She hated when he kept things from her.

Being a law major, he knew Cassidy liked to read his body

language. She was naturally suspicious of anything she didn't feel was right. She always felt the need to be in control, and for the most part, it was okay with him. However, it created problems, often leading down a trail of accusations. He was familiar with her readings by now to know how she would react after. When she wasn't comfortable with something he was doing, she became reserved.

After dinner, Andrew sat in the living room, a beer in hand, the remote in the other, and channel surfed for most of the night. It wasn't until his phone vibrated on the coffee table that he put the remote down. Glancing at his iPhone, he saw he had a text from Adam. He looked at the message in confusion. It contained only a phone number with an area code he was familiar with.

Having known Adam a long time, his confusion immediately cleared. Andrew knew it was her number. Adam had been trying to get them to talk since the fallout, so a text like this wasn't unusual for him. It was probably one of the main reasons Adam had invited him to come to the cabin in the first place. He'd always expressed his discomfort having to play both sides. He just couldn't understand why things had gone south. Andrew could never bring himself to explain why he and Mona were no longer on speaking terms, though Adam often speculated.

It wasn't like Andrew didn't want to talk to her. It was quite the opposite. More so now than ever since her father had passed. There wasn't a day that passed that he wasn't reminded of her in some capacity.

He was tired of lying to himself about missing her, talking to her, hanging with her. She had been such a massive part in his life growing up and not talking to her for the past two years, with the exception of the funeral, had weighed heavily on his mind. Often, he wondered why he had let things sour between them. There were opportunities he had missed to reconcile, but coward. He blamed himself fully. He could never take back the things he said or how he left things between them.

He missed his best friend.

His thumb hovered over the number in temptation. He wasn't sure if he wanted to make this leap just yet. Seeing her at the funeral and offering his condolences was one thing. Picking up the phone and striking a conversation with her as if nothing had happened was out of the question. But still, the urge to hear her voice had outweighed his conscious.

He dialed the number.

The phone rang twice before the receiver picked up.

"Hello?"

His breathing hitched at the sound of her gentle voice. He couldn't bring himself to answer her back. What could he say? Anything that left his mouth wouldn't have been enough, that he knew. He could hear a conversation in the background. Was she with someone right now? Was she watching TV? He couldn't help but wonder what he had interrupted her doing.

His mouth opened and closed after she repeated herself. He was so concentrated about what to say, he almost didn't catch Cassidy standing at the door of the bedroom watching him from the corner of his eye. His eyes snapped to her in surprise, causing him to drop his phone on the carpet by accident. He quickly gathered it from the floor and pressed the end button discreetly before standing.

"Are you coming to bed?" Cassidy asked as she crossed her arms.

"Yeah," he muttered as he turned off the TV and his phone. He headed to the bedroom without another word. Cassidy followed quietly, though he could feel her stare penetrating the back of his neck. Slipping into the bed, they both got comfortable, her back facing the opposite wall of his. She was fast asleep in no time. It would take another two hours before he drifted off to sleep, the sound of Mona's voice humming through his mind.

Chapter Five

Mona

SATURDAY FINALLY ARRIVED, and Mona wasn't sure whether to rejoice or be annoyed that she had said yes to the month-long trip. Several small travel bags barricaded her inside of her room after she had thrown them in a fit. For the fifth time that morning, she had misplaced the last charger she had for her phone. Down on all fours, she searched every nook and cranny for the darned thing but with no luck.

She huffed and stood back up, dusting imaginary dirt from her white jeans and stuck her phone into her back pocket. She contemplated whether it would be necessary to stop at the store on the way to Nina's apartment for a charger.

Checking her phone battery, she cursed when she realized it was on ten percent.

"So much for that," she muttered to herself.

Gathering the bags, Mona struggled to bring them to her car. Finally, she was able to close the trunk and turn on her car to head to a nearby convenience store.

Mona planned to meet Nina at her apartment so they

could take the long drive to Hunter's Creek together. Nina had suggested they share a ride because long car rides often made her sleepy.

It was true.

Parking in front of Joe's Shop, a local convenience store she frequented, she stepped out and headed in. She waved at the owner, Joe, who often worked by himself behind the counter. She didn't know him entirely well, but they exchanged light conversation from time-to-time.

Joe was at least in his seventies with a long white beard and a shaved head. From afar, he looked ex-military, although Mona had come to learn that that was inaccurate. He was just a sweet old man who immigrated from Sweden in his early teens and really loved his store.

She knew exactly where to go for the chargers as she lost one at least once every three months. She was ashamed to admit how much money she spent already for the year on iPhone chargers.

"Ah-ha!" Mona exclaimed to herself as she grabbed the two-for-one charger on sale. Grabbing a pack of M&Ms, she brought her items to the counter and pulled out a twenty-dollar bill.

Joe looked at the charger and shook his head with a knowing smile as he rang up her items. "I might just dedicate the whole section of chargers to you."

Mona laughed. "I think that would be a great idea. Might save me the time looking for one."

She handed him the bill and grabbed her bag when he

gave her change. Waving goodbye to Joe, she made her way outside. She ripped open her bag of M&Ms, throwing a couple in her mouth as she approached her car.

"You should really pay attention to your surroundings."

Mona whipped her head to the familiar voice, only to find Calvin leaning against her car. If the bag hadn't been secured around her wrist, she likely would've dropped it. Trepidation immediately overcame her at the sight of him.

Unable to speak or move from her spot, she could only stare at him in shock. He had rendered her motionless.

A knowing smirk spread across his face. The slit across the top of his lip was still there, faintly serving a reminder of a time they shared together she prayed to one day forget. She backed up slightly as he approached, only stopping when her foot hit the parking brick.

"You know, I always wondered what I would say to you when I saw you again. What I would say... I always draw a blank somehow. The only thing on my mind at this moment is the confliction of how beautiful you look, and yet, I can only imagine how tainted you are."

He spat out the last bit of words with a snare. Tainted. It was word he used before when he was in one of his jealous fits three years ago because of how much time she was spending with Andrew. Tainted to him was the equivalent of someone touching what was his.

Finally finding her voice, Mona forced out, "Y-You need to leave, Calvin. I have a restraining order. If I call—"

"Call them. I don't care, Mona. I've got nothing to lose."

He approached her further until yellow was all she could see from his shirt. Placing a hand on her cheek, he bent slightly to look straight into her eyes. Brown clashed with gray, and Mona found herself unable to look away.

All the memories came crashing back at once. His tender touch. His sweet smile. His heavy hand. She felt paralyzed in his hold. A sneaky smile crept onto his lips and just like that, she snapped out of his hold.

Mona yanked his hand from her face and created some space between them. "Don't ever touch me again or I'll call the police! I mean it!"

The smile slipped from his lips and he slowly backed away. "I've already lost you once. I've got nothing to lose... nothing. But I'm sure you do. I'll see you around, Mona. I promise you that."

With one last look, he turned and walked away, disappearing around the back of the convenient store. Mona stood for a moment trying to decipher what just happened and calm her frazzled nerves. Taking one last look around, she hurried into her car, locked the door and drove off as far as she could.

When she felt safe enough, she parked on the side of the road and finally let her anxiety and fear get the best of her. Wet sobs escaped her lips as she broke down. By the time she could gain control of her breathing, she leaned back against her seat and thought about how Calvin had known she was there.

Was it by chance?

It didn't seem like it. He waited near her car as if he were waiting for her to come out of Joe's Shop.

Had he followed her?

Mona knew she should've called the police. She still could.

She pulled out her phone to dial the number but then realized it was dead. With a frustrated sigh, she took the charger from the bag, she plugged in her phone to her car console and let it charge. By the time the phone charged enough to turn on, Mona had already changed her mind.

She couldn't let that happen again.

Wouldn't.

Pulling back out into traffic, Mona did her best to put everything behind her but failed miserably. Calvin had a way of invading her life in the worst possible way, and if she wasn't careful, it could turn deadly.

It was amazing how well he had fooled her the majority of the time they were together. Manipulative, jealous, and possessive didn't crack the list of descriptions Mona had for him. He was good at putting on a mask. He did it for the first six months.

Blinded by bliss and gifts, Calvin had meandered his way into her life, attempting to turn her against her friends, succeeding once with Andrew. His controlling and possessive nature would convert to physical harm, which she always blamed herself for. Toxic wouldn't even begin to describe their short-lived relationship.

The straw that broke the camel's back was the end of her friendship with Andrew two months before he had left. When he pleaded for her to leave Calvin like he often tried, she had dishonored their friendship to the point of no return. They never talked after that, nor did they cross paths.

Thinking about the look on his face when she had thrown his insecurities back at him, like his struggles with being ambitious like the rest of his family or his struggles with feeling accepted and loved. It was like she had slapped him.

Even now, she regretted that day. She regretted pushing Andrew to move far away from her. She regretted ever meeting Calvin, but most of all, she regretted letting him turn her into a shell of her former shelf.

As she wiped the tear that had slipped from her eyes, her car Bluetooth indicated she had an incoming call. Turning to her phone, she saw it had powered on automatically. Nina's name flashed against the screen of her car display.

She pressed the answer button on her steering wheel. "Hey, Nina."

"Don't 'Hey, Nina' me! Where are you? You were supposed to be here, like, forty minutes ago!"

Mona sniffed to clear her clogged nostrils from crying. "I had to stop for a charger..."

Mona deliberately left out the part about Calvin. Nina would insanely freak out.

"Why the sniffing? Are your allergies acting up again? I have Benadryl—"

"I'm fine, Nina. I'm on my way now. I shouldn't be too long."

"Hurry up, then! We have to leave soon. I want to pick out the best room in the cabin before everyone gets there."

Mona frowned. "Everyone? I thought it was just us."

There was a pause on Nina's end. "That's what I meant."

She could tell by the evasive tone in her voice that Nina was lying. Though she had a feeling she wasn't going to like the answer, Mona decided to press her for more anyway. "Nina... who else is going?"

There was another short pause before Nina sighed defeatedly. "Andrew might be there..."

It was like she got knocked over twice in one day. For the second time within the hour, Mona felt speechless. Suddenly, she could feel her heart pulsating in her ear, and the possibility of having to come face-to-face with her regrets made her nervous. She opened her mouth and closed it before trying to reel in her emotions.

"I'm sorry. I should've told you when Adam told me, but I didn't know how you would react. Adam said Andrew never gave him a definite yes or no, so there's a possibility that he might not even show."

But the possibility was still there, she thought.

"It's okay, Nina. I can handle it."

Could she? She'd at least have to pretend for her sanity. She couldn't just cancel the trip. She needed it more now than she realized.

"Are you sure? I can call Adam and tell him—"

"No! I can do this. I promise. We'll just have to tolerate each other if it comes to it."

"Okay," Nina started. "But if it becomes too much for you, just let me know. I don't know exactly what happened between the both of you, nor is it my business, but if he bothers you in some way or if you feel uncomfortable, we can leave. I'm here for you."

Mona wanted so badly to tell her it wasn't Andrew she was afraid of, it was herself. With how she hurt him, she was scared to face him again and seeing the look of hatred in his eyes. It was the thought that the twenty years they spent building a friendship was long gone. It was the fact that she wasn't sure if she could look him in the eyes and see a void that once held so much compassion for her. It scared her to think that she was responsible for the end of the dynamic of their group because the chronicles of Mona and Andrew were dead.

Nonetheless, she said the only thing she could to keep from breaking apart. "Thank you, Nina."

"Always. Now hurry up and come before I lose my mind!"

With a sad smile, Mona replied, "I'll be there, I promise."

Deciding it was a good idea to put her thoughts in the back of her head, she hurried to Nina's apartment. Thankfully, by the time she had arrived, Spencer was long gone at work.

"Is Spencer coming to the cabin, too?" Mona couldn't help but ask.

Nina shook her head. "He has to work, thank God. I don't need him there, cramping my style."

Mona mentally rejoiced. That was one less person to bother her during the trip.

Looking around Nina's apartment, she noted the many bags she had lying on the ground. "You're not bringing all those, are you?"

"Yep!" Nina said, popping the "p" as she tried stuffing the last bag with shoes. "Can't be too careful. I never know what I might need. Don't just sit there, help me bring them to the car."

Mona could only roll her eyes in amusement as she got up to help Nina. By the time they finished packing Nina's car, an overcast had begun to roll in. Lightning sparked from the sky, followed by a rumble of thunder.

Nina and Mona looked at each other with the same idea. "We should head out before the rain drenches us.

And so, they did.

Turning on the radio to a soft tune as they merged onto the interstate, Nina turned to Mona, who was nodding her head to a Phil Collins song. "So, what took so long getting to my apartment? You only live a few blocks from me."

Mona turned to her, the song now offering only a slight distraction in the background. Mona decided to choose wisely. "I went to get a charger."

"You lost the other one already?" Nina said, looking at her incredulously.

Mona could only shrug.

"Wow, you lose chargers like a baby loses teeth."

Mona let out a genuine laugh. "That's the oddest simile I've ever heard."

Nina wiggled her eyebrow. "Well, I'm full of them. Now, tell me the real reason you were so late because Joe's Shop only keeps the chargers in one place, and it's never full."

The smile that was on Mona's face slipped away. Looking

out her passenger window, she wondered if there was a way to avoid the path this conversation was about to take. Nina had always been good at reading between the lines and could usually tell when she was withholding something.

With a calm breath, she decided to dive in headfirst. "I saw Calvin."

"You what?!" Nina almost swerved, causing Mona grab hold of the door handle. "Mona, please tell me you're joking. Please tell me you did not meet with Calvin."

"I didn't *meet* with Calvin. He was waiting for me when I came out of Joe's Shop," she clarified.

"Did you call the police? What did he say to you? He didn't hurt you, did he? Because I swear—"

"No, I didn't call the police, and no, he didn't hurt me. He just... wanted to scare me that's all." Mona wasn't sure how much of that last statement she believed. Calvin wasn't always one for a simple shock factor. He still had a plan up his sleeves. Just the thought made her shudder, but she wouldn't dwell on it. She could only hope she was wrong.

Nina turned to her in disbelief. "Why are you taking this so calmly? Do you not remember who we're talking about? Why the fuck didn't you call the police? He's not supposed to be near you!"

Mona couldn't take the yelling anymore. "I get it! Nina. I can handle myself. I'm here now, and I'm unharmed. I was just... surprised at the moment and froze. Give me a break!"

Silence fell within the car, the tension sat palpable between the two. By now, they had reached the outskirts of Hunter's Creek. Fewer businesses and houses were in the area, and Mona was happy to see the familiar change of scenery. She had missed being able to get away from the city every summer and live free at the cabin with her friends. Fond memories of her high school days made her smile.

She remembered driving ATVs with Nina in the trail behind the cabin and being chased by Adam and Andrew. Movie nights on the patio deck. Swimming in the wee hours of the morning. The days of being carefree were long over.

Hearing the radio shut off, Mona was brought out of her thoughts.

Nina cleared her throat. "Mona, I'm—"

Mona held her hand up to silence her. Although Nina may have overreacted, she knew it was out of fear and love. "It's okay. I get it, Nina. You want to protect me. I appreciate you for it. Always will. And I'm thankful for you always have my back. Some things you must understand that I can handle. I'm not a kid. I make mistakes, but I'm not dumb."

Nina nodded sadly. She kept her eyes on the road as she switched lanes.

Mona continued, "Thank you for always having my back."

Nina turned to her briefly, eyes glistening. "I just don't want to see you hurt again, Mona. You've been through so much in the last three years. I'm not sure how you're still functioning. I would have fallen apart long ago. You're brave, and I admire you for it. I'm sorry. I know I can be overbearing but you're like a sister to me, and I never want you see you go through that kind of pain—or any kind of pain—again."

Mona smiled at her, blinking back tears. After a brief silence took over again, Mona spoke to break the ice and change the subject. "Do you plan to stay the whole month at the cabin?"

Nina nodded, pulling a loose strand of her hair behind her ears. For once, Nina had decided to straighten it, letting her full black flow past her collar. "Seems long, but you know time does fly when you're having fun."

"Don't we know it," Mona muttered.

"You know," Nina started. "They renovated the cabin a few years back."

Mona raised an eyebrow. She hadn't known.

"They had expanded the back area, reconstructed the pool, and added a small basketball court."

"Sounds more like a beach house than a cabin."

"Potato-patato."

The familiar tune of Nina's ringtone halted their conversation. She briefly looked at the screen before handing it to Mona with her nose scrunched and turning back to the road. "Here, you answer it."

With a slight snicker, Mona pressed the answer button, putting it on speaker. "Yes, Adam."

"You guys almost here yet? I just got here about twenty minutes ago. The cabin looks fantastic."

"We're about thirty minutes away."

"Well, tell Nina to put some pedal to the metal. With how she drives, her dead grandma could pass her."

"I heard that, asshole!" Nina shouted.

"Adam! That's so insensitive," Mona scolded.

Adam snorted. "Please. She cares less about the old hag than her nails. Nina and I both know that."

"Yeah, but still…"

"Well, hurry up, then. I want to get this party started!"

The call ended, leaving Nina and Mona shaking their head. "This is going to be an interesting month."

Mona nodded as she thought about possibly seeing Andrew for the first time since her father's funeral.

Interesting, indeed.

<u>You Had Me at First Fight</u>

Lawson Elementary School

"YOU'RE GOING TO do great, honey! Just smile, listen to the teacher, and always be polite. Remember what mommy told you." Andrew's mother, Linda Sumpter, knelt before him to straighten his clothes and tousle his mop of hair.

"I don't want to go!" a six-year-old Andrew whined.

"You have to, sweetie. I'm sorry."

His mother looked at him with remorse before standing and taking his hand. He struggled to release his hand from her grip, but she held tighter as they neared the front door. By the time she made it to the car, he had tears streaming down his face.

"Mommy, please! They're mean to me. I don't want to go!" he hiccupped.

She managed to give him a reassuring smile, but the sight of him crying broke her heart. Nevertheless, she continued to push towards the car and buckled him in as he struggled to settle.

She rushed to the driver's side and started the car, watch-

ing as Andrew sniffled in the back.

"Andrew, sweetie, I want you to promise me one thing, okay? I know I can't stay with you all day at school to protect you, but I want you to always remember I have your back. I believe you when you tell me those kids are mean. I get it. They used to be mean to me, too. I hated school as a kid. But I always remembered that they were never better than me. Promise me that you won't let those kids get the best of you, ever?"

Andrew didn't speak, but he looked at her with tear-stained eyes and nodded. She knew he wouldn't understand it fully at his age, but she needed to offer something, even if it wasn't much.

Andrew had been the victim of minor bullying since he began school because of his glasses and shy personality, the kids citing his intelligence made him easy to kick around. As a mom, she felt to need to hold his hand through his battles, but she knew she couldn't do it forever. At some point, she knew he was going to have to start standing up for himself, but it didn't hurt to push him in the right direction, she thought.

The rest of the ride was quiet as she snuck glances at Andrew sulking in the rearview mirror. Pulling into the parent drop-off lane at the school, she got out to open his door. He refused to get out, crossing his arms across his chest and turning away from her. With a sigh, she knelt by his side and ran her fingers through his head of curls.

"Andrew, you know I wouldn't let anyone hurt you, right?" she spoke softly.

He turned to her and nodded slowly.

She kissed his cheeks and smiled lovingly. "I promise it gets better. You're going to grow to be the most handsome man, and everyone is going to be so jealous of you. They probably already are. People fear what they envy and don't understand. Kill them with kindness. It goes a long way, trust me."

She extended her hand, which he took hesitantly and pulled him into a tight hug. "I love you so much, honey. Now, go be great."

The school bell rang as a first warning, prompting Andrew to rush into the crowd. She watched idly by as he stopped midway, turned to her, and waved before getting lost in the sea of children heading to their class.

A tear dripped from her eye, which she quickly whipped before getting inside of her car and driving off.

***

"ALRIGHT, CLASS! SETTLE down!"

Ms. Coleman tried her best to hush the class as the majority wouldn't stop playing. Turning to the chalkboard, she wrote out the title of "Verbs" and opened her textbook.

Andrew turned to get paper from his backpack on the floor but was met with an empty spot. With panic, he looked around and caught Jordan Velez's eye.

Jordan held up Andrew's backpack from across the table with an evil, toothless grin. "Looking for this, pipsqueak?

Here, have it!"

Jordan threw the bag at Andrew's face, the buckle at the front, hitting his face. Andrew's hand flew to his eye with a yelp, catching the teacher's attention.

"Jordan! I saw that! Go to the counselor's office, and I will be calling your mother today!" Ms. Coleman said. The class laughed at him as he angrily got up and left the room.

"Are you okay, Andrew? Do you need to go to the nurse?"

Andrew shook his head even though his eye was throbbing. Warily, Ms. Coleman turned back to the chalkboard with a frown but didn't press the issue. Taking a piece of paper, Andrew spent his time writing down notes. Occasionally, he would catch the new girl looking at him and offering a smile, but he shied away.

The bell rang for recess, and Andrew pulled out his lunchbox from his bag. He made his way outside alone, trailing the rest of the class as they rushed to the playground behind the portables. Sitting at a bench, he bit into his sandwich and watched a couple of kids chase each other around.

"Well, well, well, if it isn't the little hamster eating his food in the lonely corner. What did mommy make for you today? Another lousy sandwich?" Noah, a friend of Jordan's, mocked him with a couple of his other friends standing beside him.

"Please go away," Andrew whispered as he watched them step closer. Noah grabbed the sandwich from his hand, threw it to the ground, stepping on it. He picked up his lunchbox and was ready to toss it before his attention turned to

someone beyond the bench.

"Hey! Leave him alone!" the new girl yelled as she approached the boys.

Andrew turned around and watched her mesmerized as she stood in front of them, arms crossed. Her shiny brown curls reminded him of his mother's. She stood before him like Wonder Woman. He couldn't look away from her long tresses, wondering what it was like to touch it.

Noah threw the lunchbox on the floor and sneered, "And if I don't? What's a scrawny girl like you going to do about it?"

The new girl bent down and grabbed a bunch of dirt in her hands before throwing it in his face. In a split second, he charged at her, but she tripped him, making him fall and face plant next to the bench. His friends began to laugh at him.

Before Noah could get up, the new girl grabbed Andrew's lunchbox from the ground and took his hand, pulling him from the bench. "Come on! Let's find a hiding spot!"

Andrew stared down at their joined hands, wondering what that tingling feeling was. He never held hands with a girl before, and it felt weird. She dragged him to a spot under the slide and handed him his lunchbox. She took out a piece of candy from her back pocket and gave it to him.

Staring at the candy in his hand, he said, "Why did you do that?"

She shrugged and popped a lollipop into her mouth. "They are big fat meanies, and you are nice."

Andrew searched her eyes but was met with cool gray.

He blushed and looked away. "Thank you," he muttered.

"I like your eyes."

"I-I like yours, too," Andrew replied shyly. He opened his lunchbox but realized he had nothing but an apple left. He wanted to offer her something in return for saving him but wanted the apple more. Looking at the candy in his hand, he offered her the apple anyway.

She shook her head. "You can keep it. I have a lot of candy in my pocket. Do you want some?"

Andrew nodded, no longer interested in the apple. "Yes."

He stuffed the apple back into his lunchbox while she grabbed a handful of candy from her back pocket and put it between them.

"Don't tell anyone. My daddy gives me candy every day even though he says it's not good for me. You can have as much as you want. I have more at home."

Andrew grabbed a few boxes of nerds and a piece of gum. Nerds were always his favorite. He thought they described him nicely: nerdy and sweet.

"What's your name?"

"Andrew."

"My name is Mona."

That's a different name, he thought. It was a pretty name. They sat in comfortable silence as they ate candy and watched the kids chase each other around the field. Every now and then, Andrew felt the need to pinch himself. This was the most he's ever been in the company of anyone outside of his family. He never had any friends.

"We should be friends," Mona exclaimed as if she had discovered something new. "We can come here every day and eat lunch and candy. And those boys are not allowed. We can fight them together. And when we get older, we can be best friends and always have each other's backs forever!"

Andrew smiled wide. He liked that idea. "Okay."

Sticking out her picky, she gave him a toothy grin. "Forever?"

He stared at her pinky momentarily before linking his with hers, offering a giant smile. "Forever."

Chapter Six

Andrew

IT LOOKED DIFFERENT than he remembered.

Andrew pulled up into the roundabout driveway and parked behind a Corolla he didn't recognize. After a long and quiet drive, they had finally arrived at the cabin. The sun was just beginning to rise, painting a beautiful aura around the two-story wooden structure. A fountain stood off-centered in the front of the cabin, spewing water from the depths.

It looked rich.

Along with the addition of the fountain, the cabin had been extended wider. Double doors were now in place of the front door. The steps leading to the porch were polished and freshly installed. A large shed rested alongside the cabin, which looked like it could be a pool house. The windows were larger now with shades obstructing the view to the inside and vice versa. Although he was sad to see most of the familiar features gone, he couldn't say the added changes didn't bring value to the cabin.

Cassidy opened her door and stepped out of the truck

to stretch her limbs. It had been quite a while since she had gotten out of the car since they had decided that fewer stops meant an earlier arrival.

Andrew and Cassidy had decided that leaving Sunday would benefit them best. Cassidy was able to switch schedules for work while Andrew used Saturday to go over last-minute details with Dave for the restaurant.

Pulling open the trunk, Andrew lifted their belongings out and handed Cassidy her luggage, before making their way to the front door. He firmly knocked three times and waited. Nobody was likely to be up to get the door as it was only ten past seven. He looked around for a doorbell in case no one heard the knock and sighed when he didn't see one.

All the fancy updates and *still* no doorbell, he noted.

What a waste.

"Does Adam know we were coming? We need to get in. I'm hungry, and I'm tired, and I need to shower before I meet anybody," Cassidy grumbled.

Rolling his eyes discreetly, Andrew didn't bother to answer as he walked around the side of the cabin with his luggage in tow. The familiar sound of a basketball pounding the pavement was distinctive. Following the sound, he was surprised to see a small basketball court further on the land.

To Andrew's discovery, Adam stood in front of the net, dribbling a basketball. He hadn't heard Andrew approach, instead, focusing on the net, and anticipating his shot. Andrew could only shake his head at his friend's obsession with basketball—one he adamantly denied having for years, yet Adam was never far from a net.

"Stare at the net all you want, you know it won't make it in."

Adam snapped his neck to Andrew in surprise, causing him to drop the ball. The ball bounced aimlessly to the other side of the small court, now forgotten.

"What the hell! You made it!" Adam exclaimed.

All smiles, they exchanged a manly embrace. "Albeit, a little later than originally planned. Why isn't the front door open if you're out here?"

Adam pointed to the sliding door around back.

"Of course."

Adam wiggled his eyebrows. "It's really good to see you. So, where's the lady? I've been dying to see this girl."

Andrew eyed his friend suspiciously. "Why, so you can try to unsuccessfully hit on her?"

"Of course. I have to make sure she's right for you," Adam replied with a laugh.

Andrew couldn't help but feel lighter with the banter exchanged between them. It was as if he had never left, and they picked up where they left off.

"Come on, I'll take you inside."

Adam led Andrew to the back door. Pulling his luggage through the cabin, he was surprised to see Cassidy already inside.

"When did you get inside?" Andrew asked with surprise. He had forgotten she was waiting for him out front in the first place.

Cassidy glared at him. "You mean after you left me by my-self?"

Not in the mood to argue, Andrew stayed quiet for an awkward minute. Adam's eyes jumped between the two curiously before taking matters into his own hands.

"You must be Cassidy. I'm Adam, the one and only. Nice to finally meet you. Might I say, when you get tired of Andrew—like most do—my arms are always open," Adam finished with a wink to Cassidy.

Andrew punched him in the arm, resulting in a pained expression from Adam.

Raising an eyebrow at Andrew, Cassidy replied, "Most?"

Andrew hit him again.

"Ow! I was kidding, jeez. You haven't even been here for an hour, and you're already resorting to violence," Adam said rubbing his sore arm.

Cassidy smiled politely but looked slightly annoyed. "Just show us our rooms so I can get out of these clothes, *please.*"

Andrew and Cassidy followed Adam up the stairs and down the hall to their room. Adam stopped in front of the open door, motioning them in. "You can get this room. Freshly cleaned and tailored to your needs."

Andrew and Cassidy stepped into the room with their luggage. It was enough space to fit a full bed, a dresser, and a small chair near a walk-in closet. With double windows installed, there was a perfect view of the backyard. The walls were an off-white cream color and bare. The room didn't look familiar to Andrew, possibly an add-on. Nonetheless, it was perfect for him and hopefully Cassidy.

"I'm going to let you guys settle in. I'll be downstairs making myself breakfast," Adam stated as he exited the room.

The pair began to unpack their belongings into the dresser and closet, quietly moving around each other. Wondering the time, Andrew frowned when he reached into his pocket for his phone but came up empty-handed.

"Shit," he muttered to himself.

Cassidy turned to him. "What?"

He shook his head. "I forgot my phone in the truck. I'll be back."

He didn't wait for her response as he found himself outside shortly after, searching the driver seat of the truck for his cellphone. Finally, he located it under his seat. How it got there, he had no idea.

As he got ready to close the door, someone walking the trail near the cabin caught his eye. He would've dismissed it had it not been for the shirt that he recognized from a distance. The tricolored tank top was hard to miss in the morning sun and stood out against the greenery surrounding the forest. It was a top he would associate with athletic activities in the past.

It was Mona.

Paralyzed, he stood watching her fixing her shoelaces against a tree. Though he was quite a distance, he was close enough to see her face. She looked winded. She stood for a few moments as if she were trying to catch her bearings.

He willed her to look at him. To find him. He couldn't

look away until she did.

Andrew was so focused on her, he unexpectedly dropped the keys, causing the alarm to go off. Jumping into action, he quickly turned it off once he swiped the keys from the ground and looked up to see if Mona was still there, but she was gone.

Surveying the area, he couldn't find her anywhere. Hesitantly, he closed his truck and headed inside, wondering if he'd imagined her there.

Robotically, he made his way back to the room where Cassidy was still situating herself. Having changed her clothes and tied her hair into a sloppy bun, he noticed she seemed a bit more relaxed than before.

At least one of them was.

"Are you showering first, or should I?" A bit rhetorical considering she had already changed, but he felt he should ask to be sure. He needed time alone.

"I'm starving, so I'm going to make breakfast. You go ahead."

Shrugging, he gathered his belongings and got ready for his shower.

There were only two rooms in the cabin that had their own bathroom from what he remembered: the master suite and the secondary suite. He assumed Adam was taking the master suite, but he wasn't sure who was taking the secondary. They had taken one of the smaller rooms that didn't have its own bathroom; leaving him to travel to the one down the hall that he and the other guests would be sharing.

Thankfully, the bathroom still held some resemblance

from years prior. It had a small tub but a more extensive walking space than most bathrooms. The earth tones on the wall made the bathroom feel inviting. The walls were decorated with the same generic nature photos.

Placing his belonging on the counter, he stripped off his clothes and entered the shower. The heat of the water relaxed his muscles and transcended him into more euphoric state. He ran a hand through his dark curls, staring at the water swirling into the drain.

With his mind drifting, Andrew was reminded that at some point during his stay at the cabin, he'd have to confront his demons. He wondered how that scenario would go down. How would it even begin if they didn't speak to each other? How would he approach her? If there was anything Andrew knew about his former friend, he expected her to put up a fight when it came to reconciliation.

He was shocked she even agreed to come to the cabin. Knowing Adam, he would neglect to tell her of his presence at the cabin. She likely would've refused to come if Adam had told her he was staying too, right?

Did she harbor animosity towards him for leaving? He certainly wouldn't blame her if she did.

Stepping out of the shower, he reached for his towel but was startled by when the door swung open.

"Shit!"

"Close the door!" The door slammed closed immediately. Andrew grabbed his towel swiftly, wrapping it around his torso before grabbing the handle of the door and yanking it open.

"What the—Nina?" Nina stood off to the side with her hand over her face.

"I really hope you have something on because I do not want to see what I just saw again!" Nina exclaimed.

Andrew scoffed. "Don't you knock?"

"Don't you lock the door when you're showering?"

Andrew rolled his eyes. "It was an honest mistake. You can move your hand now. I have a towel on."

Nina scrunched her nose in disgust when she finally looked at him. "I'm surprised you decided to show up."

"I wasn't going to pass up on a free vacation."

"You're brave."

"Why would you say that?"

"Considering everything..." Nina trailed off.

Andrew didn't say anything, instead offering a brief silence. He wasn't sure how much Nina knew about the situation between him and Mona, and he wasn't going to explain himself to her.

"Look, I don't know what happened between you and Mona. All I know is that you better not hurt her while you're here. She's finally coming around. It's either you fix what either of you broke or stay away from each other.

Andrew nodded in understanding. Nina was going to look out for Mona no matter what. He was grateful she had someone like Nina to protect her.

"Does she know I'm here?" He still wasn't sure if she had seen him earlier or not.

Nina shrugged. "That's a question you will have to find

out on your own. By the way, you might want to put on some clothes. I doubt your girlfriend would appreciate you standing in the hall partly nude. She seems to have a bit of an attitude problem, and I am not trying to get on her bad side."

"So, you opened the door for her this morning," he stated more to himself than to her.

Nina scuffed. "Yeah, and I shouldn't have. Way to pick 'em.'"

Andrew didn't get a chance to tell her it was most likely his fault for Cassidy's attitude because she walked off and out of sight down the stairs. Frowning, he looked down at the infinity symbol on his wrist for a fleeting moment before heading back into the bathroom to finish getting ready. He left the bathroom shortly after, taking the same route as Nina.

The smell of eggs and pancakes in the air was hard to miss. Pots were still on the stove, plates around the tables, but no one to be found. Wrinkling his nose in disgust at the mess, Andrew removed the dishes and pots from their respective places and into the sink.

He always had a cleaning fetish when it came to the kitchen. It irritated him to the core to see dirty dishes and an unkempt table. Where food was kept, no mess should ever dominate. Often, he chalked his OCD on him being a chef.

The sliding door in the dining area opened and closed. Cassidy walked toward him, kissing him on the cheek though his back was to her as he scoured the pots. She frowned slightly when she saw what he was doing.

"Seriously?" She pointed to the dish in his hand. "You're

doing work away from work?"

"This isn't exactly working. My job doesn't solely consist of me being a dishwasher," Andrew answered, slightly annoyed.

"You know that's not what I meant." She took the dish from him. His eyes held defiance, but as she caressed his cheek, his eyes softened. Gliding her hands against the slight shadow on his face, she smiled.

"Relax. You're on vacation. Adam asked you to come for a reason. Go hang with him. Catch up with your friends after you eat. I'm sure they missed you. It won't kill anybody to leave the kitchen messy for at least a day."

Sighing, he removed her hands from his face but didn't release them. He gave her a pained smile and kissed her hands.

"I guess I can consider..."

"No, you *will*. For yourself and for me. I want us to have fun, put aside work. And I want to get to know this side of your life. I want to be a part of it."

He closed his eyes and nodded. This side of his life, she wanted to know. Wanted to be a part of it. The problem was, he wasn't sure if he was part of it anymore. With his two-year absence, could things ever go back to normal?

She stepped away and dragged him outside to the others. Nina and Adam were in the pool fighting over a noodle float. Scanning the area, he didn't spy Mona anywhere. He made a note of the hour that had passed since he saw her last.

Was she still on the trail?

"I had it first! Besides, you lost the round!" Nina shouted, breaking Andrew's thoughts.

"Nina, that was three turns ago! Let me have the damn thing!" Nina and Adam continued struggling for the noodle, mushing each other in the face with it while holding on to the noodle.

"You know what? Fine! You can have it. I hope it drowns you," Adam yelled, swimming away from Nina.

Nina rolled in eyes, feigning despair. "Whatever, you loser!"

Cassidy and Andrew stood idly by, watching with amusement. The familiar scene put a smile on Andrew's face but disappeared as he began rubbing his infinity symbol absentmindedly.

Cassidy looked at him, her eyes briefly flickering to his movements. "Your friends are funny. We should go to the pool before everyone else comes. I hear they're on their way."

He hesitated. As far as he was concerned, all his "friends" were present already. "Who's coming?"

She shrugged her shoulders. "I just heard that there is more to come supposedly."

He watched as Cassidy stripped out of her shirt and shorts, leaving her in a swimsuit he didn't know she had on. It was a white halter top bikini with shorts that hugged her figure in all the right places. Her belly button ring twinkled in the sun as she shifted while folding her clothes. And while he never got tired of looking at her picture-perfect figure, he couldn't help but notice that he lacked the desire to grab her like he used to.

Spying the curious look on his face, she said, "I changed

while you were in the shower. I figured I should enjoy the pool while I can."

Without another word, Cassidy jumped into the pool as Adam got out to stand beside Andrew. "She's beautiful. It's a shame I didn't meet her before you did," Adam joked, moving just in time before Andrew's elbow to connected with his rib.

"Adam, don't even try it."

Adam held his hands up in surrender. "Don't worry, I'm perfectly happy with my girl. It's just fun to irritate you."

"Where is this mystery girl anyway?"

"Her name is Symoné, and she's on her way here. She wanted to bring her cousin, Dixie."

Andrew frowned. "How many others are coming?"

Adam held up two fingers. "Just those two."

"Good."

Andrew breathed a sigh of relief. Anyone else would've been a crowd.

"We're lucky. We almost got Spencer."

Andrew scrunched his nose in disgust. He and Spencer never quite got along whenever they interacted. Spencer tended to measure dicks, in other words, he seemed to think Andrew was his competition and made everything into a rivalry. Andrew found it more than a little annoying.

"Lucky us," Andrew muttered.

The two watched as Nina and Cassidy made small talk by the edge of the pool, the noodle long forgotten as it floated on the other side. Andrew smiled as they laughed at something Nina said. Cassidy seemed to fit right in despite Nina's earlier assumptions. Or perhaps Nina was just playing nice.

"With all that bickering you and Nina do, it's a wonder you guys haven't hooked up yet," Andrew pointed out with a grin. From the moment they met, they always picked on each other like schoolyard children do when they have a crush. To his knowledge, though, they didn't seem to be interested in each other that way, but it was always fun to watch.

"Funny." Adam turned to him with a smirk. "We all used to say the same thing about you and you-know-who." He wiggled his eyebrows at him. Andrew gave him a dark look in return. He opened his mouth to respond, but the faint sound of knocking caught their attention.

Adam brightened. "Must be Symoné."

Not quite in the mood to swim or to watch the girls, Andrew followed him into the house to greet the incoming guests.

Rushing inside, Adam opened the door swiftly with a smile. "*Mi casa es su casa*! Welcome to my humble abode." He bowed with his hand outstretched. Andrew stood to the side against the stair banister, arms folded, shaking his head in amusement.

"Oh, get a grip, Adam! This isn't even your home," a girl with a ruby-red, pixie hair cut answered as she shoved her way inside. She blew past Andrew so fast he didn't even have time to give her a proper greeting.

"Don't worry about Dixie. She's just mad because I forced her to come," Symoné West said as she leaned in to kiss Adam.

"Uh, hello? I'm still here. I can hear everything you just said," Dixie snapped as she came back to the couple by the door. She turned away from their PDA with a huff.

Snickering behind her hand, Symoné shook her head at her cousin. "Lighten up, you need the vacation more than anyone after taking care of Grandpa."

With another huff, Dixie walked away from the couple, disappearing out back, an angry scowl on her face.

"That girl is going to be the death of me." Turning to Andrew, Symoné stuck out her hand with a friendly smile. "You must be Andrew. Adam talks about you all the time. Nice to finally meet you."

Symoné was beautiful and lengthy, having missed Andrew's six-foot stature by a few inches. Her hazel eyes complemented her dark skin well and her dark hair tumbled down her back pin-straight.

Though Adam had sent Andrew photos over the last year, Andrew had never met her, though Adam did try. However, his schedule and reluctance to return never permitted the meeting.

Andrew returned her smile and shook her hand. "Nice to meet you as well. If I knew Adam missed me that much, I would've visited a lot sooner."

Adam chuckled, "Whatever, man."

A loud splash and a screech from the back made them both jump in surprise. Adam and Symoné both looked at each other with slight amusement. "We better get outside before she kills somebody."

"You read my mind, babe," Adam replied before rushing outside, Symoné hot on his tail, leaving Andrew in their wake.

He made his way into the kitchen to get a snack and put the less-than-enthusiastic morning behind him. Out of all the houseguests, he was only concerned about one. And he was patiently waiting until she would make her presence known.

CHAPTER SEVEN

Mona

MONA TOOK A chance and glanced around the tree.

He was gone.

Sighing with relief, she cautiously made her way back to the trail. It was a close call.

The alarm had startled her, but nothing like seeing Andrew standing next to the truck as he scrambled to turn it off.

Had he seen her?

She hoped not.

Mona pulled her hair back once more and fanned herself with her free hand, though it was doing nothing to provide fresh breeze. The air stood stiff, and the sun boreholes in the pores of her glistening olive skin. It was probably going to get hotter later, much to her dismay, considering it wasn't even noon yet.

She had gotten up early to try and beat the morning heat for her routine jog, but it seemed the humidity was patiently waiting for her. Now an hour later, she was deciding on her next course of action.

To stay or not to stay? Her only option seemed to be going back to the cabin where her past was waiting for her.

Mona reluctantly headed back. Her headphones continued to blare her routine workout music in her ear as she walked the short distance. If she was honest with herself, she desperately needed the distraction to calm her nerves.

Throughout the night, her mind had wandered. She found herself revisiting her time with Calvin, her life before her father's untimely demise, and more importantly, the friendship she lost and the inevitable meet up. She understood the trip as a means to get her mind off things, but that would be a lot easier said than done, especially with Andrew's presence.

Checking her phone, she saw that she had a text from Nina asking where she was. But instead of answering she turned the screen off and stuck her phone back in her pocket.

She mentally beat herself up for not preparing for the prospect of seeing him. She hadn't seen him since the funeral, and even then, they had not particularly spoken. By the time he had expressed his condolences, he was nowhere to be seen or heard from. She found herself wondering if she had imagined the entire thing and the longing for his embrace thereafter.

She knew she wasn't ready to face her mistakes or Andrew. She wasn't prepared for the memories. She wasn't ready to forgive herself for her part in the demise of their friendship. She wasn't even sure if she was ready to move past their current state. If she were strong enough to let him back in after his departure wouldn't be because of him but because of her.

She had become comfortable in her bubble. She wasn't sure how having him back in her life would affect her, however brief it may be.

Maybe coming to the cabin was a bad idea. She thought about chickening out and heading home.

Shaking the thoughts from her head, Mona stopped just short of the end of the trial, willing her nerves to calm down. She needed to get it together.

Eyeing the truck warily as she neared it in the driveway, she hesitated up the steps and took a deep breath, dramatically squeezing her eyes shut before opening the door.

The cabin was rather quiet, but she could hear laughter coming from the pool area in the back. Relief settled in as she realized no one was inside, or at least not downstairs. She made her way to the stairs only to see Nina coming down in her slightly wet swimsuit.

"What took you so long? I was starting to think you got lost."

Mona shrugged. "The trail was good. I figured I would run a little longer before coming back. Did you just come from the pool? I might take a dip myself."

Nina tugged at her hair nervously, "Y-Yeah, we have some visitors as well. Look, don't get mad or anything, but—"

"—Andrew's here," Mona interjected.

Nina could only nod. "You're not surprised," she stated.

Mona didn't bother to tell her about seeing him during her run. There seemed to be no point as she was sure to see him soon anyway.

Although she felt confident that Nina was convinced of her nonchalant attitude, she still wasn't quite sure how she would approach the situation when it came to a head. Now she found herself wondering if she should isolate herself in her room until she felt more prepared.

Nina offered a sad smile. "I already warned him…"

"No need. We're adults. I can handle this."

Nina approached closer and hugged her best friend. "If you say so. I have your back either way. If he bothers you, let me know. I'll set him straight, I swear."

Mona snickered lightly. "I don't think we need to hear you two arguing for the duration of this trip. That would be just as bad as hearing you and Adam fight. I'm pretty sure we came here for a *quiet* getaway."

Nina pulled back from her and lightly punched her shoulder. "I should just leave you two alone and have you guys work out your issues if I didn't think that would end with a potential house fire and a murder."

More like she would self-destruct, but Nina didn't need to know that.

Mona rolled her eyes as she stepped past Nina to head up the stairs. Nina followed close behind despite just coming from that same direction.

"Are you really coming to the pool? You know he's down there with his girlfriend."

"Girlfriend?" Mona pivoted as she reached her room door. With her back to Nina, Mona hoped Nina couldn't see the frown that marred her face. It was stupid to think that he wouldn't bring someone, but she didn't like the unease settling at the base of her stomach over the mention of a girlfriend. Fighting it off, she pretended as if the thought did not deter her in the slightest.

"Yeah, his plus one, I guess. Adam's girlfriend, Symoné, and her cousin, Dixie, are also here. As far as I'm concerned, we're the only ones staying here. I met her at the pool... well, actually earlier than that, but you get what I mean."

Mona nodded in agreement, pulling out her favorite white halter bikini and laid it out on her bed. It was a bit revealing but not out of taste. She could've opted for the one-piece she had brought as back up, but she decided against it.

"Are you sure you're ready to go down there so fast?"

The question caught Mona off guard. She stopped what she was doing and looked at Nina questionably. "What do you mean? To face Andrew? Why do I get the feeling you don't want me downstairs?" Truth be told, she didn't want to go anywhere, but she needed to act normal regardless.

"No! That's not it, Mona. It's just... this is the first time we're all going to hang out in two years. I know what him not being around has done to you and not counting the time at the funeral, I don't think you guys would call each other friends right now. I just want to make sure you're okay mentally before you jump the gun. It's a big step you're taking."

Mona considered Nina's explanation. Everything she said was true. What may seem like a simple task to someone else, Mona found to be painful. She was on the fence if she should even greet him, although it would be the polite thing to do. It wasn't like he was a long-time acquaintance. This was some-one who knew every detail of her life. Or used to.

How do you approach someone you don't have good standing with anymore but knows how to read you like a book?

Mona offered Nina a reassuring smile despite the ongoing battle in her heart. "Nina, I can do this."

Nina returned her smile and walked to the bed, picking up the swimsuit Mona had just laid out. "Then let's do it!"

Mona quickly threw on her swimsuit and pulled a blue see-through beach dress over it. She left her hair in a bundle on top of her head, figuring it was best to keep it out of her face. Throwing on a pair of flip flops, she and Nina headed downstairs.

"I need to get something to eat before I step outside. I worked up quite an appetite," Mona said.

"Sure, I'll wait for you out back by the door. Just come out when you are finished."

Making her way to the kitchen, Mona rapidly fixed a tur-key sandwich for herself. She devoured it at the counter before cleaning up. As she turned to head outside, someone slammed into her causing her to painfully bump the counter.

"Oh, I am so sorry!"

Briefly accessing the woman that crashed into her, she hissed at the throbbing at her elbow. Examining it, she's noticed her elbow had a small but painful gash.

"I can clean that up for you."

Mona waved it off, fully turning to the girl. "It's fine. It's just a scrape."

A scrap with one hell of a sting, she thought.

"I don't think we've met. I'm Dixie, Symoné's cousin." Dixie held out her hand, which Mona politely shook.

"Mona. Adam's friend. It's nice to meet you."

"You should come out back, everyone is here, and the water is nice and cool," Dixie suggested. She made her way to the fridge and pulled out two Fanta soda bottles.

Taking in Dixie's one-piece swimsuit, her wet pixie, and the pool of water that began to form at her feet, Mona guessed that's where she'd come from. She was about to respond when she was interrupted by Adam coming from the backdoor.

"Finally!" Adam said as he spread out his arms dramatically and closed his eyes, relinquishing the air conditioning. "It's freakin' hot out there!"

Dixie snickered from beside her as she opened one of the Fanta bottles. "It's not that hot outside, Adam. You're so dramatic."

Opening one eye, he opened his mouth to respond but smiled when his gaze swerved to Mona. "Mona! You made it back. I thought we lost you for a minute there."

Mona watched in amusement as he barreled over to embrace her in a firm hug. "Adam, you're squeezing too tight," she managed to get out. Finally letting go, he stood back with a gleam in his eye.

"Why are you looking at me like that?" she asked curiously. Adam was obviously up to no good.

"You need to come outside, like, right now," Adam urged.

"Adam, let her be," Dixie answered for her.

Adam groaned. Ignoring him, Mona turned her back to him to rummage through the fridge for a cold beer.

"Come on! You've wasted enough time stalling. Hurry up!" Mona rolled her eyes as she searched for a bottle opener. There was no rush to go outside, and Adam wasn't going to make her, either.

Dixie giggled beside her. "He sure is annoying. How do you deal with him daily?"

Finally finding the bottle opener, she popped the top and tipped the beer back, taking long gulps. The cold liquid tingled her throat as it slid down but felt right for the warmth that spread throughout her body. She didn't turn back around as Dixie and Adam began to fuss at each other though she was glad the attention was off her. It seemed no matter who he was around, Adam could always find someone to argue with.

The sound of the backdoor opening caught her attention. She turned slightly to see if Nina had decided to get her, but quietly gasped when she saw Andrew instead. His face was in his phone, but he wasn't hard to miss.

With eyebrows furrowed and his fingers rapidly tapping his phone screen, he was oblivious to her silent assessment. His hair was dry, and his ever-present black-rimmed glasses were perched on his face meaning he most likely had not been in the pool yet. He had on a different outfit than when she saw him outside. Instead of pants, he had swapped for a pair of red swimming trunks and a white t-shirt that accentuated his toned body.

He seemed slightly more built than when she saw him

last—not counting the funeral as she barely had time to assess his presence. His hair was somewhat shorter, but his brown curls still made her want to run her fingers through them.

Mona mentally kicked herself out of her trance. She turned back around as he got closer to Adam, instead, busying herself by reading the nutrition facts on her beer bottle though it was more a passing thought at that point. Taking one last swig of her beer, she noticed her hands trembled as he began to speak.

"It's funny how you asked me if I wanted a drink ten minutes ago, and I have yet to see it," Andrew interrupted Adam and Dixie's bickering with his face still in his phone.

Hearing his voice made her stomach knot. She was suddenly thankful Dixie was partially blocking her view so she couldn't turn around and see him like before.

"I'm pretty sure Adam's attention span lasts less than that. I've only known him for a few weeks, and I've already come to that conclusion," Dixie said.

Andrew chuckled a little. Mona nervously fiddled with the bottle of beer in her hand. There was no escaping this, she knew.

Adam scoffed, "I'm offended. I'm sure there are some people who wouldn't feel that way, right Moe?"

As if right on cue, Mona turned to Adam with a glare. He used her nickname on purpose. No one ever called her "Moe" except the man standing in front of her with alarm clearly written on his face, his phone long forgotten and limp in his hand. Her eyes slid past Adam to Andrew, his own penetrating hers for what felt like forever.

Even before, it was always difficult to look away when his eyes captured her. He had a way of looking at her as if he were staring at her soul and could read every thought, every secret she kept hidden. His deep green orbs have been able to turn women into putty, including herself, though she kept that to herself for years.

Mona wasn't sure how long they stood there, but it wasn't until Adam spoke that she was able to rip her eyes away from him.

"Anyway, since you're here now, you might as well get your own drink. Dixie, I think I hear Symoné calling you."

"I don't hear anything..."

The smirk on Adam's face had her glaring daggers at his retreating back as he dragged a perplexed Dixie out the backdoor.

That bastard.

Tension quickly engulfed them as they stood there in awkward silence. She refused to look at him, but she could feel his eyes on her. It was a feeling that made her skin burn but at the same time, made her stomach flutter.

The silence must've nagged him because he cleared his throat, asking, "You've been okay?"

That simple question held impeccable weight. There were so many ways she could answer that question. There were many references in which it could apply.

She was anything but, especially with him still occasionally glancing in her direction. She was having a fight or flight moment. There was no possible way she could stand there and pretend to exchange pleasantries. Being polite was one thing. Having a conversation with a familiar stranger was another.

Mona could only nod and hope he saw her because she didn't trust her voice nor her actions.

"Good," he said quietly. He struggled to find his next words. "Moe, I—"

The sound of her nickname jolted her core. She had to get out *now*. Interrupting him, she trembled, "I-I should find Nina. She's probably looking for me."

Still not meeting his gaze, she quickly brushed past him and out the back door, leaving him standing in the kitchen confuddled and struggling to find new grounds.

She chose flight.

Eventually finding Nina, Mona did her best to steer clear of Andrew for the remainder of the day. Nina had bombarded her with questions about her brief absence when she finally made it to the poolside. She vaguely described the Adam incident but left out her encounter with Andrew completely. Knowing the concerns Nina already had, she was reluctant to increase her interest in the subject.

Mona lounged on one of the pool chairs in a forgotten section of the pool. She watched as everyone mingled and laughed. Nina eventually left her company to swim laps in the water as she and Dixie became acquainted. Adam and Symoné were dancing to some salsa music that was blaring through his phone.

A woman whom she assumed was Andrew's girlfriend

was also lounging on one of the pool stairs near her. With her sunglasses on, she perched her head back as her hair swayed behind her. She had yet to officially meet this woman, but she was apprehensive about doing so for whatever reason.

Her black and white bikini hugged her like a Victoria Secret model. No hair could be spotted on any part of her body, with the exception of her blonde curls. Her skin was smooth and nicely tanned. Her lips were full and naturally pink. She was the type of beauty Mona would expect to find on the cover of a magazine.

Typical for Andrew. He could get anyone he wanted with his handsome looks. It was no wonder he would find someone on his caliber.

"Cassie, I got you a beer. I think Dixie left it inside earlier," Mona faintly heard.

Mona froze as Andrew approached where "Cassie" was lounging. This was the first time she'd seen him since their brief exchange in the kitchen.

Lost in thought, she couldn't hear the rest of their conversation, instead opting to secretly study them together.

Mona watched as he laughed at something Cassie said, his voice deep and rich. Her heart ached at the memories of that same laughter being directed at her. She managed to look away.

She hated feeling so vulnerable in his presence. Back then, it was never an issue. In fact, she was only ever fully capable of being herself around him. The need to run from him was never an option. She had always felt safer in his company like no other. But even with her choice to run, she couldn't understand this feeling of nostalgia that overpowered her.

Feeling like she was being watched, she looked up again and was shocked to find him watching her. Their eyes met in a standoff, neither willing to look away. This was the closest she had gotten to a real conversation with him in over two years. Green clashed with gray as they assessed each other from afar. Her breathing became hitched and cluttered with nerves, she unconsciously rubbed the back of her neck, his eyes following her every movement.

But their silent communication was over as fast as it began when Dixie splashed into the water, sending a wave of water on both Cassie and Andrew. Mona smiled as they all began to bicker about it, Adam soon jumping in the water with the same grace.

Andrew shook his head, chuckling. The dimples in his cheeks appeared, something Mona used to love to look at. His eyes slid over to hers again, offering her a small but meaningful smile. He looked away before she could respond with her own if she had ever planned to.

She released the breath she didn't know she was holding. Deciding to busy herself and keep her mind off him, she headed to the jacuzzi area far, far away from the group.

This was going to be a *long* vacation.

Chapter Eight

Andrew

THE CABIN STOOD silent. Not even the snores of his fellow cabin mates escaped through the walls. It had been some time since coming back upstairs after getting a drink, but Andrew couldn't seem to catch that same drift as he had. His mind raced with thoughts, some haunting, some joyous, but all involving Mona.

Looking over at Cassidy's sleeping form, Andrew eased out of bed, careful not make a sound. He walked over to a pair of trousers hanging on the back of the chair, sliding out his hidden pack of cigarettes and a lighter before leaving the bedroom.

He tipped down the stairs and out the back door, lighting his cigarette and taking his first draw under the stars. It was weird listening to crickets communicating through an otherwise silent night. Most nights, he spent time at the restaurant under the bustling orders of hungry customers, pleasing the unpleasant.

Andrew rotated his shoulders and took another draw. His

mind replayed back to the events that happened the day before. As much as he tried not to think of her, his mind always seemed to trace back to Mona.

Glancing briefly at her yesterday, he could still see traces of sadness and confliction in her eyes, although she did her best to mask it. He could always read her emotions. He remembered once telling her she wore her emotions in her eyes.

She'd hated that.

He wasn't sure what to say to her, what would be appropriate. After two years of zero conversation, it was like starting back at the beginning, but with open wounds.

Their encounter in the kitchen had left him reeling. He was unaware she had been in the kitchen when he got in. After waiting several minutes for the drink Adam had offered, he had decided to find it himself. He was still under the impression she was on her jog. But seeing her in the kitchen left his stomach in knots.

He'd be lying if he didn't acknowledge the sadness that overcame him with the thought that this was their new normal. Back then, they wouldn't have hesitated to jump into the conversation, relinquishing their days and current issues. He smiled weakly, thinking about the first time they had met in grade school.

From that moment, he knew he'd found a friend. An everlasting best friend. All the teasing in the world couldn't take that away from him. He knew that her friendship was enough for him, and that's all that mattered even now with the prospects of them never being close again.

Andrew shook his head and threw his finished cigarette to the ground. He stomped on the bud, defusing the remaining flare. He reveled in the silence for a few moments before lighting another.

"Can't sleep?"

Andrew jumped. He hadn't heard anyone approach. Adam had come to stand next to him, a beer in hand.

"Do *you* ever sleep?"

Adam chuckled. "I have too much energy. I figured I'd use it doing something productive."

"Kinda like getting all of us here for a cabin stay that's sure to end in disaster?"

Adam shrugged his shoulders. "I want my time here to be memorable."

Andrew turned to Adam with wide eyes. "You're not dying on me, are you?"

Adam threw his head back in a hearty laugh. "No! Is it so hard to believe I actually miss having my friends around? *Together*?"

Adam looked at Andrew pointedly. Guilt coursed through Andrew knowing he was partly responsible for the rift. Turning his attention back to the dark sky, Andrew sighed. "I'm sorry."

"I mean, I get it. I don't expect things to be back to normal, but I want to feel like things are normal for once."

A comfortable silence engulfed them for a moment.

"I know what you were trying to do in the kitchen," Andrew muttered.

"And?" Adam pressed.

Andrew shook his head. "'And' nothing."

Adam frowned. "Did you guys say anything to each other? Or did you both just stare at one another the entire time?"

Andrew turned to him with a frown. "What do you mean?"

"Never mind. Look, I'm not going to try and pit you guys together, but I'd—no, *we'd*—appreciate it if you two could at least try and tolerate each other for the sake of everyone else in the cabin."

"I'm not here to fight with her. I'm pretty sure she doesn't even want to talk to me much less argue."

Adam sighed. "I just wish..." he trailed off.

Andrew nodded silently wishing the same as he could already guess what Adam was thinking. "Yeah, me too."

Adam shuffled back to the door but turned before getting inside. "You guys are important to me, more than anything. Like family. And family shouldn't fight. Both of you just need to find out how to trust each other again. I'll be at the court later if you need me."

Adam disappeared through the door, leaving Andrew to drown in his thoughts.

It was already close to dawn, and Andrew honestly didn't have a wink of sleep in him. Figuring he could work off the tension he was feeling, he decided to head to the basketball court after Adam. Trudging back up the steps, he slipped back into the room, quietly pulling out a pair of basketball shorts and a white t-shirt to change into.

"Where are you going?" Cassidy croaked, sitting up and

rubbing her eyes.

"Heading out to the court. You should go back to sleep."

"Why so early? Come back to bed," she said drowsily.

Without turning to her, he replied, "Can't. I'll be back in a little bit."

He finished tying his sneakers and left without another word.

Adam hadn't made it to the court by the time Andrew got there. Finding a basketball nearby, Andrew spent the next hour shooting hoops as the sun filtered the sky. By then, he had lost his t-shirt from the increasing heat. The sound of crunching gravel caught his attention as he threw one last basket.

"You started without me!" Adam exclaimed with an accusatory hand pointing at the basketball in Andrew's hand.

"I didn't know I had to consult you," Andrew returned, throwing the ball into the basket for a perfect shot. "You weren't out here."

"I got caught up."

"In what?"

Adam wiggled his eyebrows. "Wouldn't you like to know?"

Andrew looked at him in disgust. "TMI. Everyone up?"

"Yeah. They're fighting over who cooks breakfast or not. I had to get out of there!"

Andrew shook his head with a chuckle.

Adam beckoned to the cabin. "She's up, you know."

Looking to the cabin, Andrew's frown deepened. "Cassidy? Yeah, I know. I spoke to her before I left the room."

"No, I'm talking about Mona, dummy."

Andrew stared at Adam while trying to keep his face neutral. "And?"

Adam looked at him in disbelief. "What do you mean 'And?'" This is your opportunity to talk. Come on, man. You guys can't ignore each other forever."

Though he knew Adam was right, he still didn't want to discuss his issues with Mona with him. It wasn't like he wanted to ignore her. He just knew that anything he said would probably come off wrong or distasteful.

Nevertheless, Andrew nodded his head to appease his friend, putting his shirt back on and started toward the cabin though he had no intention of confronting anyone so early.

Adam walked ahead of him into the cabin where everyone was assembled in the kitchen, arguing.

"That's a stupid idea!"

"Well, I don't see anyone else coming up with a better one."

"Guys, I can't cook—"

"I guess everyone will be getting sandwiches then..."

"Guys!" Adam yelled, catching everyone's attention. "All in favor of Andrew cooking for the week, raise your hand."

All hands raised in the air faster than Andrew could react to Adam suggesting the idea.

Adam clasped a hand on Andrew's shoulder, who stood stiff with his mouth agape. With a teasing smile, Adam said, "Problem solved."

"You set me up..." Andrew watched as everyone excitedly left the kitchen in favor of his cooking. He caught Mona's eye briefly as she left giggling.

"I like my eggs scrambled," Adam yelled as he headed back out the door with the basketball in his hands. With a heavy sigh, Andrew got to work doing what he did best.

Chapter Nine

Mona

THE SUN WAS blazing again, much to her chagrin, but Mona was determined to make the best of her day outdoors. She wasn't ready to bump into Andrew yet and it was sure to happen at some point as he was on kitchen duty for the next couple of days. She was startled by the fact that he was up already playing basketball on the court when she awoke earlier that morning.

Mona had eaten a morning snack, secretly watching as he dominated the court, something she was privy to seeing once before. Back in high school, they had played together after school. He had taught her in middle school how to play so they could connect more. After a few moments of admiring his uncharted skill, she had raced into the kitchen so she wouldn't get caught.

Now sitting outside, she wasn't entirely sure what to make of his presence there, especially with his girlfriend. Cassidy was most certainly his type if his past girlfriends were any indication of one. Leggy, beautiful, and blond but with intelligence. He couldn't stand dating a girl who couldn't keep up in conversation, he had once said to her.

Having not introduced herself fully yet, Mona wasn't sure what Cassidy was like. According to Nina, they had gotten off on the wrong foot, but eventually, Cassidy had evened out. Mona wondered if Andrew had mentioned her to Cassidy.

Mona ultimately planned to ignore him for the duration of the stay if she could help it. Late in bed, she convinced herself no amount of apology would change anything. There was nothing left to say. All of that was said and done two years ago. She'd be a fool to think there was anything left to salvage. Once Andrew departed the cabin, she likely would never see him again if it didn't regard Adam or Nina.

"This seat occupied?"

Mona looked up to find Cassidy standing before her. Looking to her right at the empty lawn chair, she secretly wished it was occupied. With a slight frown, Mona murmured "no" and went back to reading the book she had been pretending to read.

While she was sure Cassidy was a nice girl, she wasn't up for conversation. Not with her anyway. Shady but, she didn't care.

"If this is where you all used to spend summer vacation, you guys are so lucky. All I ever did during the summer was babysit," Cassidy said, scrounging up her nose.

Mona, not sure how to respond, nodded but never took her eyes off the page. Cassidy glanced at her through the corner of her eyes with a frown of her own.

"I never did get your name. I'm Cassidy, Andrew's girl-friend," Cassidy said eagerly. Sticking out her hand, Mona looked at her and then her perfectly manicured fingers. Hesitantly, she responded to her handshake and offered a weak smile.

"Mona."

"Mona... that's a pretty name," Cassidy said carefully. Briefly scanning Cassidy's face, Mona was taken aback by the frown that had now deepened.

Did she not like the name? Mona couldn't help but think.

Before she could interpret the look further, she spied Andrew heading their way. Knowing who he was coming for, she stuffed her face back into the book.

"Hey, Cass," he said. "Breakfast is on the table. Everyone is already inside."

There was a moment of silence before Cassidy answered with a meek "okay" and left, the sound of shuffling footsteps moving further away. Mentally thanking him for creating an opportunity of isolation, she finally looked up but was startled when she saw Andrew still standing in front of her lawn chair.

His green eyes held little emotion, but he continued staring at her for a moment too long before he cleared his throat and scratched the back of his neck.

"I put your food aside. I wasn't sure if you wanted to eat right now since you were... busy."

More like busy avoiding him, she thought.

Mona slowly nodded at him, her heart rate picking up speed. A soft look passed through his eyes before he turned and slowly began walking back to the kitchen.

"T-Thank you," she called out, cursing herself for stuttering. He didn't turn back around but instead nodded and proceeded back to the cabin.

That wasn't awkward, she thought. Flipping the page, she got back to reading what little she could take in. The breakfast would have to wait.

***

"I SAY WE do a movie marathon tonight."

Mona made up her face in disgust. She brushed through her tangled brown curls, wincing when she dragged the brush through a stubborn knot.

Nina flopped on the made bed and played with her phone. "Oh, come on! I think it'll be a cute bonding experience, don't you?"

"What bonding experience do we need? We all know each other. Besides, it's not like we're going to be watching it anyway. With all the couples here, I'm pretty sure there will be less watching and more smooching."

Nina snorted. "Smooching? Who says that anymore? And there are only two couples here: Adam and Symoné and Andrew and his girlfriend, Cathy."

"It's Cassidy."

Nina waved her off. "Same difference."

Nina got off the bed and approached Mona as she finished brushing her hair and tying it into a high ponytail. "You're not worried about Andrew and his girlfriend, are you?"

Mona rolled her eyes. "What for? It's not like we talk, and he can do whatever the hell he wants. I don't care."

"Are you sure about that?"

Mona frowned at her best friend, wondering what she was getting at. "I'm sure."

The smirk Nina wore slowly slipped off her face. "You guys need to hurry up and hash out these 'secret' issues you guys refuse to talk about. It's getting annoying."

Irritation began to boil in the pit of Mona's stomach. She would talk to Andrew when she's ready, if ever. "It has nothing to do with you, Adam, or anyone else. Stay out of it. I'll approach the situation when I'm ready. We just got here."

"I know you miss him, Mona. You're not fooling anyone. You've been moping since he's got here," Nina pointed out.

Mona stepped to Nina, her eyes blazing with anger. "Then don't hang around me if bothers you so much. What happened to supporting my decisions? Not too long ago, you wanted me to take my time."

"I'm just trying to help..."

"I don't need it. If I did, I would've asked," Mona hissed.

Taken aback, Nina decided to leave the room without another word, slamming the door on her way out. Mona stood rooted in the same spot. It hasn't been a good thirty-six hours since she's settled into the cabin and already, she was losing her mind. Frustrated, she yanked her door open to apologize to Nina for her outburst but bumped straight into Symoné.

"You okay?"

"Peachy," Mona grumbled. She cringed at her tone and immediately felt guilty. "I'm sorry."

Symoné shrugged with a smile, making Mona feel even more guilty. "It's fine. Really. But more importantly, are you okay? You seem pretty angry."

Mona sighed with resolve. "It's nothing. I'll be fine."

"If you say so..."

Mona left a confused Symoné standing in her wake as she trudged down the stairs. The busying noise and laughter surrounded the common area as she reached the bottom of the steps.

Quietly, she shifted towards the door, making sure not to bring attention to herself as she eased her way out of the cabin.

The sun was just beginning to set painting an orange hue in the sky. Looking at the trail she had jogged not too long ago, Mona debated whether to take a long trek through the woods again.

A minute was all it took to make up her mind as she started on her usual morning path. The calming chirp of birds and vibration of crickets keep her mind at bay as the setting sun illuminated her path.

She was never afraid of the woods, partly because most of her fond memories were spent exploring them as a youth. It was like being one with nature. Coexisting with the animals and insects that inhabited a place most wouldn't find solace in. It was her time to find solitary between the trees.

Roaming around for quite some time as she cleared her

mind and refocused her emotions, Mona hadn't realized she had gone off-trail into an unknown area. The night sky was vastly approaching but she was still able to see around and far enough to feel safe. She analyzed her area to find a way back on track but paused when she noticed a clearing. Squinting, she could see a small structure ahead between the trees.

The snap of a twig caught her attention as she swung around in fright. Surveying the trees behind her, she stood frozen to hear it again. It sounded rather close. The small crunch of the leaves nearby was enough to get her to step back. Her skin began to crawl as the feeling of being watched tickled her skin, causing the hair on her arms to stand in alert.

"Get a grip," Mona chastised herself.

Mona shook her head in dismissal. It was likely just her imagination. Hunter's Creek was one the safest place she'd known. No one had access to the trail besides them. There was nothing to worry about, or so she thought as she refocused her eyes on the cabin in the clearing, unaware of the pair of eyes that followed her every move from beyond the trees.

She quietly made her way to the opening where the small cabin stood idly. A dark green pickup truck was parked along the makeshift dirt driveway. Lights illuminated the cabin against the darkening sky. All around it was vast land. It looked quiet and cozy—a place she could see herself being at peace.

Mona wasn't sure how long she stood there deep in thought, but she was startled when the front door swung open. A tall man stepped out with a basket of laundry in his hands.

He was slender and looked to be about Mona's age from where she stood, if not a bit older.

His dark shaggy hair was pulled back with a black bandana around the front of his head. Mona stood there, observing as he placed the small basket into the bed of his truck. With his back to her, she watched as he secured the basket near an open space in the back of the truck.

He hadn't glanced in her direction since he had made it outside. Mona had figured this was her time to escape. Stepping back, her foot caught a root causing her to fall back on her behind. The sound her crashing onto fallen leaves made the man turn around in alarm.

Rushing to her side, he extended a hand, which she accepted, and helped her up. "Are you okay?"

Mona dusted off her pants before facing him. "Yes. Thank you."

Her face heated with shame when she noticed he was staring at her curiously. "I-I wasn't spying for anything. I was just going for a walk and ended up here. I'm so sorry—"

"It's quite alright. Honestly," he assured with a smile. Although a stranger, he wasn't giving her creepy vibes despite their unusual meeting.

He stuck out his hand. "My name is James, by the way."

"I'm Mona," she answered as she took his hand.

"You live around here? If you don't mind me asking?"

She nodded. "Well, for the time being."

James nodded. He looked up at the darkening sky. "Do you need a ride back to your place? It's getting awfully dark.

I don't think I'd forgive myself for letting you walk back by yourself."

Mona hesitated. He seemed friendly but did she trust him enough to make him any wiser about where she'll be staying?

James must have been reading her facial expressions because he spoke up before she could give a final answer.

"I promise I won't try anything. I'm assuming your cabin is close by? It'll be a quick drop. I just... I don't feel comfortable leaving you out here in the dark. Especially in the woods. Close or not."

Mona weighed her options. The night had already begun to settle and finding her way through the woods was obviously not an option. But she also did not want to inconvenience him.

"Y-yeah, I guess you can drop me off, but only I'm not out of your way."

"Nonsense. Follow me." He led her to the pickup and opened the passenger door. She thanked him as she settled into the leather seat before he closed the door.

He got into the driver's seat and started the truck but didn't move immediately. "So, if you don't mind me asking, what brought you to my cabin anyway?"

"Just needed to clear my head. I was sort of wandering."

He chuckled. "Someone must've really pissed you off for you to walk in the woods so late." He pulled out into the main road.

"Where to?"

Mona pointed west. "Just around the bend about two miles up."

James turned to her in surprised. "You're not in that renovated cabin, are you?"

Mona nodded cautiously. "Yes, in fact. I am."

His dark eyes brightened. "Oh! So, you're friends with Adam."

"Yeah. How do you know Adam?"

James smiled as he headed west. "We go way back, actually. My parents are friends with his. We used to hang whenever they met up, though not often."

Mona felt more relaxed with that information.

"Wow, he's never mentioned you before," Mona said.

"No, I suppose he wouldn't have. We were more like acquaintances than friends, to be honest."

"Oh." A comfortable silence engulfed them before he spoke again.

"Not to pry, but he wasn't the one to make you angry, was he?"

Mona shook her head. "No, Adam's a sweetheart. He's annoying at times but a great friend. He's like a pesky younger–older brother. It's just... hard being in that cabin with everyone."

"People you don't like?"

Mona sighed but didn't elaborate. Looking out the window, she could see the cabin in the distance.

"Look," James began, "I know you don't know me very well, but if you want to talk, I'm here. You look like you have a lot on your chest."

He pulled up into the driveway, cut the engine, but made

no move, and neither did she. She rested her elbow on the door and leaned her head back.

Mona couldn't help but smile. He barely even knew her, yet he was offering something she couldn't get with her own friends. Something about him seemed genuine, and it made her want to spill her guts.

"It would be easier if you ask the questions," Mona started. "I'm not even sure where to start."

James shook his head a grin. "Ok, sure." He pondered a bit before continuing, "So how do you know everyone in the cabin?"

She turned to him, her eyebrows furrowed. "That wasn't the question I was expecting."

James shrugged. "Gotta ease my way to the problem. Sometimes it's nice to know the back story."

She nodded before answering his question. "Aside from Symoné, Adam's girlfriend, and Dixie, her cousin, I've known everyone else since grade school."

"Who did you meet first?"

She opened her mouth and then closed it.

James lifted an eyebrow. "I guess I found the problem already."

Mona smiled. "Andrew. I met Andrew first."

"Andrew... that name sounds familiar," James pondered.

"Adam's best friend."

"Ah."

James continued to press. "So, you met Andrew first, then probably Adam," he stated. Mona nodded in agreement. "Who are you closer to?"

"My other best-friend Nina," she half-lied. Technically, she was closer to Nina now. Back then, it was Andrew.

James nodded. "You're lucky. I never got to grow up with so many friends."

"Why is that?" She asked, genuinely curious.

James scrunched his nose. "My dad was in the Navy, so we moved a lot to be closer to him on the naval bases until he was discharged. The hardest part was always leaving good friends behind. It was hard keeping up with relationships the farther I got."

"That must have been hard for you. I lived in the same house since the day I was born. I wish I traveled like you have."

James shook his head. "Trust me, it's not all it's cracked up to be. You can only deal with new faces for so long."

"So, where is your dad stationed now?"

James clenched his jaw, a dark look passing over his eyes. "He passed several years ago."

Mona began to backtrack immediately, thinking she had overstepped her boundaries. "Oh! I'm sorry. I shouldn't have asked."

"It's okay. Really. I've been pounding you for personal info; it's only fair I share a few of my own." James said, giving her a sad smile. "He died a couple years ago. It was a few days before my graduation from high school, actually. He had come home on a quick leave to see my mom since she was pregnant at the time. On his way home the day he was supposed to go back, someone had broken into the house—"

James cleared his throat, obviously having a hard time finding his words. Mona could understand completely.

"You don't have to explain, James," she pleaded. She was feeling bad or turning the focus to him.

Shaking his head, he said, "No, I don't have to. But I want to."

He continued. "Someone had broken into the house while my mom and I were gone. She was at work, and I was at school. My dad was back at the house packing to leave. They held him at knifepoint as they took everything they could get out. He could've taken them on. I mean, my dad was big. But he didn't because they were just kids. So, he let them take whatever they wanted, figuring they would leave him alone if he didn't fight. Plus, he was already outnumbered five-to-one.

"But I guess they wanted more than just the valuables. They had something to prove. Apparently, he had tried to talk them out of robbing him. He was allowing them to walk away. They let him believe they were going to turn themselves in. And when he let his guard down, two of them stabbed my dad fifteen times before they left."

Mona stayed quiet. Letting the hard reality of his story settle. "I came home and found him on the floor, bleeding out and choking on his own blood. He was fighting it. He was fighting so hard," he whispered the last part and blinked a couple times to hold back a tear.

"He died later that night after an unsuccessful surgery. He had lost too much blood. After years—decades of spending time at war, serving his country, he leaves just to be killed in his own home by a bunch of wannabe thugs? It's so unfair."

Mona blinked away tears she hadn't known were threatening to leak from her eyes. Hearing his story made her feel so ungrateful for not being able to keep herself together after her father died six months ago. At least her father died peacefully.

James continued. "My mom almost lost the baby because of the stress. Thankfully, Elijah made it through. But it was hard trying to be the man of the house in just a day. I couldn't even cry. I just wanted to make sure my mom was okay because at that point, she and Elijah were all I had left, and I couldn't leave her. I needed her as much as she needed me."

He frowned when he saw the look of distress on Mona's face. "Hey, I didn't mean to make you sad. I just felt the need to, I don't know, talk about it. I've never opened up about it before," he said with a shrug. "It feels good to vent."

"I'm sorry," Mona began. "You're so brave. I wouldn't know what to do. My father died recently, and I'm still trying to get used to the fact that I can't call him when I want. Like when I'm having a bad day or even now."

She hadn't expected to let that piece of information slip, but it felt good to reveal. James turned to her with a sad smile. "I guess we have something in common, as messed up as that sounds."

Mona nodded. "I guess we do."

"Ready to tell me why you've been walking in the woods all alone?"

"I don't know to act around Andrew. I'm conflicted whether I want to ignore him or to let my guard down and pretend like nothing happened between us. I'm mentally not ready to face him."

"What happened between you two?"

Mona sighed before beginning, "We stopped talking about two years ago. Things were great until I let the wrong person come between us, and I wouldn't listen to him. Eventually, he got tired of waiting for me to come around and he left. It wasn't until after he was gone that I realized how stupid and reckless I had been. He'd been my crutch for so long that I assumed no matter what he would always be there, and I messed that up, big time.

"I'm partly angry at him for leaving, but mostly angry at myself for giving him a reason to give up on me. Things won't be the same between us, and I don't know if I want to try to open my heart again or get my hopes up or risk hurting him again. I don't know if he will either. But I miss him a lot. More than I'd like to admit."

"Sounds like you need to talk to him. Whatever is going on between you two needs to be sorted out; otherwise, those feelings will turn hate. Trust me, you don't want that."

"I could never hate him," Mona muttered but James didn't seem to hear her.

"If he's willing and he really cares, he'll hear you out. From what it sounds like, there's plenty of unfinished business between you both."

The front door to the cabin opened, catching both of their attention. They were far enough away in the driveway to not see the face, but she recognized the silhouette. It was Andrew.

"Shit," she whispered.

James frowned. "Is that him?" Andrew looked around before zeroing in on the truck.

"Yeah," she muttered. "It's him."

James looked at the time on his phone. "It's getting late. They're all probably worried about you. I'd go in if I were you."

Mona nodded but didn't make a move. "Maybe you should come inside for movie night? I'm sure Adam wouldn't mine."

James laughed. "And get strangled for keeping you hostage by the other cabin mates? No thanks."

She turned to him with a smile. "Well, at least stop by for the cookout tomorrow."

James nodded. "I'll do my best. Now go, before he comes over here—uh, too late. Welp, that's my cue to leave. Good luck. It was nice to meet you."

Mona thanked James before hopping out of the truck as Andrew made his way over. She barely heard the truck starting up and peeling back. She watched intently as Andrew stalked towards her. She could practically see the stream flying out of his ears.

"Where the hell have you been? And who the hell was that?"

Mona was taken aback by his tone. This was the most emotion he showed to her since arriving at the cabin, the anger dripping from his voice. Though his tone was harsh, she understood the worry as she had left no indication of her whereabouts to anyone in the cabin. His anger was valid, but it didn't mean she had to accept it.

Stepping past him, she started towards the cabin. "I went out for a walk."

"A walk? That looked like a truck to me," he pressed, following closely behind.

"Yeah, a walk. He was nice enough to offer me a ride back since it was dark. Not that it's any of your business." She walked up the steps, but he abruptly grabbed her elbow, stopping her in her tracks. He didn't grab her hard, though the contact of his fingers wrapped around her biceps left a tingling feeling.

Andrew was less than two feet away from her face, his eyes blazing under the trajectory of the motion light of the porch lamp. As much as she wanted to, she couldn't look away. Her pulse quickened, and she prayed he couldn't feel it.

"Do you think this is a joke? You've been missing for damn near two hours, and nobody knew where you were. On top of that, you show up with a fucking stranger, and you expect me to 'mind my own business?' You had Nina about ready to have a panic attack inside."

Mona's stomach twisted in knots. He was right. "I'm sorry. I just needed to clear my head. It won't happen again."

Andrew nodded and stepped back, but Mona stood paralyzed. In a careful and gentler tone, he started, "I-I was worried. Just... please be safe."

"I promise." And she meant it.

Mona turned to step into the house but stopped short when he asked, "Who is he?"

Mona frowned, glancing at him though he turned so she

couldn't see his face in the light. Was he hiding? She couldn't tell. "Why do you want to know?"

Andrew stood silent for a moment and then shook his head. "Because..." he paused. "Never mind, let's just go inside."

"No, what is it? Something's bothering you." Mona could feel the energy change.

Andrew shook his head, whispering more to himself, "It's nothing. I'm just glad your safe."

He walked past her, opening the front door and waiting for her to step through the threshold.

They walked inside together, gathering the attention of Adam and Symoné sitting in the living room, Symoné watching him play video games. Adam wiggled his eyebrows at the two, pausing the game to give them his full undesired attention, much to Mona's chagrin.

"Mona, where'd you run off to? You had poor Andrew over here looking lost for two hours," Adam said with a grin. Symoné frowned at Adam, then looked between the two in thought.

Andrew flipped him off and headed upstairs without another word. Mona rolled her eyes and headed up after him, leaving enough space in between them. He went into his room but not before nodding at Nina's door, which was currently shut.

Mona took a deep breath and nodded as he offered a meek smile before closing his own door. She didn't immediately go in, instead, tracing the symbol on her wrist and looking back at Andrew's door.

It was weird to think that for the first time since arriving at the cabin, they actually had a real conversation even with the slight panic and edge. It felt good to know he thought about her.

She wasn't sure what to make of the fact that he was worried about her, more than he'd let on if Adam was telling the truth. With the confusion still whirling in her head, she lightly knocked on Nina's door, prepared for the worst.

Chapter Ten

Andrew

ANDREW GRABBED THE movie from out of Adam's hand. "We are not watching this stupid movie."

"Don't be a joy killer, Drew! You haven't even given it a chance!"

With a menacing look, Andrew pointed to Adam's chest. "First of all, don't ever call me Drew. Second, I know this movie sucks. I am not watching Frozen! And who carries DVDs anymore?"

"Don't knock what you don't use."

"It's the streaming era. Why upgrade the cabin but not install proper programming?"

"Because I can watch Frozen without it buffering for signal!"

"You can watch something other than that Frozen trash without buffering!"

Adam snatched the DVD out of his hands and threw it on the coffee table. "Fine, then! Let's see you come up with a better idea."

Cassidy, who had been watching the whole debacle in amusement, decided to pick for them. "How about we all just settle on some action like Transformers or a Marvel movie?"

"Whatever!" Adam sat with a pout as Cassidy pushed a Marvel movie into the DVD player.

Symoné poked Adam's side. "You're such a baby when you don't get your way."

"I have a right to be, this is my cabin."

Dixie descended from the stairs just as the movie began the previews. "Hey, where is everyone? I thought this movie night was for everyone, not just couples."

"Nina is upstairs changing, and Mona is sleeping, I think," Adam answered from the couch.

"Well, shit," Dixie murmured. "I'm going to be the third wheel."

"Just for a little while," Symoné offered.

Dixie took a seat next to Andrew on the couch, a bit too close for his comfort. She gave him a flirty smile, which he openly frowned upon. The other side of Cassidy was empty, something Dixie chose to ignore. Cassidy threw her a glare before wrapping her arms protectively around his arm.

"Who's doing the snacks? We can't have a movie night without snacks," exclaimed Symoné.

Feeling a bit suffocated, Andrew volunteered, "I'll do it."

Prying Cassidy's hands off him, he quickly escaped to the kitchen. He gathered chips and soda as well as a bowl of cheese whiz for Adam and his strange cravings. All that was left was for the bags of popcorn to finish in the microwave.

He stood in a daze, watching the bag expand but having his mind wander to Mona for the umpteenth time that night. He didn't know why he had gone outside. He had planned to talk to her when everyone had settled down but when he couldn't find her and no one could recall her whereabouts, he panicked. And to find her in a stranger's car well after dark in the driveway just about set him off.

In the back of his mind, he urged himself to leave her alone. But his protective instinct allowed him to panic and in turn, possibly further chased her away. She had taken care of herself without his help for two years now. He lost his right to care when he left her to fend for herself. That stung more than he liked to admit.

In the years he had known Mona before, he knew that she wasn't one to easily forgive and forget. He hadn't come expecting her to welcome him with open arms. But he would be lying if he said he didn't miss the easy-going nature of their relationship. And it was all his fault.

He wanted to fix it, but it certainly wasn't going to happen overnight. He knew one thing, however; he missed his best friend, and he wasn't leaving until he mended their broken friendship.

He smiled at some of the best memories of her laughter and spark. Was he the reason that spark was now gone? He didn't doubt it one bit. He contributed among other things.

The smell of burning dragged him out of his thoughts. Realizing it was the popcorn, he rushed to remove the burned bag out the microwave.

"Shit," he said as he threw the bag away. What a waste, he thought.

"Andrew?" Cassidy came into the kitchen with alarm written on her face. "You burned the popcorn?"

He didn't answer but instead handed her the other snacks for her to carry into the living area. "Take these out to them for me, please."

Her brown eyes searched his face, registering his troubled expression. "Are you okay?"

Andrew nodded. "I'm fine. I wasn't paying attention is all."

Cassidy frowned. "I would believe you, Andrew, but you've been acting weird since we got here. What's going on?"

Andrew wanted to confide in her, but he knew she wouldn't understand. She would get jealous, start assuming things and he wasn't in the mood to argue over his past, especially when it involved Mona.

"I said I'm fine, Cassidy. Leave it alone," he replied with a harsh tone. He walked out of the kitchen, leaving her with the food, stunned by his outburst and the popcorn long forgotten.

Walking to the hall bathroom, Andrew passed Nina who looked rather down. It was so unlike her, he had to ask what was wrong.

"Hey, you good?" Nina looked at him with surprise. She was too deep in thought to even acknowledge he was even by her.

"Yeah. Fine."

Nina moved passed him without another word and into

the living room. He stared at her retreating figure with curiosity but shrugged and entered the bathroom. Staring at himself in the mirror, he took in his droopy demeanor, noting the slight irritation and confliction in his eyes. His hair looked blacker than brown as of late, possibly from working most of the time indoors. His green eyes stared back at him intensely in the mirror. He wasn't sure what he was looking for, but he wondered how Mona viewed him now.

Did she see him as an enemy? A stranger? Did she have any lingering fondness or hope for their friendship?

If she saw him in a bad light, frankly he wouldn't blame her. He let a vulnerable moment fester into a bigger problem that ruined one of the most important things in his life.

Andrew splashed some water on his face and took a deep breath. He needed to fix this soon. He hated the gnawing feeling in his chest since he got there. Shaking off the sullen sensation, he exited the bathroom and made his way back to living where everyone assembled minus Mona, he noted.

He resumed his seat next Cassidy to which she barely acknowledged his presence. A bowl of popcorn passed around the room.

"Took you long enough," Dixie whispered.

Choosing to ignore her, he focused on the movie. They went through two movies before everyone went to sleep, the only people up being Andrew and Adam.

The movie's credits rolled, and Andrew stood to stretch. The blanket that was draped over his lap fell to the floor.

Adam stood. "Should we wake them?"

"I'm taking Cassidy upstairs. She'd be mad if I left her down here. I'm not quite sure about the other two."

"Right. Maybe I should come back for Nina."

"What about Dixie?

Adam frowned. "Well, I'm not taking her up. Are you?"

"We could just wake her."

So, they did. Andrew picked up a sleeping Cassidy who snuggled closer to him as he adjusted her to get a better grip.

They both took their time carrying the girls upstairs to their room. Andrew quietly tucked Cassidy in and left the room, not quite feeling tired again. Outside, he leaned against a tree, looking up at the massive dark clouds that began to form, blocking out the crescent moon. The first raindrops hit his forehead like pellets.

Andrew sighed heavily. The weather always knew how to match his mood. He knew he should've gone back inside, but instead, he welcomed the ambush of heavy rain that followed.

He closed his eyes, feeling like he was being cleansed. Cleansed of his wrongdoings from the past and from any ill feelings that may have still lingered. He wasn't sure how long he had stood under the assault of the rain, but when he opened his eyes, he knew what he wanted to do. He was sure of it.

Tomorrow, he thought. Tomorrow things change.

***

"AH-CHOO!" ANDREW sniffed and looked at his hand in disgust.

"Baby, you're sick. Why can't you just admit that?" Cassidy probed as she handed him a tissue.

He frowned at her as he wiped his hands. "I'm not sick, Cassidy. It's just cold in here with the air conditioning on full blast."

Cassidy rolled her eyes. He even sounded stuffy. "Whatever. You need to take some medicine before it gets worse, that's all I'm saying."

"That won't be necessary considering I'm not sick, nor will I become sick. It's damn near summer outside. There's no way I can be sick."

"What were you doing outside in the rain last night, anyway? You should've come back inside."

Andrew flipped the covers off his legs and got out of bed. "Well, I was actually out jogging when the rain came down. I didn't get back in time," he lied.

Cassidy sighed and shook her head. "Kind of dumb if you ask me. Why didn't you just wait until later in the morning?"

Andrew ground his teeth in irritation. Her inquisition was starting to grate his nerves. He ignored her question and pulled off his shirt. She watched as his muscles flexed as he searched for another shirt in his drawer. Her eyes trailed to his tattoo that wrapped around his chest to his back. She licked her lips and smiled.

"Andrew?"

"Hm?" He answered without looking at her. Pulling off his night pants, he slipped on a pair of jeans and a t-shirt.

"C'mere," Cassidy demanded.

He looked up in curiosity as he finished buttoning his

jeans. "Why?"

"Just come here. Please."

Andrew cautiously walked up to where she sat on the bed. She yanked the collar of his shirt down to her level and crashed her lips to his. Surprised, he wrenched away and fixed his shirt.

"Cass, I just put this shirt on. You're going to ruin it. What was that for?" He asked a bit harsher than he anticipated.

A flash of anger appeared in her eyes. "I can't kiss my boyfriend?"

"I didn't say that. You practically ripped my shirt. If you wanted a kiss, you could've just asked. You didn't have to be so forceful about it," he asserted as he checked himself in the mirror.

She frowned as he ran his hand through his short curls. "Besides, you just said I'm catching a cold. You might catch it."

She narrowed her eyes. "I thought you didn't believe you were sick?"

Andrew shrugged his shoulders. "Look, Cassidy, I don't have time for this today. Can we not do this right now?"

"Do what? I'm not the one getting uptight for no reason."

"*This*! This game you're playing. Whatever idea you have formulated in your mind to catch me doing who-knows-what. What do you want from me?" Andrew asked angrily. He didn't quite get her game, and he certainly didn't want to be a part of it.

Cassidy got up and looked him straight in the eyes defiantly. "What is up with you lately, Andrew? You're not your-self—not since you came here. And frankly, I don't like what I'm seeing."

"Cass—"

"What is going on?" she reiterated. The determination in her eyes meant she wasn't going to give up on this conversation anytime soon.

With as much sincerity as he could muster despite his irritation, he said, "Nothing is going on. Maybe it's just the weather. Maybe I miss home. Either way, I'll be fine. I'm sorry."

Her features softened just a bit. She nodded and turned away from him. "I'm going for a swim if you need me." She grabbed her swimsuit on the bed and walked out without another word.

Andrew sighed in relief. As much as he loved Cassidy, her constant need to find something to argue about was wearing him thin. But he did admit, he had started it, though it wasn't like him to pick fights.

What was up with him?

Yawning, he turned back to the mirror and fixed his now stretched out shirt. With another unexpected sneeze, Andrew made his way outside. Adam was fixing up a small grill off the side of the patio as everyone else did their own thing. Symoné and Dixie laid under the sun, sunbathing while Nina played some music through her phone. Cassidy was already in the pool swimming from one end to another.

Andrew frowned. "Where's Mona?" He asked once he

reached Adam.

"Inside getting hot dogs and hamburger meat from the freezer in the basement." Adam looked up and cringed. "You look terrible, dude. Are you sick?"

Andrew shook his head, distracted.

"You sound a bit stuffy."

"I'm not sick!"

Adam threw up his hands in mock surrender. "Okay, no need to bite my head off."

The sliding door opened, and out came Mona and James, laughing. Andrew watched as they approached without paying much attention to where they were going. James leaned in and said something, causing her to burst out in laughter.

"Well, those two seem to be hitting it off," Adam said with a knowing smile. Andrew did his best to ignore the comment.

"Who the hell is that?" Andrew glared at them. They seemed rather comfortable together to have just met.

"That's James Lowe, his parents own the cabin just off the trail. Remember?"

No, he didn't remember, nor did he care. He didn't like how he was pushing in on Mona.

"He's the one who dropped her off at the cabin yesterday," Adam continued, eyeing his friend with knowing grin.

"We got food!" James called out before handing the packages to Adam. "Can you believe we got stuck in the basement? That door is tricky."

Mona giggled. "You were turning it wrong, James."

"You could've told me," James replied with a chuckle.

Andrew cleared his throat as the two sobered up. As if just realizing he was there, Mona's smile slowly disappeared. They locked eyes momentarily before she looked away.

James stuck his hand out to Andrew, "You must be Andrew. I'm James. I don't think we've officially met before."

Andrew eyed his hand, his eyebrows furrowed with suspicion, before hesitantly engulfing his hand in a firm shake. As much as he wanted to squeeze his grip tighter, his mother raised him better than to be sizing up strangers. Still, he offered no polite introduction.

Stepping back awkwardly and dropping his hand, James and Mona shared a look, one Andrew couldn't quite decipher, only deepening his suspicion of their acquaintance.

"Mona, you still wanted to grill these?" Adam interjected with amusement as he watched his friends.

Mona was the first to respond. "Sure."

James, who looked ready to do anything but stand in the tension, offered, "Maybe I can help—"

"I got it," Andrew blurted out without thinking.

"Uh, James, I think you can help me with something inside. I think it's best if Andrew helped her. He is a chef, after all," Adam said as he sent Andrew a knowing look.

"Yeah. Sure," James answered, following Adam to the backdoor.

As they passed, Adam whispered to Andrew, "Try not to sneeze on the food."

Andrew rolled his eyes and turned to Mona, who decided to keep herself busy by starting the fire in the grill.

She kept quiet, which was a blessing and a curse for Andrew. He couldn't explain his eagerness to be in her presence nor was he willing to. Watching her struggle with getting the grill started, Andrew picked up lighter fluid from a nearby table.

"I can start the fire if you want."

She didn't argue but she stepped back as he did his thing. With the fire lit, he placed a few hotdogs and hamburger meat on the grill.

She stepped up to the grill to take over.

"I don't need any help—" Andrew sneezed away from the grill.

"Are you sick?" She asked as she shut the lid of the grill. He shook his head. Opening his mouth to counter, he sneezed again, which gained a frown from Mona.

"No, I'm fine. It must be allergies or something."

"You don't have any allergies," she responded. A hint of a smile graced his lips.

"No, I guess I don't," he muttered.

She looked away. Silence settled upon them as they watched the smoke slip from the vent of the grill.

He watched her as she toyed with the end of her shirt, a habit he associated with nervousness. Something she often did when she wasn't sure how to express herself. Now was his chance. If there were any moment to clear the air, this very moment would be it.

"I'm sorry," he managed.

Mona turned to him in confusion, her gray eyes searching

his. "About what?"

"Everything."

She didn't respond, instead of mulling over his words and turning away. She hugged herself and took the slightest step away as if she was ready to bolt.

But she didn't.

It wasn't the way he wanted to apologize, it was the most important thing he wanted to say. Much more rested on his chest, but it would have to wait for another time if he'd ever get there with her.

He continued, "I miss us. I miss... you."

Absorbing the sincerity of his voice, she opened her mouth, then closed it before finding the courage to speak.

"I can't... I can't do this right now."

"Can't? Or won't?"

She never got the chance to answer. Adam had made his way back outside with James in tow. It wasn't until Andrew had seen Adam that he realize they had forgotten about the food.

"What the hell? You guys are burning the food!"

"Shit!" Andrew exclaimed as he opened the lid of the grill. Mona stepped back from the mountain of smoke that burst from the grill. The meat lay slightly charred on one side and uncooked on top.

Embarrassed, Andrew helped Adam removed the ruined food from the grill.

Sighing, Adam turned to Andrew and Mona. "Do I even need to ask?"

Andrew peeked at Cassie with a passing glance but was confused by the less than pleasant look on her face. She turned away and stalked inside.

"Well done, Chef," Nina laughed as she passed them following Cassie's departure. Adam silently berated Mona and Andrew as he added fresh meat to the grill, leaving he and Mona to settle in their own comfort.

"I guess my help is no longer needed," she began. "I'll see my way back inside." Mona took one last look at Andrew before heading inside, James following her.

Andrew stood, watching her disappear into the cabin, uncertain if he should congratulate himself for speaking up or scolding himself for possibly running her away.

"Wipe your drool and help me. And try not to burn the food this time, master chef," Adam quipped.

Andrew shook out of his thoughts and placed what was left of his energy into the patties on the grill.

<u>Beauty Beyond the Sea</u>

Franco Bay

MONA SAT WITH her legs stretched out in front of her, her toes dug deep into the sand. The waves weren't close enough to engulf her feet, but the passing splash from the waves was all the water she needed to enjoy. The rhythm of the waves was calming, so calming in fact, she was beginning to forget. That, she was thankful for. The sun was still high above the clouds; however, it was starting to lose its light.

She threw her hair into a top knot to keep the sea breeze from blowing it back into her face. The sounds of laughter could be heard from a distance. Children littered the beach trying to enjoy the last bit of day before the sun disappeared entirely. She smiled at the couple that passed by holding hands. The smile didn't quite reach her eyes, though.

If anything, she felt robbed of any snippet of happiness that she felt in recent weeks. The laughter, the sweet kisses, the first love; it was all a lie. There was nothing worse than knowing that someone could so easily toy with feelings with no remorse. That was scary for Mona. She couldn't stop ask-

ing herself why.

Why her? She thought she had done everything right.

Even right was wrong to some, she guessed. She had suspected things were different, but the denial that things were going to officially change was harder to grasp. And before she knew it, it all came crashing down. No more laughter, no more kisses. Goodbye to the first of many.

How women could repeat these steps over and over again, she didn't know. But if this was heartbreak, she never wanted to love again.

Mona wrapped her arms around her legs as a light breeze passed. She hadn't brought a jacket believing that braving the evening chills would better ease her mind. And while it had for some time, her mood was crippling fast, and the cold seeped further into the fabric of her clothes.

By now, the sun had finally settled with the beach becoming bare and quiet minus the sounds of crashing shores. Despite the levels of loneliness settling in the pit of her stomach, she welcomed the feeling. It was the change she needed.

"I've been watching you for about an hour now from my car. I was wondering when you'd finally leave. But I guess I'll join you instead," Andrew said as he joined her, mocking her position.

Mona wasn't even startled by his presence. She knew at some point he was going to find her after she stormed out of the school.

He always did. She was surprised, however, that he hadn't approach sooner.

"You sound like a stalker," she tried to joke, but it fell flat.

"No, I sound like a concerned friend." There wasn't an ounce of laughter in his voice. He pulled off his letterman jacket and wrapped it around her shoulders.

"Aren't you cold?" she asked as she pushed her hands through the sleeves.

His attire merely consisted of jeans and a grey t-shirt. His glasses were perched on his nose perfectly, his head of curls neat without a hair out of place.

"I'd rather get sick than to take care of you while you're sick."

Mona playfully punched him in the arm as he laughed. "I'm not that bad," she murmured.

Mona took a sudden interest in her nails as she remembered the last time she had gotten sick. He had stayed home with her that day to care for her only for her to vomit all over him. It wasn't a great moment for her.

Andrew shook his head, "Yeah, let's not go back down memory lane."

A peaceful silence passed over the two for a beat before Mona spoke, "Did you—"

"Yes, I did."

"You didn't even let me finish," Mona whined.

"I know exactly what you were going to ask," Andrew answered as he turned to her confidently.

"Okay, what was I going to say?"

Andrew smiled devilishly as he answered, "You were going to ask if I took care of him. I did, and he won't ever come near you again."

Mona's mouth hung open. That was precisely what she was going to ask. "What do you mean, you 'took care of him?' Did you hurt him?"

Andrew turned away. He played with the sand by his sandals as he muttered, "Let's just say he won't be speaking for a while."

"Andrew!"

"What? Moe, did you really think I was going to let him get away with what he did to you? I warned him before, and he obviously didn't want to listen, so he got what he deserved."

Mona looked at him incredulously. "But you don't even know the full story."

He turned to her with a sharp look in his eye. "Seeing you run out of school in tears was the only story I needed."

He was serious, and her heart swelled knowing that he was always there when she needed him most. She smiled as a tear dropped from her eye. His eyes widened, not sure what to do as she attacked him with a tight hug.

"Uh..."

She released him momentarily to look at him. "You're the greatest, you know?"

He pretended to think before answering, "Mmm, yeah, I know."

They both laughed before they settled into a comfortable silence. Leaning into him, she watched the waves brush the shore, unaware he was watching her. Feeling his gaze, she turned to him. He didn't bother to look away.

Mona felt the heat rise to her cheeks with the intensity of his eyes.

Was there something on her face?

"What?" she couldn't help but ask.

He smiled at her and looked away shyly. "Nothing. I think you're great, too."

CHAPTER ELEVEN

Mona

MONA WALKED BLINDLY into the cabin, her mind and heart left with Andrew outside. If there was ever a need for confirmation of what he was thinking, she most certainly got it. The fact that she had been stressing about how to approach everything regarding their friendship, and he turned around and apologized, was turning everything around for her.

She couldn't think of what to say at that moment. It wasn't much, if not direct, but it was all she needed to hear. She blamed herself more if anything for how things ended. Did he blame himself, too? Though a part of her still wanted to hang on to that small thread of anger for his permanent departure and leaving her when he promised he would never, she knew that anger wasn't fair.

The truth was, she feared losing him again. When all was said and done, nothing would be the same. He would still go back to a life he built without her, and she'd be left with the same memories and lost. He had his successful restaurant, his beautiful girlfriend, friends that didn't disappoint him.

Mona couldn't compete with that. She didn't fit into his circle anymore.

Maybe talking about things with him wasn't the right thing to do.

Mona sat on the couch, facing the plasma screen TV in the living room staring off into space. James had taken an interest in the contents in the pantry. Stepping out with a small bag of Cheez-It bites, he decided to join her on the couch. He took notice of her sullen face and tried to cheer her up.

"So, I hear burnt hamburgers are your favorite," he chuckled.

Mona turned to him and shook her head in amusement. "As if. It was an accident. We weren't paying much attention."

James nodded his head, stuffing his mouth with the snack before he spoke. "Did you guys talk?"

"He did."

"Did you?"

"I don't know what to say," Mona answered honestly.

"Well, what did he say?"

Mona took a breath. "He apologized." She left out the part of him missing her, figuring he might not get the reference as platonic as it was.

James nodded. "That's a start. But how do you feel about it? You don't look happy or relieved."

Mona wondered if it was the best place to talk about it. With everyone walking in and out the cabin sporadically, it wasn't something she wanted some of them to know, even if it wasn't that big of a deal.

She decided to give basics. "I'm scared, mostly."

"Why?"

Something about James made her want to spill her guts, and for that, she was thankful. It felt good to get the feeling off her chest, even if it was at the risk of him taking her secrets and feelings with him.

"Because if we reconcile this... friendship between us, I don't know if we'll last."

"Why wouldn't it?"

"Because he has a life without me now. I don't fit into his perfect life. And things won't be the same."

James put down the bag and turned to her. "Mona, that might not be a bad thing. Growing and learning are part of changing. Who's to say the relationship between the both of you won't be even better? Who cares about everything else?"

Mona turned away. "I can't ruin it again. What if I do?"

"Then, you learn and grow from that, too. And if it's not meant to be, then it's not meant to be and that's okay. Nobody is perfect, no matter how much it's presented in your face. But if he's willing to try and so are you, then I think it's worth a shot, risks be damned."

"He said he missed our friendship. He wanted to talk about it," Mona admitted.

"Then do it." James finished his bag of Cheez-It and got up to throw it in the trash before coming back to her side. "It's time to stop running, Mona. It's going to be a very long stay for you if you keep resisting it. I've only known all of you for a day and a half, and even I know he is serious about you."

"What do you mean?" Mona asked.

"If how he looks at you is any indication of how much you mean to him, then he's not going anywhere anytime soon." James left her sitting on the couch, mulling over his words. She didn't get much time to herself because Nina had come barreling from upstairs, slumping down beside her where James was moments prior, her phone her only focus.

"What's up?" Nina asked absentmindedly as she continued to type away.

Mona ignored her question. "Who are you texting?"

Nina waved her off. "Just Steph. I'm trying to get him to replace the shower head in my bathroom at the apartment." Nina placed her phone to the side, bringing her full attention to Mona. "So, when are you going to introduce me to James properly?"

"I did already, remember? You were there when I opened the door for him."

"I mean, really introduce me, Mona." Nina lifted her eyebrows suggestively.

Mona rolled her eyes. "I thought you were invested in the 'single life?' Wasn't that one of your New Year's resolutions?"

Nina huffed. "Nobody takes that serious besides you. Come on. You must put in a good word for me with James. He's quite the hottie. Unless, of course, this is your toy to play with."

"He's not an object, and no, I'm not interested in him that way. He's just a really good listener."

"More than me?" Nina's bubbly demeanor dissipated; her

tone turned serious.

While James may be a good listener, nobody would ever replace her real friends. "Of course not, Nina. He just came at the right time when I needed some unbiased advice. That's all."

Nina nodded. "I'm sorry about yesterday, again, Mona. I had no reason to—"

"It's okay, no need to apologize again. I'm over it. I want to have a good time here." Mona took her hand and squeezed it.

Nina smiled back. "Me too. But not in here we won't. Let's go back outside. I'm hoping I can catch James with his shirt off. That'll *really* make my day."

Mona wanted to plead on not going as Nina dragged her back outside but decided it was a futile effort. Not so coincidently, Nina found James and Dixie talking near the pool and decided to crash their engagement.

Mona sighed as Nina dragged her to James, who was talking to Dixie. He smiled at them both as he watched them approach.

"Ladies?" James greeted. Dixie turned around and offered a smile.

"Mona, right? This guy here is a charmer. Where'd you pick him up from?" Dixie joked.

"The woods."

Dixie's smile disappeared, giving Mona a strange look before slowly walking away from the group.

James snickered. "That wasn't nice."

"It also wasn't a lie," Mona stated matter-of-factly.

"True."

Nina interjected, "So, you live around here?"

James thought for a moment before answering. "Not so much live as I take care of my parents' cabin from time-to-time. I get a free stay out of it for the summer sometimes, so it has its perks."

"Interesting. When do you leave?"

"Whenever I want. I own an online marketing business, so technically, I don't have to go home anytime soon as long as I have internet connection."

Mona retreated to a patio table, feeling like a third wheel to their conversation. Nina was determined to keep his attention. Looking around, she wondered what else she could do while she waited for the food to finish.

Adam still maintained the grill with Andrew, the two laughing at some joke either told. Her eyes trailed solely on Andrew. He seemed relaxed in his element. She wondered if he missed being around his friends frequently. His absence was noticeably felt in their group.

From the corner of her eye, Mona spotted Symoné and Cassidy approaching her. Cassidy passed Mona a strange look she couldn't quite decipher but knew it wasn't pleasant.

Here we go, she thought.

"Hey, girlie," Symoné greeted as she took a seat at the other end of the patio table. Cassidy opted to smile instead, but it didn't meet her eyes.

Did she do something?

"Whatchu doing sitting all by yourself? You should hop in the pool with us," Symoné urged.

Mona took in Symoné's wet swimsuit. "Uh, I'll probably go when it's a little cooler later."

"Well, at least stick your foot in—"

"Hey, Symoné? Why don't you get us a drink, huh?"

Caught off guard, Symoné froze, "Uh..."

"Please?" Cassidy asked sweetly.

Symoné nodded. "What kind?"

Cassidy shrugged. "Surprise us."

Though hesitant, Symoné headed inside. With Symoné out of the way, Cassidy turned to Mona and tilted her head. "I don't think we've formally acquainted."

"I don't suppose we have," Mona answered, a bit guarded. Mona wasn't sure what the sudden interest in her was all about, but judging by Cassidy's slightly clipped tone, she could tell it was nothing good.

"Mona, right? How well do you know everyone?"

What she really wanted to ask was how well did she know Andrew, Mona knew. But she played nice. No need to stir up what could be just her imagination. Given she had been through this situation in the past many times with Andrew's past girlfriends, she highly doubted she imagined the condescending look in Cassidy's eyes, however.

"We're all good friends," Mona stated matter of fact.

"Andrew, as well?"

There it was.

Mona wasn't sure how to answer that without going into

too much detail or giving her more ammunition. "Sure."

"Funny, he's never mentioned you before." Cassidy's senile smile stirred something vicious in Mona, but not knowing who Cassidy was, she wasn't going to get out of character.

Mona shrugged. "I don't suppose he would."

"Hmm, why's that?"

"I honestly don't think it's any of your business," Mona said firmly. Perhaps she should've walked away if she had an inkling of where the conversation was headed but her interest was piqued. Who was this woman? Did Andrew know this side of her?

Cassidy was stunned by her answer but recovered quickly. With a hushed tone, she leaned in, "I beg to differ. It *is* my business when it comes to the longing stares and hushed conversations. I don't know what kind of relationship you and Andrew had, and frankly, I don't care. Just remember who had his back the last two years."

Cassidy's claws were out and ready for attack. Mona opened her mouth to fire back but closed it when she saw Symoné and Andrew approaching with Cassidy hugged to his side. Mona threw Cassidy a dirty look, which she responded with an innocent one of her own before getting up to kiss Andrew, albeit for show. Mona could tell it threw him off guard, but he responded, nonetheless. Mona looked away as Symoné placed two bottles of beer in front of her.

Noticing the scowl on her face, Symoné asked, "What's the matter? You look like you ate something sour."

Mona waved her off. "Just a bad taste in my mouth." Her

eyes flashed to Cassidy, which Cassidy ignored by picking up her beer. Symoné raised a brow inquisitively, but Mona shrugged and shook her head discreetly.

Andrew cleared his throat, his eyes briefly flashing to Mona before he focused on the other two. "Adam suggested we watch a movie out here tonight. He has a projector he's dying to test out."

"That actually sounds pretty cool," Cassidy suggested. "Watching a romance under the stars—"

"Actually, we've had our movie night, and it was boring. I say we girls go out for some drinks," Symoné suggested.

Cassidy shook her head, "I'm not feeling that kind of scene. I'll sit this one out."

Symoné turned to Mona with a pout. "You would come, won't you?"

Mona stalled, "I-uh—"

"Great!" Symoné cut in. "Then it's settled. All we need is Dixie and Nina, and we have an official girl's night. Girl, we are going to get you wild!"

Symoné left Mona speechless as she skipped inside, her head filled with ideas. Cassidy trailed after but stopped and turned to Mona, a strained smile plastered on her face for show. "It was nice to officially meet you, Mona. Perhaps we can catch up sometime. We seem to have quite a bit in common."

Cassidy disappeared inside, calling for Andrew, who still stood before Mona, a curious look in his eye. "What was that about?"

Mona wanted to laugh. If he couldn't decipher the snarky smile and tone Cassidy gave off, it wouldn't do any good to elaborate. "Nothing. Just girl talk."

Mona excused herself from the table, putting much-needed distance between her and Andrew. He didn't bother to follow, instead, following Cassidy's call in deep thought. She exhaled in relief though the day already swallowed her whole.

CHAPTER TWELVE

Mona

"ARE YOU READY yet?" Symoné asked outside the door. Mona grumbled in frustration and threw down her brush.

"No!" She stalked to the closet and rummaged through her clothes for her designated outfit. She became frantic when she couldn't find it, throwing out multiple outfits in a heap.

"I'm coming in!" Symoné burst through the door and followed the mess to the closet. "I didn't know you brought so many clothes here."

Mona sighed. "Yeah, if only I can find the outfit I picked out."

"Wear something red and sexy! Spice it up a little; you're always in some dull colors."

"Not true!" Mona fired back. She huffed and found the bed, lying on her back and staring at the ceiling. She contemplated a bit before continuing, "Yeah... maybe you're right."

Symoné laughed. "I know I'm right. Look, I want to see the fun in you tonight. I'm tired of seeing gloomy Mona. I know there's a fire in you, and I want to see you burn!"

Mona stared at her quizzically. "Yeah, yeah, I know. Wrong terminology, but you get the point. I want to see you get wild tonight. We're not just going out to gossip. We're going out to party and have some fun. Throw all your stress and trouble away tonight, please?"

Mona looked away from her, sitting up and running a hand through her hair. She smiled to herself. "Have I really been that bad?"

Symoné shook her head. "No, sweetie. And perhaps I'm exaggerating a bit, but I see the sadness in your eyes. I already consider you my friend, and I want to see you have fun. Let loose. Throw all your priorities in the trash for the rest of this trip. Be free. That's the most important rule."

Symoné took a seat next to her on the bed. "I want to see you happy. I want to see a permanent smile of that pretty face because your smile is beautiful, and the world deserves to see it."

Mona smiled before embracing Symoné. "You sure know how to throw a speech."

Symoné replied, "Don't I know it. Now let's find you something to wear and do something with that hair."

Mona touched the top of her head self-consciously. "Good luck with that. I don't even know what to do with it."

"You need to switch it up a little. Let your curls flourish. Let it be wild. No more buns, okay?"

Symoné went to the dresser to grab a brush before turning back to Mona. "Just let me put together your whole ensemble, and I promise you won't be disappointed."

For the next hour and a half, Symoné paraded around Mona like her personal project. She went from doing her makeup to her hair, her outfit, and her shoes. By the time Symoné finished, Mona was sure she was bordering a drastic Michael Jackson type of change. Opting for a full-sized mirror, Symoné forced her out of the room down the hall to the bathroom.

When Symoné turned on the light, Mona's jaw dropped. Her dark curls fell around her face, full and defined. Her outfit consisted of a form-fitting spaghetti-strapped lavender dress that reached just above her knees. The dress, although simple, accentuated her curves nicely. Her breasts looked full and perfect in the dress, not too busty, not too conservative, to which Mona approved. Her makeup was natural, with just a few highlights to her eyeshadow and dark red lipstick. Mona stepped out a bit further to examine her lacy black heels. The whole fit was perfect.

Mona gave Symoné a thumbs-up through the mirror. "This is perfect."

"Yay! I'm glad you like it. Now, it's my turn to get ready. I want to leave in thirty, so we can get back around midnight. And I beg of you, please don't mess up the hair."

Mona waved her off. "I know how to conduct myself, Symoné."

Symoné skipped away to her room to prepare. Mona decided to wait back in her room and clean up her mess but was spotted by James, who was coming up the stairs.

He whistled as he approached, causing Mona to blush.

"Wow, you sure do clean up nice."

Mona giggled. "Well, under every mask is a swan who flourishes."

James traced her curves before meeting her eyes with a smile. "I'm sure that's very true. But you always look beautiful, so I only ever see a swan."

Dixie wasn't kidding. He sure was a charmer.

"Thank you but I'm sure you didn't come all this way to tell me that."

"No, actually, I came to tell you goodnight, and thank you for inviting me to a lovely barbeque with your friends."

Mona nodded. "It was my pleasure. It's nice to have a friendly face around here."

James raised an eyebrow. "Glad I could be of service."

"So, any plans to come back soon? We still have about three weeks left here."

James thought for a moment. "Tell you what, give me your number, and we'll keep in contact. I can't guarantee anything, but I'll give it a try. Maybe switch some plans. For you," he added with a friendly wink.

Mona couldn't help but blush though she knew he was just being nice. She read off her number to him as she didn't have her phone to text him.

"I hope you have fun tonight. Get him off your mind," James suggested with a knowing look.

Mona shook her head. "I don't know if I can. Fully. But I got some sound advice tonight, and I plan to make the best of it."

"Thatta girl. I guess I'll see you when I see you then?"

"Yeah," she murmured. He placed a kiss on her cheek before heading down the stairs.

"You are one lucky son of a bitch; you know that?" Nina said as she came out from her room down the hall.

Mona jumped slightly, not expecting her. Nina came out fully ready for the occasion. She had on a high-waisted black leather skirt that reached her knees with an electric blue crop top that show a sliver of skin. Her hair was swooped to the side which showed off her chain earrings. Her blue pumps highlighted her calves nicely as she strutted down the hall.

"What do you mean?" Mona asked.

"I mean, you always got somebody fawning over you. I wish guys fell from heaven and landed on my lap, too."

Mona scratched her head in puzzlement. "I'm not sure I follow."

Nina sighed. "You're so clueless. Anyway, where are the other girls? I'm ready to start drinking."

Symoné popped out of her room right on cue. "Someone rang? I'm ready to get this party started!"

Symoné's attire consisted of a black embroidered flannel tank with skinny blue jeans and black boots. Her hair tied into a top knot. Her makeup was modest with eyeliner and red lipstick. She's was dressed simpler out of the trio, but still looked dazzling.

"Where's Dixie?" Nina asked.

"She decided to be a traitor and stay with the guys. Well, she and Cassidy. Something about playing pool."

"So, just the trio? Who's going to be the designated driver?" Mona asked.

"I know it's not me because I plan to get stoned tonight and hopefully find prey," Nina stated.

Symoné shrugged. "I guess I can drive. I'll drink, but I'll stop maybe two hours before we head home to sober up enough to drive."

"Then it's settled!" Nina presumed. "Let's head out."

Mona grabbed her belongings from her room then followed the girls to the common area. Adam, Andrew, and Dixie were surrounding the pool table and collecting their cues. Adam was the first to spot them. He whistled at the trio, causing the other two to turn around.

"Well, I'll be damned. Don't you ladies look like a snack?" Adam joked.

Symoné eyed him. "Keep playing, and I'll be someone else's snack tonight."

Adam laughed. "Just bring me back another girlfriend, and I'm sure I'll be fine." Symoné slapped him on the arm playfully. The two bantered on the side while Dixie approached.

"I'm sorry I can't come," she apologized.

Nina waved her off. "That's just more drinks for us. Besides, I'm sure Mona will be enough to handle. God knows Mona can't handle her liquor."

"Hey!"

They all laughed at that.

While Dixie and Nina branched off into a side conversation, Mona noticed Andrew staring at her from the pool table.

His cue in front of him, he shifted his weight on it as he drank her in. He smiled at her slightly, which she returned in the same manner. His eyes were so intoxicating she couldn't even look away. She subconsciously bit her bottom lip, which his eyes zeroed on before they flickered away from her entirely.

Her body felt heated in ways she knew it shouldn't. Looking around discreetly, she wondered if Cassidy was around.

"We'll catch ya later!" Symoné announced as they collectively shuffled to the door.

Adam gave Symoné a loving kiss before he and Dixie headed back to the pool table. Being the last to follow out the door, Mona made a move to close it behind her but was stopped by another hand on the door. Andrew emerged, closing the door behind him. She could feel his body heat radiating off him and as she looked up at him.

She began to ask what he needed before he spoke. "Sorry, um, I just... I wanted to wish you guys a good time. Please be careful."

Mona caressed her hair behind her ear. "Always."

They stared at each other for a beat before Andrew stepped back. "So... goodnight, I guess. That is if you guys get home and everyone is asleep, well, not me per se—not that I'll be waiting up you all to come home or whatever," he rambled.

If she weren't so caught up in the moment, she would've laughed at his rambling. Instead, Mona nodded. "Yeah, night."

She couldn't think of anything else to say. All she could do was feel swallowed by his stare, his eyes entrancing her. She could tell he wanted to say more but was refraining. She stood there for a beat, allowing him the opportunity to speak.

The car started up which Mona took it as a sign to hurry up. Ripping her eyes from his, she turned around and headed to the car.

"You look beautiful, by the way. Just thought you should know that," Andrew murmured the last part. Mona looked over her shoulder and smiled shyly, catching his eye and mouthing "thank you" before hopping into the car.

***

"WHAT WAS THAT all about?"

"Nothing," Mona shied away, hoping the line of questioning would end.

She wasn't quite as lucky as she'd hope.

"Didn't seem like nothing. He came outside like a lost puppy looking for its owner. For someone in a relationship, he sure looks smitten by you," Symoné muttered the last part, but Mona heard her.

Nina shook her head at Symoné for her to stop, which she obliged by changing the subject.

Mona's face was warm with embarrassment from the back seat. She was thankful it was dark, and they couldn't see her face through the rearview mirror. Mona was still trying to process what happened between her and Andrew. They shared an intense moment, but she couldn't wrap her mind around the look he was constantly giving her. Was he trying to tell her something? Why chase her outside to tell her she looked beautiful?

Mona caressed her wrist and the infinity tattoo. Her heart hammered against her chest at the possibilities. That look in his eyes was borderline hunger, she concluded. Mona shook the thought from her head quickly. What was she thinking? He was in a happy relationship, and their friendship wasn't even officially reestablished.

Yet.

Mona watched the girls laugh about something Nina said, and she couldn't help but feel a little jealous. Here she was, about to potentially have the time of her life, and she stuck thinking about *him*. As always, her mind seemed to wonder about him. A simple smile would have her overthinking her every move. She thought she was done with the handle he had over her life.

Old habits die hard, she guessed.

The car pulled up to the Foxy Bar just an hour later. Hopping out the car, the girls freshened up, fixing their makeup and adjusting their bras before strutting inside the establishment. The place wasn't quite a bar, but it also wasn't solely a club. However, it was rather lively considering the town they were in.

The establishment was big enough and was currently bustling with a decent crowd. The girls entered, Symoné and Nina swaying to the music as soon as they walked through the door. Mona could feel the beat of the music thumping through her chest. Most of the crowd was dancing in the center of the room.

Symoné and Nina dragged her to the bar, where several people sat chatting. "This place is a lot better than I thought," Symoné remarked.

Nina nodded while thrumming her fingers on the bar counter. "From the outside looking in, I was expecting a rinky-dink."

"At least the music is upbeat," Mona chimed in.

"Now, we just test the drinks and hope to God it does the trick," Symoné said. "I plan to get tipsy tonight, at least. I'm hoping for a drunk moment. Mona, I hope you're ready because you're getting plastered."

"I second that!" Nina said.

"Wouldn't you getting drunk all night hinder the driving plans?" Mona asked.

"Nothing water can't fix," Nina answered for Symoné, who was too busy trying to get the bartender's attention.

Mona groaned. There was no way to talk either out of the notion, and she honestly didn't plan on it. But she knew these two were up to no good.

"What can I get for you beautiful ladies?"

With Mona's back to the bar, she had to turn around to greet the bartender. His brown eyes were the first to greet her along with a warm smile. She took a moment to check him out. He was quite handsome with a lazy smile and light brown shaggy hair. He winked at her before turning to Symoné, who had begun to speak.

"Three shots of tequila, please?"

"Starting with a hardball, I see," the bartender joked as he began to fill three shots for them.

"Quick and easy, that's how I like 'em," Symoné replied after taking her shot. Nina downed her drink, followed by Mona. The bartender watched them with amusement.

"Quick and easy, eh? There's more where that came from," he said.

"Why do I feel like this conversation is about to go left?" Nina asked.

The bartender laughed. "No left turns here. But how about a second shot for you beautiful ladies on the house?"

Nina eyed him warily. "What's in it for us?"

"Yeah, and no kinky shit either. I'm in a happy relationship," Symoné added.

He laughed again before shifting his gaze from Symoné to Mona. "Just a dance. With you. Unless you're taken, too?"

Mona eyed him and the girls warily, who began to smirk. "How about free drinks for the whole night, and she's all yours?" Nina quipped.

"You can't just pimp me out to the bartender!" Mona exclaimed to her friends.

The girls were enjoying her obvious embarrassment. "Our *friend* Mona is certainly single and always ready to mingle."

"Not to mention, you seem like a chill guy. I'm sure she's willing to take one for the team," Symoné said.

Mona stood with her mouth agape, not believing her own two friends—one whom was her best friend—would throw her to the woods for a couple of drinks. "Uh, I'm standing right here."

The bartender and the girls laughed wholeheartedly. "Girl, we're just fucking with you. Although those free drinks would be a great start to what we are hoping to be an epic night," Symoné pointed out to the bartender.

"Absolutely! On the house," he said as he poured another round of shots for them. Leaning over the counter towards Mona as she took her shot, he stated, "But a dance with the most beautiful girl here really would be nice."

Mona pulled the shot from her mouth and searched his smiling face to see if he was serious. He didn't give off any creepy vibes, and he seemed friendly enough. Not to mention, the compliments didn't hurt any.

It's supposed to be a fun night, after all.

"Don't you have to work the bar all night?" Mona asked, genuinely curious.

The bartender shrugged. "My uncle owns this place. It wouldn't hurt to have someone else man the station while I play the field."

Mona felt her face heat up. Symoné and Nina turned to her and asked if she was ready to hit the dancefloor. She nodded before turning to the bartender.

"One dance."

"I can dig it," he replied with a lazy smile before she got whisked away by the girls.

They spent most of their time between the dancefloor and the bar. The tequila coursed through Mona's veins quickly once she initially hit the dancefloor. Grinding between Symoné and Nina, Mona welcomed the bold feeling that took over and let loose.

Her mind felt free. She laughed more. She'd begun to get a little flirty. She was enjoying herself. Eventually, she made her way back to the bar with Symoné and Nina. The bartender was still there serving drinks to a couple of guys a few chairs down. He came right to her when he was done with them.

"Ready for that dance?" he asked as he leaned on the counter across from her.

"Not quite. I don't have enough liquid courage just yet," Mona replied with a flirty smile. She was talkative when tipsy or drunk, a trait she hated and was often teased about. Tonight though, she was welcoming the effect.

"I can fix that for you."

"Mmm, I think you fixed enough so far."

"Not nearly as much as I want," he said, eyeing her.

"Are we on the same topic? This sounds sexual," Mona asked, scrounging up her face.

He laughed. "I don't know. Do you want it to be sexual?"

"I'm not sure anymore," she said innocently, causing him to laugh even more. "I like you. You're cute."

"I like you, too. And I'm still waiting for that dance."

Mona shook her head. "How about your name first? I see you don't wear a nametag."

He looked down at his shirt then back at her. "There's no need to. Most people who come here are regulars."

"I'm not a regular," Mona pressed.

The bartender shrugged. "Then, I guess it gives me a reason to talk to someone as pretty as you."

Mona rolled her eyes. "You're a little cheesy. The compliments can only get you so far."

He laughed. "It has gotten me far enough. That's all that matters. But you can't fault me for stating facts."

Mona smiled and took the drink he offered her. Spying the girls back on the dancefloor, she watched as Nina grinded against a guy she had taken a liking to earlier. Symoné being the dedicated girlfriend she was, decided to dance by herself off to the side.

The bartender looked over at her friends on the floor before returning his gaze to her. "They're having the time of their lives."

Mona looked at him. "Because they don't let anything bother them, unlike me."

"What's bothering you then?"

Mona shook her head and smiled flirtatiously. "Isn't that a little personal?"

He winked at her and said, "I was hoping we were past that phase by now." He served two guests at the counter before walking back over to her. "I'm taking a break, so I can cash in on that dance you owe me."

He rounded the counter and sat beside her. Mona turned to him. "I still didn't get your name. I can't dance with someone whose name I don't know."

He stuck out his hand and smiled bright, a small dimple in his left cheek showing. "I'm Ralph."

Mona took his hand. "I'm sure you remember from earlier, but my name is Mona."

"Mona... that's a beautiful name," Ralph complimented.

"Thanks. I would compliment your name, but I'm not sure I like it."

Ralph laughed. "Trust me; I don't like it any more than you do."

"So, why don't you change it? Or use a nickname?"

Ralph shrugged and turned back to the dancefloor, placing his elbows on the counter behind him. "Then I wouldn't be me. I may not like the name, but its who I am."

Strangely deep but funny at the same time. The tune of the song changed to a slow tempo. Mona got up from her chair and stood in front of him with her hand out.

He watched her with amusement before taking her hand. "I shall."

She led him to the middle of the dimmed dancefloor, far from Symoné and Nina. She swayed as he came behind her, chest to back. He was so close she could feel the bulge in his pants. She ignored it as she closed her eyes to feel the rhythm of the beat, grinding against him. She transcended into her mind; the alcohol further awaking her system and confidence.

She pictured another pair of strong arms wrapping around her waist with a needy grip. The breath on the nape of her neck from someone else. The feathered touches from the hands of another, making her quiver. Her hands snaked around the nape of his neck. His hair, instead of straight, she imagined it was curls that she was twirling her fingers through.

His lips brushed the spot between her ear. She opened her eyes and twisted in his arms, staring at him. By now, she had stopped dancing. She stared into his dark eyes, but her drunk induced mind could only see green. Deep forest green orbs staring at her with such lust. She could feel the heat between her legs intensify gradually. The hands around her waist crept slowly up her back, leaving a heated trail until they cupped her face.

Mona closed her eyes, her heart pounding, as his lips descended on hers. Leaning into him, she swiped her tongue across his bottom lip. He granted her access, deepening the kiss. She craned her head to the side as she played tonsil hockey with him. She moaned as his hands made their way below her waist, grabbing her backside.

"Oh, this is hot."

Mona ripped herself away from Ralph immediately. Symoné and Nina stood in front of them, wide smirks on their faces.

"Just a dance, huh?" Nina directed to Ralph, who could only stand there with an amused look on his face. Mona, on the other hand, was embarrassed. Granted, nobody around them cared what was going on. Most were making out or two seconds away from throwing caution to the wind.

Mona cleared her throat. "Are we heading home? I can't drive. I took a shot not too long ago."

"I thought I would be able to, but I'm about ready to fall over my own feet at this point," Symoné said as she rolled her neck from side-to-side.

"Yeah, I'm out," Nina chimed in. "Maybe we should get a ride and then come back for the car tomorrow?"

"A ride from where? Uber?" Symoné asked, a displeased look on her face.

Ralph interrupted, "I could take you ladies home. It's no problem."

Mona turned to him quizzical. "What about the bar? You can't just leave it."

"I'll get one of the workers to watch over it."

Nina shook her head. "No. As much as the offer is nice, we barely know you."

Symoné thought for a moment. "On second thought, maybe an Uber or Lyft would be better."

"Uber and Lyft drivers are just as janky," Mona added.

"But trackable," Nina replied.

Ralph shrugged and held his hands up. "It's up to you. I'm just trying to help."

Nina fished for her phone in her purse. Ralph stood awkwardly to the side, rubbing the back of his neck. Mona shook the thought of his lips from her mind. It was a momentary lapse in judgement. She blamed the alcohol and her overactive imagination.

"I should get back to the counter. Would you like another drink?" Ralph asked as he approached her.

Before she could respond, Nina piped, "Maybe one last shot for the road. By the way, we didn't mean to come off as rude for indirectly calling you a potential creep."

Symoné laughed and Mona shook her head. Ralph, who didn't seem offended in the slightest, smiled. "No worries at all. Safety first." He looked at Mona before turning away.

"Three shots, coming up."

It was twenty minutes after their two last shot that an Uber finally arrived. By then, the girls were at the bar counter, laughing about a story Nina had told. Symoné and Nina headed out ahead of Mona, who decided to give Ralph the courtesy of a good-bye.

She walked over to him as he was coming from around the counter. He saw her and smiled. "I had fun tonight," he said, standing close to her.

Mona looked down at her hands before looking at him. "Yeah, me too. Look, I—"

He held up his hands to stop her. "I get it. It was nothing serious. No hard feelings, okay? Besides, I had fun." Mona wasn't sure what to say, considering he beat her to the punch. "I'll be here in the morning for whoever wants to pick up the car out front. I'll wait. Hopefully, I get to see you again? Under friendly circumstances?"

He offered her a smile, which she returned. "I can't promise that, but thanks for a good time."

He nodded as she started to walk away. The girls were already in the car waiting for her. With her mind still fuzzy, she tried to suppress the thoughts that were running through her mind from the dancefloor. Instead, she spent the car ride home laughing and joking and having the time of her life.

Chapter Thirteen

Andrew

THE HOUSE WAS deathly quiet when Andrew decided to go downstairs for a bite to eat. It was past two in the morning, and the girls still hadn't made it back. Andrew's inability to keep his eyes shut disabled him from a peaceful sleep.

He was worried.

Who was he kidding? It was a lame excuse for wondering what Mona was doing at the hour. The other ladies barely crossed his mind in the last few hours.

Andrew shook the thoughts from his head. He shouldn't be thinking about her. Not right now. Nothing good ever comes of it. It didn't when she came down those stairs wearing that outfit. It didn't when she walked away, and all he could do was follow her outside like a dog in heat.

For much of the night, Andrew did his best to distract himself by playing pool with Adam and Dixie. Cassidy had found a way to ignore him, which was fine by him. He was happy he didn't have to entertain her or James, though he left before the girls.

What was James's deal anyway? He fit right in with everyone, and that nagged Andrew more than it should have. He and Mona got along well, but that was a problem. Were they capable of developing a friendship like Andrew shared with her or worse, were they compatible in a romantic way?

That didn't sit well with Andrew.

"Fuck," he mumbled.

Taking a solid breath to clear his mind, he made his way to the kitchen. He had a sandwich in mind, but considering his unrelaxed state, he decided to busy himself with something more. Taking out all the ingredients he needed, he started the stove. By the time he turned off the stove to prepare a plate, he could hear the front door opening.

The girls were back judging from the laughter Andrew could hear as they closed the door.

The giggling from the girls grew louder as they made their way to the kitchen. Andrew couldn't help but feel relieved to see Mona laughing with Symoné and Nina.

Her hair was a little wild, her curls less defined than when she left. The straps of her dress fell off her naked shoulder. Her eyes were red, almost bloodshot. She looked tired but alert. And even with all that, Andrew could only admire how beautiful she looked. How beautiful she always looked.

His eyes followed them as they made their way to the kitchen bar. Symoné was the first to notice him as they settled in the bar chairs. "Andrew? What are you doing up?"

"Got hungry. How was your night?"

"Loads of fun. Although I think some of us had more fun

than others," Nina said, turning to Mona, who groaned and put her head down on the counter in embarrassment.

Symoné snickered. "Oh, she certainly had more fun than us."

Andrew frowned but didn't bother asking. He wasn't sure he was interested to know. Instead, he focused on making his plate.

"What did you make? It smells good," Mona asked as she leaned back in her chair.

"Stir fry."

"Is there enough? I'm kinda hungry." She groaned and leaned her head back. He watched her hair fall from her shoulders over the back of the bar chair.

"Yeah, seriously, that smells fucking delicious," Symoné added.

Andrew looked at his pot of food. He had made enough, but he was little peeved he had to share, considering he was planning to save some for later in the evening. However, saying no was not an option. "Yeah, sure. I'll grab you both a plate. Nina, do you want any?"

"Yes, please!"

He fixed their plate with a glass of water and set it in front of them. They dug in hastily. Mona moaned as she took her first bite. "This is so good."

There was only one seat left at the bar next to Mona, but he decided not to take it. He didn't want to invade her space, for her sake and his. Instead, he hopped on the countertop facing them and ate his food with a bowl in his hand.

"You know, this reminds me. Don't forget we have to pick up the car tomorrow," Nina said in between bites.

"How does the food remind you of the car?" Mona frowned.

Nina sighed. "It doesn't matter. Don't bust my chops miss 'let's make out on the middle of the dance floor.'"

"It was a lapse in judgment, and I was drunk, okay? He asked for a dance, and things just got a little heated," Mona explained abashed as she finished the last of her food.

By now, Andrew had already lost his appetite and could only stare at Mona as she got up from her seat to place her plate into the sink. The other two sat laughing, and Andrew couldn't bring himself to lift his fork.

"You damn near fucked him on the dancefloor," Symoné included. Mona flicked her off.

Not wanting to hear anymore, he hopped off the counter. "You know, I think it's time I call it a night."

"What? No dessert?" Nina asked. She got up and placed her plate in the sink also. "I guess I'll call it a night, too."

"Yeah, it's way past my bedtime. If I don't get at least two hours' worth of sleep before the sun, I will die," Symoné announced as she followed Nina out the kitchen.

"Goodnight!" They shouted, leaving Mona and Andrew awkwardly standing around.

"I guess I'll wash the dishes then," Andrew muttered defeatedly as he walked to the sink after gathering the plates left at the counter. With her standing unusually close, he could feel her eyes on him as he lathered the dishes with soap.

Why wasn't she heading upstairs? With her watching him like that, it was unnerving.

"The food was excellent. You're a good chef," Mona said softly. Having hopped on the counter herself, her legs bounced against the cabinets, her heels still attached to her feet, her dress slowly riding up her thigh modestly. The straps of her dress still slipped, leaving the front of it droopy and exposing a small portion of her chest. Andrew averted his trance.

What was his problem?

Andrew forgot she had said anything until she spoke again, "I'm proud of you. With your restaurant and all. You've come a long way, and you chased your dreams and actually caught em'. I admire that."

Andrew froze and let her words sink in. Mona hopped down from the counter and took the last plate out his hand and placed it on the dry rack. He could smell her perfume from her proximity. Because of her heels, she was closer to his height than usual.

"You're not talking to me. Did I say something wrong?" Her question was warranted, though not valid.

Her grey eyes bore into his own with question and underlying hurt. She was borderline drunk. She was always talkative and blunt when she had liquor in her system, he remembered. Not a typical mean-spirited drunk, more extroverted and introspective. They used to talk for hours following a drink.

He didn't want to give her a cold shoulder, but her being so close and hearing about her escapades was driving him crazy as much as he didn't want to admit. And that fact that it was bothering him was making him feel ashamed. Here he is, having thoughts about someone he couldn't call his friend anymore while his girlfriend lay above sleeping. That smile she gave him before she left for the girls' night out had him ready to throw caution to the wind.

Not that he was going to try anything with Mona. Drunk or sober, he would never allow it. It always remained untouchable fantasies.

"You didn't." He finally got the courage to speak. "I'm just tired. You should head upstairs and get some sleep. It's late—or early, depending on how you want to interpret the time," Andrew suggested, murmuring the last part to himself.

Mona didn't say anything back but stared at him for a moment before going back to her seat around the bar. She fumbled with her heels before a *clunk* was heard as she dropped them on the floor and placed her head into her arms on the counter, her hair fanning around her.

Andrew looked around in confusion, not quite sure what she was doing. She seemed tired but obviously wasn't ready to go to her room. Andrew looked at the clock on the opposite wall.

4:10 A.M.

Should he leave her? He was done with the kitchen, but he did feel right leaving her there.

"Moe?" He was surprised she hadn't corrected him yet for calling her the nickname he gifted her as kids.

"Moe," Andrew tried again. "Don't you want to go to your room? Your pillows are likely more comfortable than the counter.”

She groaned but didn't move. Andrew shook his head and chuckled.

“I don't think I have the energy to make it up the stairs.”

“Do you need help?”

“Mentally or physically?”

“Both.”

She lifted her head and stretched with a yawn. “I'm going to crash on the couch.”

“I can help you to your room if you want,” he said carefully, watching her as she slipped from the chair and laid on the couch in the living room. “I guess not.”

Following her move to the living room, he watched in slight amusement as she struggled to get comfortable, one pillow discarded on the floor in the process.

“I bet that offer is sounding real nice right now.”

“I don't want to go upstairs.”

Andrew sat down on the other side of the couch where she laid, careful not to touch her. “Why not?”

Mona shrugged, not meeting his eyes. “It's nothing. Shouldn't you be going to bed? I thought you said you were tired?”

“I am, but I don't feel right leaving you here by yourself. Why don't you want to go to your room?” he probed. She didn't look scared, if not, more forlorn.

She looked away but didn't answer.

“Did something happen? Are you afraid of something?” The amusement he had earlier was now gone and replaced with worry. She continued staring at the ceiling for a moment before she spoke again.

"I had fun tonight. I finally let loose. My mind was clear. Mostly, anyway. I... felt normal," Mona explained.

"But?"

She sighed and sat up, clasping her hands together and looking down. Andrew couldn't help but want to comfort her, but the sudden change in mood was concerning.

"You can tell me anything, Moe."

"I'm alone, and I miss my dad." It looked as if she wanted to say more but decided against it. Mona turned to him, her eyes shimmering. "I just feel like I don't have anyone on my side."

Andrew was taken aback by the tears and confession. She was hurting more than she'd let on. "What do you mean you don't have anyone? What about Nina and Adam?"

What about him? He wanted to ask.

"Never mind. Just forget I said—"

"No, I'm not going to drop it. Obviously, you're hurting, and you're not telling anyone. You need to talk about this, Moe. Before it eats you alive."

Mona looked away. He scooted closer to her, taking her hand. He half expected her to reject him, but when she didn't, he settled next to her.

"You can talk to me. I'm here, Moe. Regardless of what became of us, at the end of the day, you are still and forever will be my best friend. Nina will never leave you no matter how much you guys fight, and Adam will always have your back.

"I get that you may feel alone, but there are people around you ready to support, including me. You gotta let us do our job as friends. You've been through a lot with your dad, and you're still healing. It's okay to be sad. It's okay to cry about it. But don't push us away. Please don't push me away."

If he weren't sure that her brain was still foggy from her night out, he would've expected her to correct him on the friend part regarding him. He was pushing it, but he didn't care. She needed to hear it. He just hoped she wouldn't fight him on it.

Andrew placed his hand under her chin so she could face him. Her eyes were red as was her nose, but she had yet to shed a tear. She refused to look at him, however. Even with her face red and her eyes puffy and her hair out of place, she was still taking his breath away. He removed his hand from her face as if it burned him, hoping she didn't notice.

"Look at me, Moe."

She looked up at him as she bit her lip. His eyes flickered to her lips before forcing himself to focus on her entirely. Her eyes began to drupe with her leaning forward on his shoulder.

"I'm so tired," she mumbled.

Andrew sighed, not sure if she was still listening or not. She was about two seconds away from falling asleep.

"I'll get you a blanket." He excused himself from her embrace, needing to get away from her presence before he did something he regretted. Leaving her on the couch with her eyes closed and head back, he rushed to get a blanket from the closet upstairs and brought it back down.

Mona was now resting her head on the arm of the chair, snoring lightly. He hesitated as he stared at the rising and falling of her chest. She was on her side, her arms under her head with her hair covering her face. He maneuvered closer, gently caressing her hair from her face. She moved a bit before snuggling into her arm.

Andrew smiled. He thought of how cute she looked when she slept. He missed seeing this peaceful side of her.

Gently, he covered her with the blanket and sat down on the other end of the chair where her feet didn't quite reach. He yawned and looked back at the time. It was nearly on the brink of dawn. He wasn't sure if he had the strength to make it back upstairs. Instead, he leaned his head back on the chair and closed his eyes for what he thought was a second.

CHAPTER FOURTEEN

Andrew

BY THE TIME he woke up, the sun had already risen with sunlight reflecting directly in his face from the window near the couch. He stretched, the blanket he had no idea was on him falling to the floor. Looking around, he realized he was alone. The spot that was occupied by Mona only hours before was now void of any existence of her presence.

Was it all a dream?

There was some chatter in the kitchen. Recognizing Cassidy and Adam's voice, he picked up the blanket and made his way to the bar.

Their back turned; they didn't hear him approach until he greeted them.

"About time you woke up," Adam said as he took his eggs out the pot into his plate. "Thought you were going to sleep in all morning."

Looking up at the clock, he realized it was ten minutes past eleven. Sleeping in late always made him groggy through-out the day. It was going to be a while before the sleepy feeling left him.

Andrew didn't say anything else but focused on Cassidy, who seemed hell-bent on ignoring his presence. Instead of speculating, he tried to clear the tension.

"Morning, babe," he said with a lazy smile.

She didn't look up at him, nor did she stop what she was doing at the blender. She threw back a meager, "Morning." He frowned and looked at Adam, who was watching them. Adam shrugged as if to say he wasn't sure what her deal was.

Deciding that he wasn't helping his case, Andrew announced he was going upstairs to put himself together. With one last glance at Cassidy, he made his way to their room to fish for clothes and a towel for a shower.

He paused before going in the bathroom to stare at Mona's door, wondering if he should check on her, considering things were left unresolved between them. It could wait, he decided, putting it in the back of mind until he was fully prepared later.

It didn't take long for him to shower and dress in a black shirt and dark jeans. He took out his contacts that were now drying his eyes and put on his traditional black-rimmed glasses.

Making his way back downstairs, he grabbed a bite to eat. Though he was hoping to catch Cassidy in the kitchen, a feeling of relief quickly escaped his body. Instead, he was greeted by Symoné.

"Good morning," Andrew greeted her.

"You mean afternoon? The day is going by fast, isn't it?"

Symoné inquired as she buttered her toast. She was nursing a cup of hot chocolate in her hands soon after as she leaned against the counter next to him.

"Oh, right. How did you sleep?"

Symoné sighed. "I woke up with a massive headache. I'm sure Nina is sporting one as well. But your food did help, so thank you."

Andrew smiled. "No problem."

Looking around the corner, he tried to see if he could catch a glimpse of Cassidy.

Seeming to have read his mind, she offered, "I think she's getting ready, I haven't seen her yet."

Confused, Andrew turned to her, assuming she was talking about Cassidy. "Getting ready? For what?"

"To get the car," Symoné said between sips of her hot chocolate. "We agreed last night that she would drive the car back from the club this morning and have the bartender from last night drive the other car."

Andrew frowned. "Wait, what? Are you talking about Mona?"

Then it clicked. The bartender she was referring to must be that guy they mentioned that Mona was into at the club. No way in hell was that happening on his watch.

"No shit, Sherlock. Who did you think I was talking about? Do you not remember anything from last night? And I thought I was drunk," Symoné muttered under her breath before taking another sip of hot chocolate.

Forgetting all about Cassidy and ignoring her question,

he turned back to Symoné, "How did you guys get home last night?"

Symoné shrugged as if it were no big deal. "Uber."

"Why didn't you call one of us? You guys were all drunk when you got here."

Symoné waved him off. "Don't get your panties in a twist. We arrived safe and sound."

Andrew rolled his eyes. "That's not the point."

"It's not a big deal, Andrew."

"To you," he pointed out. "I still don't get why you're making her go alone. Wouldn't it just be easier to tag along and make one trip or why not just take another Uber there and get the car? And who the hell is this guy?" Her responses were starting to piss him off.

Symoné was taken aback by his outburst, to the point that she stood idle with her mouth slightly agape without any inclination of how to respond.

Andrew shook his head, muttering, "Forget it," as he proceeded to make a small meal. He settled for a ham sandwich and waited for Mona to make an appearance while Symoné quietly ate her food.

Finally, Mona came down, looking fresh-faced and awake. Wearing jeans and a grey t-shirt with her wallet in hand, she looked like she was ready to head out. She approached Symoné, still seated at the bar eating. She threw Andrew a weak smile in greeting.

"You have the keys, right? And whose car am I taking? I came without one."

There was no way in hell Andrew was going to leave her to handle taking back two cars on her own. Nina and Symoné needed a head check. He found himself blurting out, "I'll take you."

He could already see the defiance in her eyes. She began to shake her head as he approached her. Grabbing the keys from her hands after Symoné fished them from her pockets, he said, "I'm not taking 'no' for an answer."

Mona sighed heavily and turned to Symoné for help, but she just shrugged and turned back to her phone and food. "He's been bitching this whole time until you came down. If you don't take him, I might kill him."

"I guess you have to take me, then," Andrew gleamed.

Mona rolled her eyes and grabbed the keys back from him. "Or I just take an Uber." He followed her out of the kitchen to the front door.

"Please, don't be obtuse. Let me take you."

She craned her neck to look at him but backed away when she realized just how close he was. "Why? I can do this on my own. I don't need a savior."

"I didn't say you did. I'm just trying to be a friend."

Mona thought for a moment and deflated. "Fine."

Andrew did a small victory dance in his head as they headed out the door and stopping at his truck.

Mona looked at him, puzzled. "I thought we were taking the car?"

Andrew opened the passenger door, gesturing for her to sit inside. "Not on my watch." He shut the door and made his way to the driver's side. Thankfully, his truck was a push start, and his remote was already in his pocket when he came back from his shower.

Before starting the truck, he dug into his pocket for his phone. He shot Cassidy a quick text saying he was leaving and would be back later. His phone dinged as he pulled out of the driveway.

"Can you check that for me?" he asked. He motioned to his phone in the cupholder between them. Mona looked at him quizzically before picking it up.

"What's the passcode?"

"What it's always been," he answered, throwing her a quick look. "Am I going the right way?"

"Yeah," she answered, distracted. "There's no way you've kept the same passcode for over ten years."

"Why don't you try it and see? I don't change it even when I get a new phone. It's the only set of numbers I'll probably remember, and my credentials are too easy." Andrew watched from the corner of his eye as she unlocked his phone.

"My birthday?"

Andrew shrugged. "As I said, it's probably the only set of numbers that I'll always remember. What does it say?"

"'K.'"

"No, what does it say?"

"It says 'K.' That's all she wrote," Mona said as she placed his phone back in the cupholder.

Andrew tightened his hands on the wheel. "Just the letter K? Are you sure?"

Mona turned to him with a frown. "I know how to read letters."

"I'm—that's not what I meant, Moe. You know that," Andrew scrambled to correct himself. Cassidy's nonchalant answer was bothering him more than he thought it would. What did he expect? Cassidy was mad about something, and more than likely, he was sure to be the cause for her foul mood. He made a point to talk to her when he got back.

The air around the two had changed over the week since they got to the cabin. Maybe even before then, if he was honest. He noticed but had been so focused on other things, like approaching Mona, he neglected to talk about it with Cassidy. But he couldn't just leave the potential to patch things up with Mona. Not when he's come this far.

Mona cleared her throat. "Not that it's any of my business, but are things okay between the two of you?" She struggled to get the words out. She fiddled with a piece of lint from her jeans. "I couldn't help but notice she seems... apprehensive nor does she seem that fond of me."

Had Cassidy said something to her?

The thought angered him though he didn't show it. Cassidy could be mean-spirited when she wanted or felt threatened but if she had attacked Mona for no reason, that would cross a line.

Staring blankly at the road before him, he answered, "Honestly, I don't know. Maybe she's mad that my focus shifted."

"Shifted, how?" She asked she rolled down the window,

her hair dancing wildly around her face.

His focused shifted, indeed. He diverted the question, preferring not to explain something he wasn't entirely sure he could articulate. Instead, he asked for further directions, even though he was sure where they were going by then. They stayed silent until Andrew parked beside the car the girls drove in front of the club the night prior.

"I'm going inside for a minute. I'll be right back."

Andrew looked at her quizzically but nodded. He waited patiently in the truck as she made her way inside.

From the looks of the parking lot, it wouldn't seem open. Andrew wondered how lively the place got in the wee hours of the night in such a secluded area.

Andrew blankly stared the door to the club, wondering if he should go inside and see what Mona was up to, but he decided against it out of respect.

Maybe she needed a moment away from him.

"You can't control everything," Andrew said aloud to himself. Defeated, he decided to start the other car for when she returned. The car wheezed but didn't turn over. He tried again but got the same result. Opening the hood, he checked what he could but doesn't see anything wrong. The lights were still on in the car, and all the necessary car fluid levels were filled.

Frustrated and hot from the blazing heat, Andrew continued to fight with the car until Mona came back outside with someone Andrew was unfamiliar with. With the hood still up, Andrew couldn't quite see his face where they stood. He frowned as he watched her laugh with him.

Was this the guy the girls mentioned?

As if just realizing the hood of the car was up, Mona approached Andrew. "Something wrong with the car?" she asked, looking a bit concerned.

"I don't know. The car isn't starting. Could be the ignition switch, but it's not the battery or the starter."

The words came out curter than he'd meant. "Should we call a tow truck?" Mona suggested carefully. Perhaps she had picked up on his sudden mood change, Andrew wasn't sure. She shifted her weigh a bit uneasily.

Having yet to acknowledge her "friend," he took it upon himself to make his presence known.

"I can probably look at it if you want." Andrew and Mona both turned to him, prompting him to clear his throat and stick out his hand politely. "I'm Ralph, by the way."

There was a bit of awkward silence as Andrew stood without taking his hand. Mona looked between the two, waiting for a response, disappointment marred on her face. Eventually, Ralph got the message and put his hand back at his side.

Andrew knew deep down, Ralph was just being polite, but he couldn't help acting as if he had a chip on his shoulder. "I know what I'm doing. I don't need your help."

"Andrew..." Mona began. She shook her head and turned to Ralph. "I'm so sorry. He's probably just frustrated, especially with the heat and all—"

"I can talk for myself, Mona. I don't need you being my interpreter," Andrew snapped. The fact that she was acting as if he wasn't even there was pissing him off.

"Hey, don't talk to her like that," Ralph said interjected with a glare.

"How about you stay out of my business?" Andrew retorted as he got closer.

"Enough!" Mona said, pushing Andrew back. "Andrew, please just call the tow truck?"

Andrew stared at her incredulously. He knew he was acting ridiculous, but that fact that she was making him out to be the bad guy instead of taking his side was riding on his conscious. Then again, did he expect her to take his side given their current relationship?

With an exasperated sigh, Andrew said, "Fine." He made his way into his truck and dragged his hand down his face in shame.

The green-eyed monster had reared its ugly head again, and he didn't like the feeling.

Why did he let things go so far?

He pulled out his phone and dialed a tow truck from a friend of his that lived in the area. As he gave him the address of the bar, he watched as Mona hugged Ralph and headed for the truck. Ralph glared at his truck, not able to see him through the tints before heading inside.

Andrew ended his call as soon as she entered the truck. She sat in silence, gathering her bearings before turning to him with intense and angry eyes. Her gray orbs were so intense; he leaned back, knowing she was about to unleash.

"What the hell was all that about? He was just trying to help!"

"I didn't need his help," Andrew grumbled as he watched a few cars pass through the rearview mirror.

"There was no reason for you to act like an asshole!" Mona continued.

Andrew sighed. "Look, I'm sorry, okay? But I don't know the guy from Adam and Eve and I didn't need the help. This could've all been avoided if you hadn't brought him outside."

Mona scuffed. "So, now it's my fault that you don't know how to act when you feel threatened by another male? Grow up, Andrew. I don't have to consult you every time I meet a guy."

He snapped his neck to her so fast he also cricked his neck. "What the hell is that supposed to mean? And for the record, I am not, nor will I ever be threatened by another male. For your information, I've only ever tried to protect you. It has nothing to do with being threatened. Don't insult me."

Andrew felt offended she would even say that considering her track record with guys and him always saving her in the past.

"It means that you don't change. It also means that you still are and will forever be overbearing and bit of an asshole." She turned away from him to stare out her window. "I can't believe I even considered we'd stand a chance."

Those words hit him like a slap to the face. He couldn't help but outburst. "A chance? You mean the hot and cold attitude you've been giving me since we got to the cabin? That's what you call a chance? I'd hate to know what you call 'nice.'"

"I was 'nice' last night," she recalled.

"Yeah, because you were probably drunk and tired."

"Well, I guess you'll never find out, then," she retorted, ignoring his last statement.

Andrew chuckled grimly. "Wow. You know, you talk about chances, and that same nasty attitude of yours has only manifested."

"Fuck you, Andrew. Maybe if you grew the balls to try to learn something about me instead of holding me back with this bullshit excuse about 'protection,' we'd actually get somewhere. And I have changed. I've changed a lot, not that you would ever know," she spat.

"So, all the times I've saved your ass is bullshit? No, you haven't changed, Mona. You always have to be the victim. I may be an asshole, but I own up to it. You expect everyone to kiss your ass just for you to be comfortable. And you're ungrateful because I've always been there for you."

"Excuse me? I don't expect anyone to kiss my ass. You're one to talk, Mr. 'I-run-away-from-my-problems'. And I never asked you to protect me. I can handle myself!"

Andrew shook his head angrily. "No, you never asked for me to be there, but as a good friend, I was anyway. Maybe if you didn't chase everyone away, I wouldn't have left."

"I never intended to chase you away, Andrew. You walked away all on your own." Mona glared at him.

He searched her face, wondering where all this was coming from. It wasn't just him that was the cause of their demise. It takes two to tangle. "You're not the only one that's hurt, Mona. I had a right to protect myself. I got tired of paying for my mistakes, and after all that, still, I came here wanting to make amends, but you're like a chained door!

"You don't give chances. You shut everyone out and wonder why everyone walks away at some point. I've done you wrong, and I'm sorry. I get it. I fucked up. And two years later, I'm still paying the price. But I can't correct my mistakes if you continue to shy away from me. I don't know how you expect to heal if you push everyone away."

Andrew took a breath he didn't know he needed. He wasn't even sure where that had come from. But it needed to be said, that much he knew.

Silence befell the truck, only the sound of the air conditioning running sustaining the air. Mona, who had turned away from him, wiped a tear that had escaped her eye.

Immediately, his anger dissipated. A lot needed to be processed on both ends. True feelings were expressed, and they both were hurting. Still hurting from a failed friendship that was once so tightknit, they thought it would last forever.

Andrew opened his mouth to say something but closed it when he noticed the tow truck pull up next to the car. Instead, with one last glance at Mona, he opened his door and greeted his friend. They talked for a bit before Andrew handed him the keys to the car.

"You mind just dropping it off? I got somewhere to go, so I won't be able to guide you there," Andrew explained. Coming up the plan last minute, he decided to it was best not to head home just yet.

"Sure, man. Just give me the address, and I'll put it in my

GPS."

Andrew gave him the address, stating what he should do with the key when he got there. Heading back to the truck, he waited for the tow truck to leave with the car before backing out of the parking lot and heading in the opposite direction. If Mona noticed, she didn't say anything. Instead, they continued to stay silent; the air tense between the two until Andrew parked the car some twenty minutes later.

It was a park that Andrew remembered coming to with Adam back in high school. It sat just off the main road near the lake across the street. Considering it was still mid-afternoon, and the sun was still blazing, many kids were outside playing and having the time of their lives. People jogged around the trail that circled the outskirts of the park.

Andrew sat there for a minute, wondering if it was a good idea. His resolve was broken, but he was determined to make the situation right once and for all before they headed home. He couldn't go one more day without either of them clearing the air. The park, he was hoping, would lighten the mood and involve fewer outbursts in case it came to that again.

He really hoped it wouldn't.

Taking a deep breath, he opened his door and stepped out. The sun sat right above his head, blinding him momentarily. He hesitated and peaked at Mona through his open door. She sat stiff as her fingers fiddled with her chain. He hadn't noticed she had it on before.

The chain, which was rose gold with an infinity symbol, was given to her on her seventeenth birthday. He gave it to her before the tattoos they got together when they were drunk a few weeks prior. It was reason he bugged her for the tattoo from the beginning. He smiled at the memory.

Mona must've felt his eyes on her because she turned to him, looking straight in his own, her eyes red and slightly puffy. The intensity of her eyes drew him in. He could see pain swirling in her orbs. She turned away, most likely not wanting to encourage him to talk.

Tough luck.

After closing his door, he made his way to hers to open. He gripped the handle, but it didn't give.

She had locked the door.

Andrew leaned his forehead on the window to peer through the tint. She sat facing forward, refusing to look at him.

"Mona..." he began. He tapped on the glass three times to get her attention. She didn't budge.

He decided he wasn't going to fight her. Leaning against the truck, his back facing her, he shielded his eyes from the sun with his palms on his eyes.

"You know," he started. "I'm surprised you didn't fight me more when I invited myself to get the car. To be honest, I was slightly expecting this fight early on."

He could hear movement behind him; however, she didn't say anything.

Andrew continued, "The truth is, as bad as I want things to go back to normal, I think it was in our best interest during that time to really see what it was like not being glued to each other's hip. I mean, we practically did everything together. Maybe it was a problem long before it became a problem, and we couldn't see it."

He craned his neck to peek at her in the car. She was gnawing on her lips and still refused to look at him. At least she was listening, that much he could tell.

"Last night, you said you were proud of me. And whether you were drunk or meant it, it meant a lot to hear you say that." He kicked a rock near his foot and stuffed his hands in his pockets.

"I did mean it."

Although it was muffled, he turned to Mona.

Nodding as he gave her a thoughtful stare, he said, "Good. Because I wasn't giving the compliment back, my pride can't take it." He chuckled a little.

He stood a moment, remising on last night's events. It was closest they had gotten in years. Turning back to the rock, he shook his head. "Those two years apart were the best and worst times of my life. I threw myself into creating something of my own. Something that couldn't be taken from me. I'm living my dream with that restaurant. But I feel... hollow. I feel hollow without the people I wanted to share my success with the most. Especially without you."

He cleared his throat, his throat feeling dry. "I could stand here all day and apologize, and it won't change the past or the damage that's already been done. But I'll continue to say it until you understand just how sorry I am. I mean it, Moe. I'm sorry for treating you the way I did, smothering you. I'm sorry for not trying harder to fix something I broke. I'm sorry for running and for not being there for you when your dad died or during the times when Calvin had you in his grasp."

Sneaking another glance her way, he caught her eye. "I'm sorry for being a terrible friend."

Not able to hold his gaze, she forced her eyes to her hands that were fiddled in her lap. "I want a chance to start over. I want to give you a reason to forgive me, and I hope you find it in your heart to let me in because you mean a lot to me. Always have. God, you don't even know how much—" he stopped before he got carried away.

After a momentary silence, he gave up and made his way to the curb and sat. Suddenly, the door of his truck opened, and Mona stepped out. He watched as she slowly made her way over to him, taking a seat beside him. Her eyes were no longer red but looked like she had rubbed them quite a bit. Despite her lack of smile, he couldn't help but admire her pure beauty.

He waited for her to say something, but she opened her mouth and closed it as if she were trying to find her bearings. Finally, she turned to him. "You're right. You're not the only blame in this, and I'm sorry if I ever made you think so. I'm sorry for pushing you away and refusing your help. But I forgave you a long time ago, Andrew. I just... I don't know how to move on. I don't know if we will ever get back to the way we were. I don't even know if that's a good or a bad thing. We have our own lives now. You don't even live here."

"We don't have to go back to the way things were, Moe.

We won't get anywhere trying to live a past life. We can only start over and hope for the best. Try our hardest." He grabbed her hand, bringing it to his chest. "But you have to let me try, Moe."

"Andrew..." she breathed.

"I don't care whether you want me to or not. I'm going to be here when you come around. I'm not going anywhere."

A single tear escaped her eyes. "Maybe...maybe I don't want you to."

Andrew offered a smile. "Good because I refuse to let the last two years define a friendship. We've been friends for fifteen years. We've grown together and learned together. I'm not letting you go that easy. Not again."

His eyes darted to her lips as she gnawed at her bottom lip, the urge to do something stupid coming on very strong. He pushed the thoughts out of his head and focused on her instead.

"Let me in, Moe."

"You never left," she muttered.

Andrew engulfed her with a tight hug, which she surprisingly returned. Her tension seemed to dissipate, to which he was grateful. He took in her natural scent and the feel of her dark curls as they caressed his cheek. He couldn't help but inhale. It was a scent he was familiar with, one that never left him, and one he missed deeply. She wrapped her arms around his neck, his hands fastened around her waist, and he couldn't help but think how perfect they fit in each other's arms.

"No more shying away?" he muttered with his mouth

pressed against the top of her head.

"No more shying away."

"No more hiding from me?"

"No more hiding."

CHAPTER FIFTEEN

Mona

SHE COULDN'T BELIEVE it had been a week since the whole fiasco with Andrew. After they had called a truce, they had spent a little time walking the trail at the park, catching up on all they missed with each other. It wasn't until her phone rang, interrupting their heart-to-heart, that they realized how long they had stayed out. By the time they got home, it was already past 2 P.M.

Things had been smooth since then—more than smooth. It was almost like they had picked up where they left off.

Almost.

Their argument in the truck had brought on feelings of guilt and shame. Mona was forced to reflect on her behavior, her self-pity, and her inability to move on from the past. Hearing the hurt in Andrew's voice had crippled her spirit. She was so focused on being a victim and hadn't realized the amount of pain she was causing him.

His plea to get back into her life had finally weighed heavy when he briefly left the truck, her tears exploding. Yes, she was tired, too. She wanted him back in her life. She wouldn't forget the past, but she wanted to forgive. She needed to finally allow herself to enjoy what was presented to her: friendship.

She had to pinch herself to make sure that she wasn't dreaming. It was like things had fallen into place where they needed to be.

It was almost a bit overwhelming, but she welcomed the change. It was necessary.

By all means, she needed to live by her father's words: "Learn to live. Learn to let go. But never forget how it changed you." Forced to look at herself, she realized that she was doing more harm than healing.

Since their reconciliation, Andrew has made a point of including her in his plans in every way. It made her happy to see that giant smile on his face again. She hadn't realized how much she had missed seeing it, especially directed at her.

Mona also felt lighter, like the weight had been lifted from her shoulders. She had started to actually enjoy herself. Even Symoné had commented on how much fire she'd seen in her since she came back from the club. Slowly, Mona could feel herself let go. She just hoped it was the right decision in the end.

Mona looked at her bikini before throwing on a short beach dress and walking out of her room. She met Nina in the hall, who was already about to head downstairs. She did a double-take at her beach dress. "Nice! Where did you get that? I need one of those," Nina commented.

Mona looked down at the aqua mesh material. "It was imported to the shop before I left. I figured I should keep one for myself. It's very comfortable."

"I. Have. To. Have. It. Please tell me there are more colors?"

Mona winked at her. "There certainly is. Don't worry. I'll hook you up."

Nina squealed. "Thank you! You headed to the pool this late?"

Mona noted the time at 10 P.M. before she left her room. "More like the hot tub. I just want to relax, look up at the stars. Where is everyone?"

Nina shrugged. "I think Adam and Symoné went out. I'm not quite sure what Andrew and Cassidy are doing. Or Dixie, for that matter."

"Where are you headed?"

"To watch a late-night movie in the living room. Party of one. Looks like you've got company." They stopped at the glass sliding door, seeing the hot tub was already occupied by Andrew. Nina blocked the door, turning to Mona. "You're okay to go out there with him? I've noticed you guys have been getting rather... close again, lately. Not that I'm not happy to see you guys cordial, but are you ready to move on from whatever issue you guys had? Are you ready for him?"

Mona smiled at Nina reassuringly. "We've come to an understanding. We know that things will never be completely the same, but we at least want to try and make this friendship work. I'm ready to accept him back into my life."

Nina nodded understandingly. "I've got your back, always, and I trust your decisions. But if he hurts you again, which I pray he doesn't, I'm stomping him in the nuts."

They both burst out in laughter as Nina opened the sliding door. Andrew, who had his head back, eyes closed with a cigarette in his hand, had looked up alarmed. He settled and took a drag of his cigarette as they made their way toward him.

"I thought you quit smoking?" Nina gave him a pointed look. He looked between them and crushed the cigarette butt on the edge of the tub.

"I did. I just..." he paused, looking at Mona, who stood in front of him with a frown on her face. She was disappointed. Especially with how long she had helped him to kick the habit long ago when his health was taking a beating.

"You promised you wouldn't smoke again." She remembered that day, too. As he laid on the ground after one of many bad asthma attacks directly related to his smoking habit, he had promised to start working on healthier habits.

He looked away, ashamed. "I was stressed. Am stressed. Old habits die hard, I guess."

Nina shook her head in disbelief. "You must not remember what happened last time, do you? You're going to kill yourself, giving in to *habits*."

He threw Nina a glare. "I get it. I'll work on it." He turned to Mona with pleading eyes. "I'm sorry."

Mona stuck her foot in the hot tub and sat on the edge facing him. "Don't be sorry. Just quit before something bad happens. Again."

"I'll try. "

Nina scoffed, "I'll leave you two at it. Catch me inside when you can, yeah?" Nina nodded to Mona and threw Andrew a glare before heading inside. They waited until they heard the click of the sliding door closing before turning to each other.

"I feel like she's going to stab me in my sleep one day. As a matter of fact, I'm surprised she hasn't run me over with her car since we started hanging out."

Mona snickered. "She won't. Nina's all talk, and she loves you. Deep, deep, deep down."

Andrew looked at her incredulously. "That's not love I saw in her eyes."

Mona rolled her eyes. "Nina is trying to make sure there is peace at the end of the day. That we are as good as we say we are."

Andrew moved a little closer, holding her gaze. "Are we?" he asked.

Her breathing hitched when he brushed her foot. She covered with a small cough. "Are we what?"

"As good as we say we are?"

She stayed silent for a moment, even though she already knew her answer. The way her week has been spent getting to know him again, she was as good as she'd been since before they split.

"We're not perfect, but we're better than good."

Andrew smiled and returned to his side. He spread his arms over the top of the tub, motioning her to come in. "You should get in. You're missing out on these jets."

She didn't respond, but instead, took off her dress and

slide in. The jets hit her back forcefully, spreading warmth throughout her body. She closed her eyes as she listened to the calm of the night. She was at risk of falling asleep if she had decided to stay the way she was. With her eyes still closed, she asked Andrew how long ago he had started smoking again.

"Can we not talk about it right now?"

She lifted her head and met his eyes. He looked uneasy. "If we don't know, will we ever?"

Andrew shrugged. "We'll talk about it. Just not right now. Right now, I just want to enjoy your company."

She couldn't argue with that. They had all the time in the world to talk about it. But she wouldn't let him get away it. She cared about his health, even if he didn't. She would be damned if she lets him throw his life away on cancer sticks.

Deciding to change the subject, she asked him a question that had been nipping her. "Where's Cassidy?"

He looked at her, opening his mouth and then closing it as if he was debating whether he should answer or not. "I don't know," he finally said.

Mona looked at him curiously. "You don't know where your girlfriend is? I find that hard to believe."

Andrew sighed, sinking deeper into the hot tub until the water was just under his chin. "She left after we had an argument. She's probably driving around in my truck somewhere."

"And you didn't think to follow her? Something could happen to her. You're a terrible boyfriend," Mona joked. He didn't laugh, making Mona want to recant her words.

"I was just kidding, I'm sorry," she apologized when he

didn't say anything. He wouldn't look at her, but he didn't seem mad. Just deep in thought.

"You're probably right," he finally said. "I'm probably way past that by now."

"What do you mean?" she asked thoughtfully.

Andrew didn't answer. Instead, he settled back and closed his eyes. Mona decided not to push. Obviously, there was way more to the story, and he wasn't in the mood to talk about it. It was none of her business, but she was curious.

For a time, they didn't talk. They kept their distance, but it wasn't awkward. Mona stared up at the stars, getting lost in memories of all the summers she'd spent at the cabin; before they had all grown up and found new meaning to life.

Life was so carefree back then.

She felt a brush of skin on her right side; she turned to find Andrew beside her. He mirrored her position, staring at the stars. She laid her head back, ignoring the burning feeling she felt in the pit of her stomach.

"I'm not shutting you out, I promise. I'm just not ready to face the reality of Cassidy and me. What I know in my heart might happen. My relationships are like glaring failures, and I have no one to blame but myself."

Mona understood that completely.

"I know. It's none of my business, but if you ever need to talk, I'm always here," Mona offered, turning her head to the side. He was already looking at her, but she hadn't anticipated how close they really were. Unconsciously, she shifted away.

"I'm glad I decided to come here," he muttered. His eyes

flickered to her lips so quick, she almost missed it. But she couldn't bring herself to move. Not with the intense look he was giving her. That he always gave her. And she could never figure out what it meant.

"Me, too." She took a deep breath and turned her head, breaking their moment. She felt him move from beside her, standing at his full length before getting out the tub. She watched the water drip from his chest, her eyes tracing his tattoos. Her eyes stopped on the infinity symbol on his wrist they both shared.

"Well, I'm going to head in. You'll be okay out here by yourself?"

Mona nodded. "Yeah, I'll probably head in a few minutes."

Andrew grabbed his towel that was thrown over a lawn chair. He ruffled it through his hair and then wrapped it around his shoulders. "Cool. So...I guess this is goodnight?"

Mona looked at him, gnawing her lower lip unconsciously. His eyes zeroed in them before bringing his eyes up to hers. He had a pensive look on his face. His tone was light, but his eyes completely opposite. "Yeah, I'll see you in the morning."

Andrew pivoted for a second before scratching the back of his head and chuckling to himself.

"Goodnight." He didn't wait for an answer.

Mona didn't take a breath until the click of the door was heard. And suddenly, she felt cold in the hot tub.

What was that? She wasn't sure, and she didn't delve into it. At all. After a few minutes, she got out and turned off the jets, grabbing a loose towel on a chair. She headed inside shortly after with her beach dress back on. She spied Nina on the couch, lights off, with a bowl of popcorn and a chick flick on the big screen.

Nina turned to Mona as she closed and locked the sliding door. "You okay? You look troubled. Something happen? The fucker didn't even say goodnight."

Mona shook her head. "No, I'm fine. We had a great time. He was probably just tired or something. It was nice out there. You should've come out there," Mona tried to steer the conversation.

Nina smiled. "And interrupt the Mona and Andrew show? No, thank you."

Despite the light tone, the comment rubbed her the wrong way. "What's that supposed to mean?" she asked carefully.

"Look, I really don't mean any harm with what I'm about to say, but in a room full of people, you and Andrew always act like you're in a room by yourselves. I don't even think you guys notice that you do it, but it leaves the rest of us feeling like we are outside of your bubble. And now that you two are talking again, it's bound to happen."

Mona wasn't sure what to make of what Nina was telling her. Did she really shut people out before when she and Andrew were talking? Nina said he did it, too.

Nina continued, noting the look of disbelief on Mona's face. "I'm not offended by it. I've—we've learned to accept it for what it is. Don't take this the wrong way, but there's a reason neither of you could hold a relationship."

Taken aback by that last comment, Mona frowned and

shook her head. "We just make bad choices. That's it."

Nina shrugged, not at all moved by what she said. "I love you, Mona. But I wouldn't be who I am if I didn't tell you the truth. Like I said, I'm not in any way offended by it because you've known Andrew longer, and I know you guys have this... bond that the rest of us will never quite understand. But we know better than to put ourselves in the third wheel position."

"Wow," Mona began. "Well, I think I've heard enough for tonight. Goodnight, Nina." She practically ran to her room. She wasn't mad in the slightest, but what Nina said resonated with her. Had she and Andrew always done that? She couldn't think of a time they solely ever focused on each other unless they were alone.

Mona threw off her dress and bikini and gathered supplies for a shower with a towel and robe wrapped around herself. As she made her way to the bathroom, she heard a grunt from behind Andrew's closed door. Curiosity got the best of her, and she tiptoed to the door pressing her ear to it, but the floorboard creaked pretty loudly. She jumped back when she heard him say, "Hello?" and made her way to the bathroom, shutting the door lightly.

With her heart pounding, she threw off her garments and entered the shower, holding to wash the embarrassment away. What processed her to think it was okay to press her ear to his door, she wasn't sure. She wasn't sure if she wanted to know what was going on in there. Perhaps Cassidy had come home, not that it was any of her business.

After finishing in the shower, she carefully made her way

to her room, locking out the world. She drifted into a fitful sleep, not quite able to get Andrew off her mind.

***

Andrew

"HELLO?" ANDREW SAID as he paused at his door. The shadow from the door moved, and he could hear the door to the bathroom shut, followed by the shower coming on. He leaned his head against the door, his heart pounding in his throat. He wasn't sure who it was, but he could probably guess. Cassidy would've come in the room before a shower.

If Cassidy had walked in, he would've had a lot of explaining to do. He couldn't quite lock the door because that would look even more suspicious if she had come back. Andrew sat on the bed, somewhat flustered, and painfully aroused. His night with Mona in the hot tub had taken its toll on him both physically and emotionally. He wanted to slap himself for the thoughts he was having about his *friend.*

Adjusting his pajama pants, he wiped his hands with cleaning wipes and put the lotion back. At this point, he figured it was a bad idea to even attempt to ease his tension. He waited until the bathroom was unoccupied before making his way in there and washing his face with some cold water.

It worked to calm himself down, and he went back to his room to occupy himself. Even though it was late, he called the restaurant to make sure all was well. David sounded like he had everything under control, thankfully. After he hung up,

Cassidy finally walked into the room.

"Hey," he offered.

She looked at him blankly for a moment before saying, "Hey."

He watched her take off her shoes and dress. "Where've you been?"

"Out."

"I know that. Where?"

She turned to him with exhaustion in her eyes. "Andrew, can we not fight tonight? I have no more energy."

"It's a simple question, Cass," he continued to urge.

Cassidy turned to him as she pulled on pajamas. "Why even pretend you care? You didn't call me to see if I was okay, you never came after me, nor do you even remotely look concerned. As of matter of fact, you don't even look mad. That tells me everything I need to know right there."

She had a point, but he wasn't about to admit that. He didn't want to admit to himself how much he lacked the drive to even try and figure out what was going on between them. "I do care."

Cassidy scoffed, "Yeah, you care. You care about the wrong person."

"What's that supposed to mean?" he asked. He could already feel where the conversation was headed. Like so many of his other relationships around the years, it was like an automated system. In true fashion, she went there.

"It means that you're too busy eye-fucking this woman you've never mentioned before I got here. It means I'm tired of being your back-pocket girlfriend. It means I want out. You have no time for me, and I have no time for this bullshit."

The room stood still as she threw her hair into a small ponytail. The tension was palpable. Andrew was unsure of what to say. She had said it. She didn't want to be with him anymore. He wasn't surprised, but as someone who had watched him make something of himself in those two years he spent away, he now felt the need to at least try and fight for someone who was on his side when no one else was.

Andrew could feel a guilty knot twisting in his stomach. He got up from the bed as she reached for the door, ready to leave, but he beat her to it. He stood in front of it with pleading eyes.

Cassidy sighed. "Andrew...move."

He shook his head. "Not until we talk. A real talk. Not a screaming match. No fighting. Just talk. At least give me a chance to explain myself."

"Andrew..."

"*Please*? Obviously, I'm doing a shitty job of showing you that I care about you, but I do. You were there for me when I needed you, and I will always love you for that. But I had unresolved issues here, and it took up my time because it was important to me."

She looked at him sternly. "Is *she* important to you?"

Andrew took a breath before answering, "Yes, but—"

Cassidy tried to bypass him, but he grabbed her hands and held them. "Just listen! Please!"

"Let go of me, Andrew! I don't want to hear it because all

you do is tell me one thing, but your actions are what's bothering me!" She yanked her hands from him. "Stay away from me until I calm down. I don't want to talk. I've heard enough, and I'm done."

Cassidy pushed him out of the way to open the door and slammed it on the way out. He yanked the door open after her, ready to chase her down but was pulled back by Adam.

"Leave it alone, dude. Let her calm down," Adam advised as he guided him back to the room.

"But—"

"She doesn't want to talk. Trying to force it is going to make it worse, trust me."

Andrew sat on the edge of the bed, his head in his hands, defeated. Adam sat on the bed beside him, offering silent support. "When did you get back?" Andrew asked.

"A couple of minutes ago. You guys were loud enough to hear from downstairs. I'm surprised the whole house didn't wake up. What happened?"

Andrew shook his head. "Cassidy wants to break up. I can't even pinpoint exactly what's wrong. All I know is that things between us have been spiraling slowly, even before we got here. I guess it's just..." Andrew trailed off, not sure how to describe it.

"Blowing up in your face in the worse way possible?" Adam offered with a chuckled. Andrew shook his head with a meek smile. Adam patted him on the back before standing. "You should get some sleep. Get your thoughts together. Come up with a plan to win over your girl."

Andrew sighed. "I think we're kind of passed that point."

Adam waved him off. "Nonsense. If you and Mona can get over a two-year hump, you and Cassidy can get over a week setback, or however long this has been going on. You just gotta prioritize."

"But she's not Mona."

Adam smirked before saying, "Maybe that's the problem." He backed out of the room, leaving Andrew more puzzled with even more questions than answers.

Chapter Sixteen

Andrew

"WE'RE ALREADY STAYING in a cabin. Why go camping outside of it?"

Andrew followed Adam as he led him deeper into a wooded area he had already set up from the night before. Adam turned back to him, a smirk on his face. "Why else? We need to have fun. What are we going to do? Sit down in the cabin, watching movies all day? That's boring."

Andrew rolled his eyes. "This just seems unnecessary considering we're already in the woods."

Adam dropped the items in his hands in the clearing. "That's because you have no imagination."

"Whatever."

Adam and Andrew spent the remainder morning setting up several tents and making a makeshift bonfire. Andrew sat on one of the logs they had found as Adam finished the last tent.

"How did things go with Cassidy?" Adam asked.

Andrew played with a fig he found on the ground, reminiscent of the last few days. "Steady, so far. But I'm not so sure anything is going to change. She was willing to listen, but…"

"But what?"

"But I think the damage is done."

Adam sighed and walked over to Andrew, sitting beside him on the log. "I'm sorry, man."

Andrew shrugged. "It is what it is. Can't change how she feels. Two years down the drain."

"That's probably your longest relationship." Adam laughed, trying to brighten the mood.

Andrew reciprocated his laugh and shook his head. "Yeah, I think it is."

"You know, for what it's worth, it probably wouldn't have lasted much longer anyway."

Andrew turned to him with a frown. "Why do you say that?"

Adam looked around as if trying to find the right words to say. "Given your history, the relationship with Mona probably would bug her more if you guys got… closer."

Andrew was taken aback. "So, you think Mona is the problem in my relationships? I've held plenty of relationships when we were best friends. I mean, I know Cassidy was bothered by it, but there's no way that it was the overall issue. We've been distant a lot longer than that, I just haven't realized it until now."

The notion of Adam thinking that Mona was the root cause of his relationship problems was ridiculous to him. Sure, Cassidy alluded to having a problem with his reconciliation with her, but not enough to want to end a two-year relationship.

Adam got up and went back to setting up the tent. "If you say so."

Andrew was getting a bit annoyed at Adam's tone. "You don't know my relationship, Adam. With either of them. Please, don't pretend like you do."

Adam threw up his hands in surrender. "Look, I'm sorry. That was out of line. I was just giving you an honest opinion."

"Well, you can keep your honest opinion. Mona is not the root of my problems."

"No, she isn't. Your feelings for her are."

"I don't—"

"—Either way," Adam interrupted, "one of them was bound to get hurt because, in your heart, you can only give your all to one person. And it wasn't Cassidy. You and I both know that. Now, I'm done giving you my honest opinion."

Adam finished setting up the tent and got a lighter from his pocket. Andrew watched as he set ablaze the bonfire, not able to clear his mind.

He loved Cassidy. That he knew. And Mona will forever be just a friend. He knew that. He was okay with that. He wasn't entirely afraid to admit his eyes lingered on her more than it should. Or that he sometimes imagined what her lips tasted like. Or that he found her extremely attractive. He'd be blind not to. And that night—he just had a weak moment. But that didn't mean he had feelings for her. There was no way of that ever happening.

He was sure.

They watched the fire cackled in silence, an unresolved tension between the two. "I don't have feelings for Mona. Like that."

Adam turned to him with his eyebrows raised in question. "Okay... I believe you. But do *you* believe you?"

Adam didn't wait for an answer. Instead, he shuffled back to the cabin, probably to gather more supplies. Andrew followed, determined to get his point across. "Yeah, I believe my words. I just don't get where this is coming from? I thought making up with Mona would've been better for everyone."

"Oh, it is, don't get me wrong. I love Mona like a sister, you know that. Honestly, if it meant I didn't have to see you sulk another minute, I'm all for it. I'm just trying to let you know that there is a direct correlation to your relationship issues and your friendship with Mona. You guys may not notice it, but you two are the reason why your relationships don't last. You guys are *too* close to be friends, and I can understand why Cassidy would find an issue with it. If Symoné had a guy friend and they interacted the way you and Mona do, I would have an issue with it, no doubt."

"So, once again, Mona is the problem?" Andrew reiterated.

"No." Adam sighed. "The competition is the problem. The competition that Cassidy may feel is a losing battle. You only have eyes for Mona. Whether you realize it or not, Mona has always been your 'one.'"

"My *what*?" Andrew looked at him incredulously. His 'one?' What the hell did that mean?

Adam gave him a pointed look. "I can try and explain it and promptly confused the hell out of you, but honestly, you're not going to understand until you see it for yourself. And when you do, everything, from then and now, will make complete sense."

Adam continued without him, Andrew being completely frozen in his spot. Andrew sighed in defeat. What was he failing to see? Everything was happening too fast for his liking. Just when he got closure on one issue, another one opened.

One thing he knew for sure was that he was not giving up his friendship with Mona. Not with everything that's happened within the last week and a half. Not after he just got her back in his life. He wasn't going to let her go. Not even for Cassidy.

Andrew started back toward the cabin, pulling his hair in frustration. He patted his pocket for a cigarette but grunted in frustration when he realized he threw out his last pack after Mona caught him smoking that night in the hot tub. He leaned against a tree, inclining his head to the sky.

Thinking back to the last few days spent trying to make up with Cassidy, he remembered the sour look on her face whenever Mona was in the same room. If they talked, Cassidy would walk away. Her mood never improved over the past week. He had taken her out one night, hoping something would spark, but she was mundane.

Truthfully, he was fishing to find some of that spark in him as well. It was almost forced, the way they interacted. Even before they'd come to the cabin. He still hid things from her, primarily where Mona was concerned. What kind of relationship was that? What was he afraid of?

Andrew grew more bothered by the questions he couldn't answer anymore. He heard someone's throat clear, and he turned his eyes from the morning sky to face a grey pair of eyes that haunted his dreams.

"Everything okay?" she looked concerned, rightfully so. He stared at her for a moment, noting her hair pulled back in a bun and her shorts that hugged her just right and her tank top that exposed a sliver of skin. She was beautiful, even when she wasn't trying.

"Andrew?" Mona repeated. The smile she was sporting started to fade, and he couldn't help but want to keep it on her face. She had a beautiful smile. He could stare at it all day if it weren't weird.

Coughing a little, he replied, "Yeah, I-I'm good. Just… thinking."

"About?" She shook her head and smiled at him. His heart picked up a beat. "Never mind. It's none of my business. I was going to go for a walk, you want to come?"

"Uh…"

He spied Adam coming through the back door with kitchen supplies. Adam looked between the two with a suggested raised eyebrow before moving past them to the campsite. "Um… actually, I should probably go help, Adam. Raincheck?"

She nodded in understanding. "Sure. I can help if you guys want. The walk can wait."

"No! I mean, we got it. By the time you come back, we'll

probably be completely done anyway," he urged. It was probably best he clear his head before doing anything with her. He had to play his cards right around both she and Cassidy.

Mona looked unsure but replied, "Okay. I guess I'll see you when I get back?" It came out more as a question than a statement. Like she was waiting for assurance.

He gave a sincere smile, his eyes penetrating hers with honesty. "Of course. Maybe when you get back, we can make our famous s'mores?"

Mona laughed. "I haven't eaten that since—"

"High school, I know. I got some ingredients, maybe we can get started when you get back. Maybe finally share some of the delight with the group," he offered.

"I'd like that." Mona gave him another smile before heading on her trail, his eyes trailing after her.

"Stare too hard, your eyes might fall out," Adam said as he passed by.

"Whatever, man."

By the time night fell, everyone had gathered in front of the fire, laughing and enjoying each other's company. James had joined sometime in the evening, fitting right into the group as if he had been there all along.

Andrew observed him as he struck up a conversation with Nina, who looked wildly attentive in his presence. They seemed flirty, much to Andrew's shock and relief. He surveyed the rest of the group, his eyes trained on Cassidy as she laughed at something Dixie said. It was the first time he's seen her smile in a week, if not more. Adam and Symoné were lovingly enjoying each other's company near the trees. Andrew looked away in minor disgust, not wanting to accidentally catch them doing something. Knowing Adam, it was bound to happen.

He took a sip of his beer as his attention swayed to Mona sitting cross-legged against a tree reading a book. She caught his eye unexpectedly, probably feeling his stare. She smiled and brought her eyes back down to the book in her lap. He made a resolve to get her a beer and sat next to her, temporarily distracting her. She took the beer he offered and set it aside with gratitude.

"Took you long enough," she said as she turned a page.

"I didn't know you were missing my presence. I should've come sooner and blessed you with entertainment," Andrew said as he took another sip of his beer.

Mona picked up hers and made an effort to open the bottle with a pair of keys from her pocket. "Yeah, you should've," she said through clenched teeth as she tried to force the bottle open.

Taking it from her, he used a lighter butt from his pocket to pop it open effortlessly before handing it back to her. "Sorry, I should've opened it before I gave it to you."

"No worries."

As she turned her attention back to the book, Andrew spied the front of the cover and snickered. "Erotica? Really?"

Mona gave him a pointed look. "It's not erotica! It's has a clear plot, thank you very much." She moved the book out of his eyesight and glared at him when he laughed.

"Yeah, sex. That's the main goal of the story. It's basically a race to see how many times the characters can fuck each other per chapter."

"That's not true, and it's a nice book," she stressed.

"Yeah, to play with yourself. Fifty Shades of Grey is erotica designed to make women, in particular, think sex and wealth is the answer to all their problems." He took another sip and challenged her with his eyes.

Mona hit him playfully with the book. "You suck, you know that?"

Andrew shrugged. "Just stating facts. I've seen the movie adaption trailer. There is no real drama in that 'storyline,'" he said using air quotes.

"The movie adaption doesn't represent the masterpiece of the book. They don't capture the essence."

"The essence of sex," he mumbled. She hit him again with the book on his shoulder.

Andrew rubbed his shoulder with a frown. "Violence doesn't make it any less true."

"Okay, since you have such a vast knowledge of literature, why don't you suggest a good book, then?" Mona crossed her arms with a daring look.

He frowned. "Books aren't my thing. That hasn't changed."

"Obviously," she joked.

Shoving her playfully, he grabbed her book to sift through. "If I do read, I get an audible book. I don't have time to sit and read."

"That defeats the whole purpose of reading," she said as she tipped her beer back. She eyed him as he flipped through the pages of the book like it was a flipbook. "Hey! Don't ruin it."

She grabbed it back from him swiftly, causing him to chuckle at her concern. "See, if you had an Audible or eBook, you would have no wear and tear. Get with the program," he taunted.

Mona turned her back to him with a huff. "Go away."

Andrew smirked as he drank the last drop of beer left in his book. With her back to him, he caught a glimpse of a wing on her shoulder that was covered by the strap of her shirt.

He hadn't noticed it before. It was rather small, and with straps on her shoulders, it would likely disappear.

Without thinking, his hand traced it, causing her to noticeably shiver. She moved away and turned to him. "What are you doing?" she asked carefully.

With his hand still suspended in the air, he hesitated before speaking, "I was looking at the tattoo on your shoulder. I didn't mean to make you uncomfortable."

Mona eyed him but moved to sit back beside him. "You didn't. I got it after my dad died," she began as she picked at twig near her crossed legs. "It's supposed to be symbolic of heaven or something, I don't know. At the time, I just wanted to feel closer to him. It was spontaneous. I was feeling reckless." She laughed softly and turned to him.

"Can I see it? Fully, I mean?" He knew it meant she had to move the strap of her shirt for a better look, but he really was curious. Besides the infinity tattoo they shared, he never thought she would get another one. She hated needles. But he imagined the pain she was in during the early months of her father's death. He swallowed the guilt that began to rise at the thought.

She turned her back to him and moved her strap. It was a tattoo of a dove mid-flight with an olive branch in its mouth. The words "Higher" were written along the belly of the bird. It didn't have any extraordinary coloring, nor was it huge, but was a simple, yet meaningful, tattoo.

Andrew had to refrain himself from wanting to retrace it. "It's beautiful. I'm sure he would've loved it."

Mona turned back around and fixed her strap. She was about to reply when Nina approached them. "What have we here?"

"Two individuals who were better off before you came to disturb our peace," Andrew said innocently. He smirked at her, but she flipped him off and took a seat on the ground in front of Mona. She spied the book Mona was reading and picked it up.

"Really, Mona? Erotica?" Nina said with disgust.

Mona's mouth hung open while Andrew couldn't hold in his laughter. "It's not erotica! They wouldn't make a movie about it if it were," she defended.

Nina tossed the book to the side. "Yes, they do, and it's called soft porn."

Andrew continued laughing, not able to catch his breath as Mona pouted. "You and Andrew are such an ass."

Nina turned to Andrew with a victorious smile. "Well, at least we agree on something." She high-fived him, a rare occurrence for the two.

"Whatever." Mona rolled her eyes as Andrew finally controlled himself.

"Anyway," Nina said. "I actually came over here to see if you wanted to perhaps play a game as a group. I was thinking Truth or Dare."

"Way to go the high school route."

Nina glared at Andrew, causing him to shrug indifferently.

"It's not high school. Hide and seek in the deep woods is high school, not to mention dangerous," Nina defended.

"What about Never Have I Ever? We can add our own rules and make it more fun," Mona suggested.

Nina thought for a minute before nodded slowly. "Yeah… yeah, that actually sounds like a plan." Nina shot up, clasping her hands. "Okay! So, it's settled. That's what we're playing. I'll let Adam in on it." She left the two and headed to Adam across the campsite.

"I guess it could've been worse," Andrew commented.

Mona shook her head. "Come on, party popper, let's get this over with."

The whole group collectively gathered around the bonfire, Adam particularly looking excited to play. Andrew eyed him suspiciously, knowing Adam all too well. He passed around a fresh beer to everyone in the circle, a glint in his eyes.

"A shot of vodka would've made this even more interesting," Dixie commented as she settled next to Nina.

"Vodka is for a special occasion. It is off-limits tonight,"

Adam answered cryptically as he opened his beer and sat next to Symoné.

Mona gathered next to Adam and Dixie. Andrew winked at her when she looked in his direction, and she smiled before turning to Dixie to say something. Cassidy sat quietly next to him on the log while James settled on the ground between Dixie and Nina.

Cassidy leaned over to him. "Should I be worried about this game?"

"What do you mean?"

She hesitated before answering as if she changed her mind about what she really was about to say. "Adam just looks like he's up to something."

Andrew frowned but shrugged. "I guess we'll find out."

"Okay, everyone! We added a couple rules to the game to make it a little more interesting. Whoever has to drink the most at the end of the round—no cheating—has to stand in front of everyone and sing the national anthem after inhaling helium while naked."

"Where the hell did you get a helium tank?!" Nina asked as Adam pulled a helium tank from his tent.

"I'm not taking off my clothes!" Dixie exclaimed. Everyone else collectively groaned.

Adam held up his hands to quiet everyone. "Now, now! You won't be completely naked. Just down to your garments. And just to make sure no one is tempted to cheat, we are allowed to say we've never done something knowing someone in the group has actually done it and you can call them out for it if they don't drink. And if you feel like telling a backstory, by all means, have fun with it."

Andrew groaned, knowing that this may be one of his worse or best nights yet. Mona tried her best to stifle a laugh across the bonfire as Adam brought the helium tank beside him like a safety net as he took his seat.

A hush fell over the group as Adam appointed Dixie to go first, followed by James. "Never have I ever—shit ...stolen a car," she finished, throwing a sassy look at Symoné, who evidently rolled her eyes before taking a drink.

"Oh, I definitely need the backstory on this," Adam wiggled his eyebrows at her.

Symoné sighed, knowing he was going to push for it if she didn't throw him a bone. "It was high school, and I gave into peer pressure. Case closed. Next!"

"Wait! Did you get arrested?" Nina asked curiously.

Symoné grinned. "I guess you'll have to find out."

James cleared his throat before beginning. "Never have I ever slept with a teacher."

Andrew looked around carefully before taking a sip. Adam's mouth hung open. Andrew shook his head before Adam could even say it, but it didn't stop him anyway. "It was Ms. Kreaton, wasn't it? Dude, you had the biggest crush on her in high school! Though, pretty much every guy did."

"It just... happened. It's not a big deal. And for the record, it was after I graduated," Andrew shied away from the conversation. He forgot he hadn't told Adam about it, he wasn't sure why he drank if no one in the circle knew, but too late. Briefly, he looked over at Mona, who looked surprised but was mute.

"You mean the young English teacher senior year? The one that had all the guys practically jerking off to her picture? How the hell did you pull that one off? Not even you have that much game," Nina said.

Andrew glared at her. "That's for me to know and for you to never find out. And you're next."

"We are so talking about this later," Adam urged. Andrew rolled his eyes and spied Cassidy, sitting motionless. He sighed as he turned his full attention to Nina.

Nina shushed everyone so she could begin. "Well, never have I ever dined and dashed."

Symoné, Adam, and Andrew took a drink. "Man, Symoné is badass!" Dixie exclaimed. They all laughed collectively.

"Peer pressure. That's all I've got to say. What's your story?" She pointed between Adam and Andrew.

Adam shrugged and looked at Andrew with a grin. "We forgot our wallet on a double date and pretended to pay for it when our dates went to the bathroom. Fun times," Adam said, his eyes glossing over in reminisce.

Symoné shoved him. "You better not do that on a date with me because I'm not paying."

Andrew chuckled at the two before the group waited for Cassidy to start. She looked around before taking a deep breath and starting. "Never have I ever... used a sex toy."

All the girls drank. Andrew raised an eyebrow in Mona's direction, and she blushed and shook her head. He laughed softly, causing Cassidy to turn to him with a frown.

"What?" he asked, confused. Why did she look so angry?

She rolled her eyes and turned away. All eyes fell on him, signaling his turn. He took a moment to think before he began, "Never have I ever lost a bet." Everyone drank to that notion. Andrew pointed a finger at Adam. "You still owe me two hundred dollars, by the way."

Adam looked confused for a moment but sobered and nodded. "You'll get it, you'll get it."

Symoné cracked her knuckles as she prepared for her turn. "Never have I ever kissed the same sex."

Mona and Nina both looked at each other before taking a drink, much to Andrew's surprise. Adam looked rather intrigued as he looked between the two who were blushing. "Oh, this is something I gotta hear, like, now."

Symoné hit him on the back of the head, causing James and Dixie to laugh. "Leave them alone."

"No! Nina." Adam motioned for her to get on with the story.

She scratched the back of her head in nervousness. "It was our sophomore year at college, and we had tequila for the first time during a frat party. We just got curious and kissed."

"Uh-huh, go on," Adam urged attentively. Symoné shook her head and hit him on the back of the head again. "Ow!"

"Nothing happened after that," Mona explained. "I believe it is your turn."

Adam huffed. "Okay, okay! Never have I ever...." He looked around, then stopped at Andrew. He groaned, knowing he was going to be a target of this one. Why was he friends with this guy, again? "Slept non-sexually— I think— in the same bed with someone I called a best friend of the opposite sex."

"That was oddly specific," Dixie commented. Adam ignored her, his grin widening.

Andrew gave him an evil eye, but Adam just sat there and smiled at him. He turned to Mona and said, "Come on! Drink up."

Andrew looked at Mona, who slowly raised her bottle at the same time he did. "Cheers," he mumbled as he tipped his head back.

"I'm intrigued. So, did you guys ever 'sexually' sleep together?" Dixie asked as her attention swayed between Mona and him. Mona choked on her beer, earning a pat on the back from Adam.

"Dixie, that is so rude to ask in the circle," Symoné scolded as she motioned with her eyes to Cassidy. Andrew looked to his feet, afraid to look at either Mona or Cassidy. He was sure of the expression on Cassidy's face, but he was worried Mona would die of embarrassment.

"Oh, shit. Sorry," she said, even though it came off indifferent.

It wasn't like it was a secret, but they knew how it looked from the outside looking in. There was a time he was always at her house during high school to escape his full one, and he sometimes fell asleep beside her on the bed. Well, more than occasionally. It became so frequent, it was like second nature. They didn't think much of it, but when Adam caught them one morning, and they realized the negative connotation, they stopped swiftly. It honestly was just a friendly jester turned negative.

Adam, who was clearly having too much fun with this and possible already drunk from the beers he had earlier, gave Andrew a thumbs up which, Andrew returned by flipping him off. He was going to kill Adam when he got the chance.

"How about we keep this moving, huh? Mona, if you would like to do the honors...?"

The round came full circle, ending with Mona. She cleared her throat nervously, obviously not liking the attention she was getting at the moment. It took her a minute to think of something to say. "Never have I ever been asked out on a date."

Everyone drank. "That's impossible, you've been on plenty of dates," Nina interjected.

"I have, yes. But I've always asked them out. They've never asked me out," she corrected. Andrew was shocked to hear that, and so was apparently everyone else.

"They're crazy," James said.

"Nope, just assholes," Andrew mumbled to no one in particular. Cassidy heard him and shot him a dark look. He didn't bother commenting on it.

"Wow, I never knew that. No wonder I hated them," Nina said matter-of-factly.

"It's not a big deal," Mona stated. "It builds confidence."

"Now that's a wave I can get on," Dixie said as she drank the rest of her beer.

Symoné got up to stretch. "So, who lost this round?"

"Well, technically you," Adam said. "But so did Mona and Andrew. Shall we break the tie, or do all three of you want to do the honors of sucking on helium air half-naked?" Adam's mischievous grin indicated how much he was enjoying making a fool out of them.

"I say we break the tie," Mona suggested.

"I second that," Symoné added.

They turned to Andrew, wondering what route he wanted to go. He shrugged, not particularly caring. "Whatever you guys want to do."

They agreed to do one last bonus round with just the three of them. Whoever had to drink twice would lose. Mona started off, "Never have I ever played an instrument."

Both Andrew and Symoné drank. Next, it was Symoné, "Never have I ever skied on a slope."

Mona was the only one to drink. It came down to Andrew, knowing he was clear from doing the last challenge. It was now between both of them. He looked between the two, giving Mona a slight unnoticed head nod, which she recognized and acknowledged. "Never have I ever... skinny-dipped."

Symoné looked at the two, Mona not raising her drink, between sighing a taking a large gulp. Andrew gave Mona a sly smile that she returned before turning her attention to Adam and the helium tank.

Symoné was the lucky loser.

"I hate it had to be you, babe, but you know the deal." Bringing the tank in front of her, she bowed her head before braving it out and bringing the tube to her lips. She had performed her best with a helium-laced voice and half-naked which had a couple of them wheezing with laughter. It would take another six rounds before they all called it quits. It was past 2 a.m. at that point, and half of them, if not all, were drunk.

"It's probably best we call it a night," Nina said as she struggled to hold her stance.

"I agree, I'm beat. Night y'all," Symoné added. She took Adam's hand and disappeared into their tent together. Nina and Dixie were getting helped by James into their respective tents before bidding everyone goodnight and disappearing into his own. Cassidy had already left mid-game during round four, so all that was left was Mona and Andrew.

They both were buzzed, but not entirely drunk as they had been secretly cheating throughout the game. Considering no one knew everything they used to do together, they had an advantage and wouldn't call out the other if they chose not to drink for that round. He felt terrible that he had inadvertently roped her into it when he signaled to her in their bonus round in round one, but she didn't seem to mind.

"You're not going to bed?" he asked as he watched her roll her neck with her eyes closed.

She shook her head. "I'm actually hungry."

Andrew thought for a minute before remembering the s'mores they had made plans to make but had forgotten about. "I don't have the honey, but we can make the s'mores we were supposed to make earlier," he offered.

Her eyes opened bright, and she smiled. "Oh, yes!"

Andrew chuckled at her enthusiasm and gathered the graham crackers, chocolate, and marshmallows by the bonfire. He also gathered some shish kabob sticks for the fire. He sat on the ground next to her and handed the stuff to her. They sat in comfortable silence for a while, enjoying the sound of the crickets and the cackling of the fire. They downed one last beer for the night as they almost completely finished their pack of chocolate and graham crackers.

"Thanks for helping me out during the game," Mona said quietly. She leaned back against the log as she finished eating the s'mores in her hand.

"No, thank you. I would've been doomed if you hadn't agreed," he replied.

She started to giggle to herself, causing him to turn to her in question. "I can't believe you slept with our English teacher."

Andrew looked away, embarrassed, and unsure if he really wanted to explain that to her, but he knew she would push for it anyway. "It really was just a one-time thing."

She shifted to look at him, her eyes slightly red but alert. "How did it happen?"

"Mona—"

"I promise I won't tell," Mona cut him off.

It wasn't the telling part he was worried about.

Sighing, he said, "It's not that. It's just something I really don't care to talk about. I thought it was a cool thing at the time, but I regret doing it."

Mona deflated but nodded. "Sorry, I'm just shocked. You

never told me. I-I mean, not that it's really any of my business anyway...forget I said anything," she clammed up.

He chuckled. "You didn't tell me about the dating thing. I knew all your boyfriends were pansies, but that confession took the cake."

Mona looked at him indifferently. "They just always thought that since I was friends with you and Adam, I was taken. So, I always asked them out first, but look what good that did me."

He watched as she picked at her perfectly manicured nails, feeling bad that he probably—he was—the reason a lot of her relationships went sour if that were true. It also put what Adam had said earlier into perspective. "They didn't deserve you anyway," he encouraged.

"No, they didn't," Mona agreed softly. She went to make more s'mores but noticed the chocolate bag empty. "I think we ate all our supplies," she said as she showed him the empty bag.

He took the bag from her and threw it in the fire. "That we did." He watched as she leaned back against the log, closing her eyes. "Tired?" he asked.

"A little," she mumbled. "I had fun tonight. I missed this."

"Sucks that this will be the last time we enjoy this place."

"Yeah. We've had a lot of memories here."

That they did. All their high school summers were spent there. It was sad to know that part of their history would be gone. "We're going to have to find a new hangout spot."

"That's if you come back."

Andrew turned away from her and stared at the bonfire. When would he find time to come back? He lived hours away, his restaurant also hours away. Visits like this were sure to be scarce. He hadn't thought that far. But now that he was, it frightened him knowing that he might drift from the group again. He didn't want that, not with him and Mona being on good terms.

"I'll be back," he whispered, his mind far away. Leaning his head back on the log, he closed his eyes and soon started to drift. He distinctly recalled Mona saying, "You better" as she placed her head on his shoulder, but he could've imagined it as he struggled to stay awake.

Night Whispers

Louise Residence

"WE SHOULDN'T EVEN be down here! My dad will kill me! What if he finds out?" Mona whispered as Andrew dragged her down to her father's wine cellar.

"Maybe if you stay quiet, he wouldn't." He stopped to give her a pointed look before tugging her hand again.

Her hands were searing from his touch as he held tight to ensure she wouldn't leave his side. She quietly let him guide her through her house. She snorted at the fact that he seemed to know more corners of her household than she did.

Andrew stopped in front of the French section of wine and turned to her with a wicked smile. "I think we found the one."

She watched as he carefully pulled out a bottle of Chardonnay from the shelves.

"Don't drop it," she warned.

Andrew rolled his eyes. "Yeah, like I'm an amateur. Come on, we should get out of here before he really finds us."

"Wait, you're not taking the whole bottle, are you? He's

going to know it's missing!" Mona refused to follow him up the stairs.

Andrew sighed, a serious look on his face. "Have I ever failed you before, Mona? Do you trust me?" he challenged her.

Mona had trouble answering, a part of her was scared that her father would be disappointed in her for agreeing to this, but also knowing that Andrew never backed down on his word. He had promised he would replace it before her father even knew it was gone, and she believed him. "Yes, but I—"

"Then, don't worry."

Andrew smiled and held out his free hand, which she took without another thought, and quietly followed him up the stairs and to her room.

After a night of complete chaos, they had headed back to her house to get away from it all. Andrew didn't want to go home as his house was filled with siblings and didn't want to leave her side. Somehow, he had talked her into going down to her father's cellar and getting wine to kickback.

Mona sat on her bed and watched him open the bottle to pour it into the glasses that were already in her room. He handed her a glass, and they both took a gulp.

She scrunched her nose at the taste. "This is... different." She struggled to find the right words as she placed her glass on the nightstand.

Andrew finished and poured himself another glass. "It's exactly what I need."

Mona got up and took the glass from him. "You should take it easy."

He took the glass back from her and drank the full glass. Mona glared at him as he took a seat at her desk and poured another glass. This time, she took the entire bottle from his hands before he could finish.

He groaned when some splashed om his jeans. "Ugh! Come on, Moe!"

"I'm serious! Take it easy, or we won't drink at all!" Mona walked over to her nightstand and put the bottle down. He got up and sat beside her on the bed, his glass still in hand.

Leaning his head on her shoulder, he muttered, "I'm sorry."

Taking the glass from his hand without struggle, she finished its contents and placed it next to the bottle. She leaned her head on his and asked, "What am I going to do with you?"

"Love me forever?"

She giggled. "Too late for that."

He removed himself from her shoulder and stared at her with an intense and strange look. He wouldn't look away as she felt forced to return his gaze, which was somewhat unnerving. Finally, he broke their staring contest and laid back on the bed to stare at the ceiling.

"Is the room supposed to spin like this?"

She also laid back beside him, their shoulders touching. "If you keep staring at the fan twirling, I'm sure it won't help your case. And that's what you get for drinking so fast."

They were silent for a moment, both enjoying the com-

fort of each other's presence. She felt him shift beside her, and when she turned to him, he was on his side facing her, his head leaning on his arm. Briefly, he took her necklace in his hand and twirled it.

His fingers accidentally brushed her chest, but he either didn't know or didn't want to acknowledge the mishap. She would've too if her skin didn't tingle from the contact. Nonetheless, she let him focus on the infinity charm necklace he had given her for her birthday the year prior.

"We should do something," he said softly. She looked up at him, but he refused to meet her eyes.

"Like what?" she asked.

"I don't know. Tonight's been crazy, and I think we deserve to have a little fun," he concluded. He locked eyes with her briefly before focusing on the charm once again.

"Like go out? Isn't it a little late to go anywhere?"

"Not really. I know one place that's still open…"

"Andrew—"

"I won't take no for an answer," he said as he sat up.

The missing warmth of his hand wasn't lost on her.

Mona could almost guess what he was suggesting. He had brought up the topic a week ago but had told him he was crazy.

Mona shook her head. "We are not getting tattoos!"

Andrew gave her a sad face, which made her groan. "Please? I promise it won't hurt. Just a small one."

She continued to shake her head as she got up from her bed and headed to her desk to sit. "I hate needles, you know *that."*

He followed her and dropped to his knees in front of her, his hands controlling the chair from swinging on the armrest. "I know, but I promise it'll probably take less than hour. And we can do it at the same time, or I can hold your hand—"

"No!"

"Pleeease? Do this for me?" His eyes were honest and desperate, and she found herself sighing with resolve. She didn't understand why he was adamant about getting a tattoo. He already had three. Why did she need to get one with him?

"Okay," she gave in.

Andrew gave her a dimpled smile and wrapped his arms around her midsection and brought his face to her stomach. Because he was in front of her, he had to force her legs open a little just to do that, which caused her to blush. She could feel the heat rising from the contact. But instead of acknowledging it, she pushed the growing feeling in the pit of her stomach down.

Andrew finally loosened his grip and sprung to his feet, much to her relief. Holding out his hand, he said, "We should go now if we want to catch them before they close."

She eyed his hand before hesitantly taking it and allowing him to pull her from the chair. "Shouldn't I change or something?"

She had on a pink tank top and black capris. Though it could pass, it was an outfit she typically liked to wear in the house rather than outside.

Andrew chuckled as he led her down the stairs quietly.

"No, it's a tattoo parlor, not a Met Gala."

Once out of the house, they decided not to take the car since the tattoo parlor was close and they had been drinking. Living in the city, they were about a block away from every-thing.

Andrew did his best to ease her mind on the way. The owner of the tattoo parlor was a friend of Andrew's older brother, Aiden, and had done all of Andrew's tattoos under the table since he was minor. He had gotten his first one on a dare two years ago for his fourteenth birthday.

By the time they walked through the doors of the parlor, Mona hadn't felt any less nervous about getting her first tat-too.

The sound of buzzing made her heart pump faster, and suddenly, she wasn't sure she wanted to be anywhere near the place. Andrew could tell how unnerved she was and gen-tly guided her by the shoulders to the counter.

"Don't be afraid. I've got you," he whispered in her ear.

Mona shivered from the contact his lips made with her ear. She nodded and stood before the man at the counter. An-drew stood behind her with his hands still on her shoulders as if to prevent her from bolting.

The man, who was covered in tattoos and piercings and sported an impressive man bun, nodded to Andrew in recog-nition. "What's up, Drew? You're here pretty late."

Andrew threw him a not-so-serious glare. "I told you don't call me Drew, Will."

Will waved him off. "Whatever you say, Drew. Don't tell

me you're drawing this fine woman here to get a tattoo. She looks terrified." He pointed to Mona.

Granted, she was terrified.

"As a matter of fact, I am. And we both are getting one."

Will nodded. "Ah, like a matching couple tattoo? Don't tell me you two are getting your names on each other? That usually never ends well."

"We're not a couple," Andrew stressed. "We're getting something… meaningful to our friendship."

"Andrew, we haven't even picked out what we wanted," Mona turned to him in question, his hands falling from her shoulder.

He thought for a moment. "Do you want color?"

Mona shrugged. "As long as it's not something I won't regret later considering I can't wash it off."

Looking around, Andrew already knew there wasn't anything in the parlor's portfolio that he wanted. His eyes fell to the symbol on her chain again and brightened with an idea.

"We can get the infinity symbol," he suggested.

Mona looked down at her chain with uncertainty. "I don't know… it seems a bit plain."

"Well, you don't like needles, so plain is good, trust me. Plus, it's a popular symbol with so many meanings."

"What would be our meaning for it?"

Andrew smiled, genuinely at her. "That no matter what, we'll never let anyone come between our friendship, and we'll always come back to each other. Our friendship is forever."

Mona couldn't mistake the intensity of his eyes. Though she knew the answer, she wanted to hear him say it to match her own feeling.

"You mean that?"

"With all my heart."

A smile crept onto her face. Looking at the raw emotion in his eyes, she could tell he meant every word. He wouldn't lie to her. Suddenly, she felt the courage to get the tattoo.

With determination, she said, "Then, infinity it is."

CHAPTER SEVENTEEN

Mona

A CRY ESCAPED her lips as Mona kneeled in front of her father's grave. She covered her mouth as she struggled to control her emotions. This was the first time she had visited since his passing. Until now, she couldn't bring herself to face his grave.

As she sobbed and gripped his headstone, she felt a hand squeeze her shoulder in comfort. Looking up at the source, she gasped and fell back, her tear-stained eyes wide with shock and disbelief.

It was her father. Michael Leo Louise.

He hadn't aged a day since she had last seen him alive. He was even in the same clothes—a white t-shirt and his house jeans with his favorite black Nike sneakers. His short dark brown hair was still slightly grayed at the front as was his beard and mustache. His gray eyes stared at her with sadness.

"Dad..." she managed to breathe out.

"Why so sad, my love?"

Mona looked back at the headstone then at him to make sure she wasn't hallucinating. "I-I don't understand. How is this possible?"

Her father knelt in front of her, using his thumb to wipe a tear from under her eye. "I am always with you, my love. No matter what, I'll always be there to protect you. Even when you can't see me."

"Dad... I have so much to say..."

"Shhh, I know everything. What matters now is you learn to move on and let yourself be happy."

Mona pushed herself up to wrap her arms around his neck. "I miss you so much, Dad!"

He rubbed her back and kissed her cheek, his facial hair fanning her face. "Open your heart to happiness, Mona. I promise everything will be okay. I love you."

"I love you, too." Mona felt him slowly slip away from her fingers like liquid. Before she knew it, he had disappeared as if he was never there.

Mona jolted awake and wiped the tear that escaped her eyes. That was the first time she had dreamt of her father since his passing. She usually put off thinking about him before bed but taking a trip down memory lane during the game at the campfire had opened the vault.

Not wanting to be sad for the morning thinking about him, she brought herself back to reality.

She wasn't sure when she dozed off, but by the time she woke up, the sun had started to peak between the trees. She blinked a few times, confused. It took her a moment to realize that what she was laying on—or rather who. The steady rise and fall on her head on his chest indicated he was still soundly asleep. His right arm wrapped around her waist, very snug. Gently, she removed herself from his grasp to sit up. He shifted slightly but didn't wake.

Mona recalled their game just a few hours before, the s'mores and bonding moment. There was still a steady quiet amongst the camp.

Turning to Andrew, she watched as he lay crocked against the log. His lips slightly parted, and his hair was wild with curls she desperately wanted to run her hands through. He looked so peaceful as he slept; she could stare at him all day. Her eyes trailed down to his black t-shirt and jeans.

"I can feel your eyes on me." Mona jumped, startled at the sound of his groggy voice. His eyes opened slightly to peek at her.

"I didn't know you were awake," she said, her cheeks growing warm.

"Would that make you admire me less?" he teased with a crooked smile.

Mona blushed and looked away. "I wasn't admiring. Were you uncomfortable?"

Andrew sat up and stressed his arms and neck. "Mostly," He turned to her, "but it was worth it."

The sound of one of the tents unzipping caught their attention and they watched as Nina emerged. Her hair stood wild on her head, and her nightclothes was twisted haphazardly on her body. Rubbing her eyes, she paused when she spied both Andrew and Mona sitting by the fire pit. "What are you guys doing up so early?" Nina said in between a yawn.

"Just enjoying the sunrise," Andrew answered.

Nina didn't look like she believed him but shrugged anyway with indifference. "Whatever. I'm heading back to the cabin to freshen up and make breakfast. Are you coming?" she directed to Mona.

Mona nodded and stood. "Yeah, I'll be there in a sec."

They watched Nina head to the cabin before speaking. "She's probably going to ask me why I didn't sleep in the tent," Mona commented.

Andrew got up and extended his hand, which she obliged. "Tell her you wanted a real camping experience by sleeping outside and you wanted a real man to protect you," he said with a knowing smile.

Mona gave him a pointed look. "Yeah, like that would cause her to be any less badgering."

"It's Nina. When is she not?"

Mona hit on his arm playfully, causing him to bark with laughter. "I'm heading inside. You want to come?"

Andrew shook his head and motioned to his tent. "I should probably check on Cassidy."

Her smile faltered slightly. "Of course. I'll see you in a bit, then." She didn't wait for him to answer and headed back to the cabin without another word.

She headed up the stairs and straight to the bathroom for a shower. She needed to wash off the feeling she had. What was up with being in Andrew's company that made her want to throw caution to the wind?

That feeling in the pit of her stomach wouldn't go away. She wanted it gone because she couldn't ignore it for much longer. She washed up quickly and brushed her teeth before wrapping a towel tight around herself and leaving the steam-filled bathroom. In a rush to get back to her room, she crashed into someone who fell to the ground.

"Oh! I'm sorry," Mona extended without realizing who it was as she looked up.

Cassidy glared back at her. "You should be."

Taken aback, Mona asked, "Excuse me?"

"You heard me."

Mona was already annoyed and trying to keep her anger at bay. "It was an accident. There's no need for the attitude. Now, if you'll excuse you."

Mona side-stepped her but stopped short when she heard her say, "Why can't you leave Andrew alone? He was better off before he came here and started talking to you."

Mona turned to her, no longer able to keep her anger at bay. "I'm doing nothing wrong. If you have a problem with our friendship, maybe you should look at your insecurities."

"Ha! That's what you call it? You need to stay away from him," Cassidy snarled as she stepped closer.

Mona was in her face by now. "I will do no such thing. If he has a problem with it, Andrew can speak for himself."

"Well, I have a problem with it. You've become a pest in my relationship."

"I thought you weren't together?"

Cassidy looked startled that she knew about the status of their relationship. "I requested a break, but that doesn't mean you should be pushing on him anyway. He's not yours."

"You must not understand how friendships work. It's probably why you need an excuse to attack me because you can't fathom what a real connection is. It's not my fault you can't make your relationship work. I'm not your problem, *you* are," Mona fired back.

Mona hadn't mentioned it to Andrew, but she had heard their argument from the other night while she lay in bed. Cassidy had a big problem with their reinstated friendship and thought there was more going on, when there wasn't. She knew that no matter what she said, Cassidy was going to have a problem with her presence in Andrew's life. She had dealt with this same scenario many times in the past and it always ended the same way.

Cassidy stood stunned by Mona's retort and instead of engaging further, had twirled and stomped to her room, slamming the door behind her. Mona stood in triumph for a moment before heading to her own room to get changed.

The victory smile on her face didn't last very long; however, as she began to feel bad about the whole situation. As someone who often liked to put herself in others' shoes, she understood the feeling of constant competition and fighting for something that didn't seem like it would ever work.

Cassidy, in a lot of ways, was justified for how she felt, but that didn't mean that her accusations and her nasty attitude were the way to deal with the situation. It would only push

Andrew away, and in the end, there wouldn't be anything left to fight for.

Mona envied Cassidy because she didn't know how good she had it. She had Andrew all to herself for two years and watched him grow in ways Mona couldn't. She missed out on the vital part of his life—his struggle and triumph of opening his restaurant and being a successful chef. Cassidy had the opportunity to be there for him when Mona couldn't, and she'll always feel some way about that.

What was supposed to be a quick dress and go, Mona spent almost an hour between fighting with her tangled mess of hair and finding the right clothes. After some time, she finally settled for black gym shorts and a yellow crop top as the day had begun to grow hot. She pulled her hair in a tight ponytail, letting her curls spring free in the back.

Heading to the stairs, she paused in front of Cassidy's door, shaking her head at the audacity of the woman, and headed to the kitchen. Nina and James were in the process of making breakfast, Nina shamelessly laughing at something he must've said. Mona raised a brow but didn't intervene as it wasn't the time or place to inquire, but it was nice to see Nina brighten with happiness. They barely acknowledged her when she entered the kitchen to warm up a bagel and leave.

On the way out, she heard a squeal from the back door and watched Dixie and Symoné jumping in joy. Curious, she headed toward them.

"Hey, what's going on?" Mona asked as she took a bite out of her bagel.

Symoné smiled and flashed her left hand at Mona. Mona stepped back in surprise at the rock on her finger. "Adam proposed!" Symoné exclaimed.

"Oh! Congratulations!" Mona replied, taking her hand to examine the ring closer. She was completely winded that Adam had proposed. She had no idea they were that serious or that Adam was ready for that step.

"Thank you!"

"When did he find time to propose?" Dixie asked. Mona had wondered as well.

"This morning," Symoné answered excitedly. "He sorta did it half asleep. He said he was supposed to do it during the game last night, but he got too drunk, and it slipped his mind."

"Sounds like Adam," Mona snorted.

Adam suddenly made an appearance around the bend heading toward the ladies with a large smile on his face. "You see the rock I got?" He bumped shoulders playfully with Mona to get her attention.

She turned and hugged him, which he returned. "I'm so happy for you! Congrats!"

"Yeah, I felt it was time. Plus, I want a kid before the year is over. My mom would kill me if I didn't do it for the traditional route."

Mona was shocked. A wedding and a kid? Adam was full of surprises.

Symoné slapped him upside the head, causing the other girls to laugh. "Don't listen to this man. Clearly, his brain hasn't woken up yet."

Adam fake pouted and rubbed the back of his head. "Okay, so I exaggerated a bit."

"So, have you guys actually set a date yet?" Dixie inquired.

Symoné shook her head. "We haven't talked. But I do want a summer wedding, so if things go my way, it'll be another year." Symoné gave Adam a pointed look.

Adam shrugged. "Whatever you want, babe."

"He's playing the good husband already," Mona joked. Adam pinched her on her arm, making her jump.

"Ow!" Adam moved away quickly before she could retaliate.

Watching the two with amusement, Dixie pointed in the direction of the campground. "Shouldn't we be occupying the campground? I mean, we are staying another night, right?"

Symoné turned to her in shock. "You want to go back? I thought for sure you'd be running for the hills on this one."

Dixie rolled her eyes. "It's a simple question. Plus, it wasn't as bad as I thought, okay?"

Symoné patted her on the back proudly. "Look at you! You'll be a park ranger in no time!"

"Kiss my ass, Symoné!"

The two began to bicker like siblings. Mona turned to Adam amused, spying the joy his eyes as he watched the two go at it. She elbowed him to get his attention, and he turned to her quizzically.

"I'm happy for you, Adam. I wish you guys nothing but the best." Mona meant it from the bottom of her heart. Adam was like a big brother to her and seeing him finally be ready to settle down made her proud.

He wrapped an arm around her shoulders and leaned some of his weight on her, much to her chagrin. "Thanks, Moe. That means a lot. I wish I could make you my best man, but that spot's reserved. However, I fully expect you to be a part of my wedding."

Mona chuckled. "Of course. Who's your best man?"

"Andrew."

"Have you told him about the engagement?" Come to think of it, she hadn't seen him since she left the campground hours ago.

Adam shook his head. "I haven't seen him since I got up. I thought he was here. That's why I came."

Mona looked around. He wasn't in the house because Cassidy was in the room by herself. Had he gone off somewhere? "Maybe he went for a walk or something," Mona mainly uttered to herself.

"Yeah, maybe," Adam said absentmindedly. "So, when do you plan on finding a husband?"

The question caught her off guard. Dating was nowhere near her vocabulary, let alone marriage. "Not anytime soon."

"Still waiting on him?"

Mona paused, puzzled. Him? "What are you talking about? Who's 'him'?"

Adam sighed and removed his arm from her shoulder. "You guys are so freaking stubborn and clueless."

"What the hell are you talking about?" Mona asked, annoyed that he wouldn't stop talking in code.

Adam shook his head and a shadow of a smile on his face. "Never mind. Forget I said anything. Symoné! We should head back to the campground," Adam dragged Symoné in the direction of the campground without any explanation. Mona could only blink at their retreating figures.

"Those two are perfect for each other," Dixie muttered before heading for inside.

Mona silently agreed but was still jilted by what Adam had said. What did he mean? Who was he talking about?

Mona shook the thoughts from her head. Instead, Mona focused on finding Andrew. She started for the camp area but hadn't seen any signs of him. She walked half of her morning trail to see if he decided to go for a walk but got frustrated and started back for the cabin. She paused, spying a lone figure on the basketball court far behind the cabin.

As she approached, she realized it was Andrew sitting on the ground with his knees up and his head back against the basketball pole. His eyes were closed, and he seemed zoned out as he didn't flinch when she sat next to him on the ground.

"I've been looking for you. Did you hear the news?"

Andrew turned to her with a frown. "No. What news?"

"Adam proposed to Symoné this morning."

Surprised, he sat up. "No, shit!"

Mona nodded with a smile. "He was looking for you to tell you but couldn't find you."

Andrew got a faraway look in his eyes but smiled. "That's great. I'm happy for him. I had no idea they were that serious. At least someone can make their relationship work."

Mona shot in a concerned look. "You okay?" she asked.

He seemed lost in thought and not all there. His eyes held a certain weight she couldn't quite decipher. "Yeah, just… thinking," he answered.

"You can talk to me if you want," Mona extended. She didn't like that sad look in his eyes. His mood had drastically changed since she left him earlier in the morning. She thought back to Cassidy in the cabin and wondered if that was the problem.

He gave her a weak smile. "It's hard to admit, but I don't think I'm in love with Cassidy anymore. I love her, but it doesn't feel the same. It hasn't for quite some time now."

Mona wasn't expecting him to say it so bluntly, but she nodded in encouragement for him to continue. "We argued— again—when I went to wake her up from the tent. She questioned me about why I didn't sleep in the tent, and I told her that we—" he motioned to the both of them "—were enjoying the campfire, and she stormed off, pissed. I tried to talk to her, but she's just not having it and honestly…" he took a deep breath. "I'm tired of this. I'm tired of the competition. I'm tired of feeling guilty for not giving her the love she deserves. I'm tired of forcing it. I'm not going to choose between my friends, family, and my girlfriend. I did that already, and I was miserable."

He bit his lip and looked down at his hands, refusing to meet her eyes. "I got a chance to live out my dreams, but at the cost of staying away from everyone, including you. I'm grateful for the time I spent with her because she did help me, and

I'll always love her for that, but I'm happy being who I am right here. I feel like this is where I belong. This is where I want to be."

Andrew shrugged. "If I'm being honest, this was probably bound to happen, whether here or there. Being here just made her—us—realize it sooner. I feel like the right thing to do is fight for her, but a part of me doesn't, and that's what scares me. I just feel guilty."

Mona was unsure how to respond. She took his hand and squeezed it reassuringly. "You shouldn't feel guilty for not wanting to force something that may not be there anymore. People fall out of love all the time. Sometimes it's gradual. Sometimes it doesn't hit until it's too late, and hate begins to manifest. Did you tell her how you feel?"

Andrew shook his head. "She let me have it, though. Cassidy is hot and cold right now. I think she's scared of it, too. Though, it is worth noting she had technically broken up with me already." He chuckled softly.

"For what it's worth, I'm sure whatever you decide to do about Cassidy will be for the better. You have to follow your heart and stop being so afraid to live your life the way you want to."

Andrew withdrew his hand from hers, making her miss the warmth of his hand. "You're right. You're always right." He turned to her with a smile. "Right now, how about we forget everything and everyone and have a one-on-one match in basketball?"

He got up to retrieve the basketball at the other side of the court, dribbling as he made his way to her. He extended his hand to her to help her up. "I'm rusty. I haven't played since high school," she said as she took his hand.

Andrew brightened. "So, an easy win for me?"

"I didn't say I wasn't going to try," Mona said as she dusted dirt from her shorts. Andrew stopped and looked at her outfit up and down, an odd look passing over his face. She could feel the heat rise to her stomach as she looked down at her crop top and shorts, trying to figure out what was wrong with her outfit. "What?"

He shook his head. "Are you sure you're going to be able to play in that?" he said, pointing at her outfit.

"Uh, yeah. What's wrong with my outfit? It's practically gym clothes."

He ran a hand through his hair as if he wanted to say something. Instead, he shook his head and said, "Nothing." He walked back to the middle of the court and shot a basket. "Just don't come crying to me when you get thrown to the ground and scrape your skin," he joked.

She huffed and jumped to grab the ball as it swished through the net. "Won't happen. But I would be worried about that balance you're struggling to keep when you shoot the basket."

"Oh, it's on!"

He dropped the ball and chased her to the other side of the court, her laughter filling the air between them. He caught her and grabbed her by the waist, knocking the wind from her lungs. His palm flattened against her exposed abdomen, sending a siring heat throughout her body. The laughter died at her lips as she turned back to him, catching his heated emerald stare.

Before she could get wrapped up in his longing gaze, she jerked from his grip. She picked up the ball and shot it into the net. She turned to him with a smug look when it went through smoothly. "And that's how you score."

Andrew stood there, stunned. "You got me. But not again."

They played frivolously with each passing glance and laughter, relieving the tension and bringing about a sense of comfort between the two. They played three games before they collapsed with exhaustion next to each other on the court.

"You're better than I remember."

Mona smiled smugly. "Never underestimate the little one."

"You are anything but little," he retorted.

"Are you calling me—"

"Big-headed? Yes." He laughed as she hit him on his arm. "Seriously, you play well. Have you been practicing?"

Mona shook her head. She hadn't played since he left, considering it used to be their 'thing.' "No, I guess you just bring out the best in me."

"That's good to know. Too bad your best still can't beat me," he said with a hint of a smirk. "What else?"

Mona turned to him, confused. "Huh?"

He leaned back on his elbow and started toying with a loose strand of her hair. "What else does my awesome presence bring out in you?"

"You are so full of yourself."

"You said it, not me."

He had a point.

Mona pretended to think with her finger tapping her chin as if she were searching in the stars for answers. "Nothing comes to mind."

"Bullshit. You're a terrible liar, you know. I can see right through you." He grabbed her sides and started tickling her.

"Okay! Okay! Stop!" she managed to get out through fits of laughter as she struggled against him. He finally stopped his attack but hadn't removed his hand from her waist. The laughter died at her lips as the air shifted around them. Knots began forming in her stomach, but she tried to ignore it. He was much closer now, his full body planted against her side.

It took him a minute to gather his wits before separating himself from her personal space. Andrew cleared his throat and got up. "We should probably head inside."

She nodded but didn't say anything. The awkward tension was palpable as he helped her to her feet. He opened his mouth to say something but was cut off by the shrill of his cellphone.

Mona watched as he pulled it out of his pocket and answered. She wasn't sure whether to wait for him or not.

"Hey, Mom... Mom? Slow down, slow down. What happened to him?"

The unnerved tone of his voice sent a feeling of panic through her. Andrew had a bunch of siblings that she was very familiar with. She prayed nothing bad happened to either of them. His back was turned to her, so he couldn't see when she crept behind him.

"Okay, I'll be there... No... I'm at the cabin... I'll explain later. I'll be there shortly. Love you, too."

"What happened? Is everything okay?" Mona asked, worried.

Andrew shook his head as he jammed his phone back in his pocket and started toward the entrance of the cabin. "It's Ant. He collapsed at school today. My mom needs me at the hospital. I gotta get out of here."

Mona struggled to keep up with him. "Let me come with you."

"No, Moe. Stay here," he urged as he pulled his keys from his pocket.

She knew it was best to stay and offer answers about his disappearance, but her gut was telling her otherwise. She wanted to support him.

Mona continued following him to the truck. "I'm not letting you go alone. I don't know how bad it is, but I want to be there for you. Please?"

Andrew stopped short of hopping in the truck and sighed. "Mona—"

"They're my family just as much as yours. Please?"

Mona cared about the Sumpters. They were like her second family growing up, and he knew this. His shoulders sagged as he got in and closed the door. He started the truck and rolled down the window.

"Get in."

Quickly, she hopped into the passenger seat, and they took off before she could get buckled in correctly.

"Thank you," she said as she watched him tap his fingers on the steering wheel nervously.

"Don't thank me yet."

Mona understood clearly. His family meant everything to him, especially Anthony, as he was the youngest and most vulnerable of the group. If anything happened to any of them—well, she hoped this wasn't one of those moments.

Reaching across the console, she grabbed his hand for comfort. He surprised her and intertwined their fingers, shooting a warm tingle to her spine. She didn't say anything. Instead, she smiled to herself as she watched the trees zip by, wishing that the moment could last forever.

CHAPTER EIGHTEEN

Andrew

ANDREW PULLED INTO the parking lot some forty-five minutes later. It didn't take them long to check-in at the information desk and head up to the right floor. When the elevator doors opened, Andrew's mom was sitting in the waiting room by the window.

"Mom!"

She looked up, startled, before rushing over to embrace him.

"You made it," she said, stepping back.

"Of course, Mom. How's he doing?"

She looked away momentarily, sadness overtaking her features. "He's stable, but he may need to stay for a little while. Maybe a day. He's really low iron, and with his anemia and the heat, it's likely why he passed out. He hit his head, too, so he may have a concussion, but he's talking and seems normal. I'm just glad it wasn't worse. Sorry to scare you over the phone."

Andrew had to take a seat, both worried and relieved. His

mother followed suit, sitting beside him and wrapping her arms around his shoulders.

"No, Mom. Don't be sorry. I should've been here."

"Well, you are now and that's all that matters."

His mother sighed, got up, but paused when her eyes met Mona's. She had been standing out the way to give them privacy. "Mona... honey, it's been so long! You look beautiful."

Grabbing Mona into a tight hug, Andrew's mother took a good look at her, her mood lightened. "Hi, Mrs. Sumpter. I'm so sorry we have to meet again under such circumstances."

She waved it off. "It's always a pleasure to see you. I much appreciate your support. It's been a couple of years, yeah? I was beginning to think my poor Andrew had lost you for good."

Mona blushed and snuck a glance at Andrew, who looked uneasy.

"And please, call me Linda, honey. Mrs. Sumpter makes me feel like an old woman. I know it's been a couple years, but you will always be like a daughter to me. I'm also sorry to hear about your father, dear. He was such a good man."

Mona nodded solemnly. "Yes, he was. Thank you."

Mrs. Sumpter embraced her once more, this time whispering in her ear, "Don't let my boy run you off again."

Giving her a pointed look, Mrs. Sumpter went to pick up her purse from the seat. "I'll be heading to the cafeteria, since you guys are here. Would you two like anything?"

Andrew and Mona shook their heads. Mrs. Sumpter turned to address Andrew, "Your father and two of your brothers should be on their way. If the doctor comes back before I do, ring me immediately."

"Yes, ma'am," Andrew answered.

They waited until Mrs. Sumpter disappeared behind the elevator doors to speak. "I wish I had grabbed a jacket if I knew it was going to be so cold in here." Mona rubbed her arms, her right leg jumping up and down nervously.

Andrew didn't have a jacket on, but he did have one in his truck. "I can go downstairs and get you the one in my truck if you want."

She shook her head. "I'll go. You have to stay in case the doctor comes out."

Andrew sighed and handed over the keys. Mona took them but waited a moment before making her exit. He looked up at her, confused. "What?"

She offered him a meek smile. "He's going to be okay. He's strong just like his big brother."

She didn't wait for a response. Andrew watched as the elevator doors closed after her.

Leaning back, Andrew let all the guilt of not visiting home more often weigh on his mind. His lack of enthusiasm for returning was also contributed by his need to feel like he was doing something with his life. His brothers and sister had their lives figured out and doing what they loved—even the ones in school had a direction they were heading in. All he ever wanted was to have something of his own.

Being the middle child meant he often felt lost and unappreciated. Though it never was a negative feeling toward the family besides wanting his own space, he needed to get away to find himself.

Andrew always had a plan, but his situation with Mona had pushed him over the edge, and he felt like he had lost control. Moving away for peace of mind, at the time, seemed like his only option.

Nervously, he sat and watched doctors and nurses pass by in a blur, his mind wandering to negative corners he desperately fought. Although she hadn't quite look it, he knew his mother was going crazy with worry internally. But like always, she dared to be strong. She often smiled in the face of adversity.

He wondered how his little brother felt in the hospital room by himself. Did he feel alone? Was he scared? Did he understand what was going on?

The ding of the elevator snapped him out of his thoughts. Mona emerged with his jacket on, his older brothers, Aaron, trailing behind her.

"Look who I found!" Mona pointed a thumb at Aaron, who threw an arm around her shoulders, a grin on his face.

"Aren't I the lucky one? What's up, bro! Long-time, no see." Aaron removed himself from Mona to gather him in a bro hug.

Andrew gave him a side-eye. "You're awfully chipper. Who else is coming?"

Aaron shrugged. "I think Dad is coming. Maybe Aiden, too, though I have no idea where he is. Alex is out of town and Audree is on call, so Mom told them not to come. The twins are still on their road trip and Amir is at home. I think Mom wanted to keep fewer people here until she knew for sure it was serious. How is he, by the way?"

"I haven't heard anything yet. Mom just went to the cafeteria. She was waiting on the doctor. Ant is low on iron and the heat and his anemia may have contributed to him fainting. He may have a concussion from fall."

Aaron ran a hand through his hair, sucking in a breath. "Damn."

"I know. I hope he's okay," Andrew murmured sadly.

Aaron took the seat next to him and motioned for Mona to come beside him. She shook her head. "I'm fine, thanks."

"Man. It's crazy seeing you here. It's been like... two years, right?" Aaron asked. "You guys finally stopped being boneheads and kissed and made up?"

Andrew shot him a glare. Aaron threw up his hands with a grin. "I'm just joking. But seriously, it's good to see you guys have gotten past your issues. Whatever it was, anyway."

Andrew took a glance at Mona. "We're cool now."

The shrill of Andrew's phone made him pull it out. Cassidy's name popped up on the screen, but instead of answering, he put it on silent and stuffed it back in his pocket. He would deal with her later.

"Mona! Offer me some company, will you, please? Your standing is strangely irritating," Aaron said, patting the empty seat next to him.

"That makes me want to stand even longer," she replied.

Aaron grinned, "If you insist. By the way, sexy pair of legs you got there. I sure missed seeing them around our house."

Mona rolled her eyes playfully and took the seat on Andrew's left instead. "Better?"

"Not quite where I wanted you, but if I get to see those beautiful legs closer, I'll take it." Aaron wiggled his eyebrows at her suggestively.

"Aaron..." Andrew warned. Aaron had always been the jokester of the family alongside Aiden. However, Aaron was also a terrible flirt, especially when Andrew used to bring Mona home to study or hang out. He looked a lot like their dad with his wide smile though his hair resembled Andrew's but a little longer and his eyes were greenish-brown. With his olive skin, he could pass off as an 80s model and he knew it. For the most part, Mona never seemed to take him seriously or minded the banter much. Andrew, on the other hand, found his nerves getting irked more often than he'd like to admit.

"What? I can't tell her she looks beautiful? You always have to have her for yourself. You never share."

Andrew chose to ignore his last statement, hoping Mona had as well. "Leave her alone, seriously. That's not what we're here for."

"Whatever, you cry baby. I'm just trying to lighten the mood," Aaron joked. He leaned over to Mona with a grin. "Sorry, my little brother is such a pain in the ass. I meant every word," he whispered with a wink.

Andrew facepalmed, giving up his efforts to stop his brother. His brother was relentless. The positive side of it all, if he could call it that, Mona seemed more amused than annoyed.

Great. Just great.

Thankfully, before Aaron made him do something stupid, a doctor approached them in their direction. Considering they were the only family in the waiting room, the doctor waited until he was in front of them before he spoke.

"Sumpter family?"

All three of them stood, Andrew shook his hand. "Yes, sir."

The doctor nodded. "I'm Dr. Fraises. Anthony is officially done with his testing. He shows no signs of a concussion, just minor scrapes. He does have low iron, so we are medicating him in order to stabilize. We will prescribe something he can go home with and under supervision. Thankfully, he should be okay with mild activity. Any questions?"

"Can we see him?" Aaron asked, his playful demeanor completely diminished. His eyes were bugged out. He was probably feeling the same way Andrew was.

"Yes, you can. He is up and alert now."

Andrew pulled out his phone and texted his mom to hurry back up while Aaron asked him a few more questions. Dr. Fraises guided them to the room shortly after. Andrew's mom caught up with them just before they entered. The doctor explained once more what was going on, and the look of relief on his mother's face was calming. They crowded around the hospital bed.

Seeing all the strings attached to his small frame almost made Andrew's eyes water. The guilt began to creep back in, but he pushed it away. Now wasn't the time to feel sorry for himself.

Mona must've sensed his despair because she laced her fingers with his and squeezed reassuringly. As much as he wanted to linger in the moment, he focused his attention on Anthony.

Anthony's eyes lit up when he saw Andrew. "Andy!"

He stretched his arms out, waiting for a hug. It melted Andrew's heart to see the big smile on his face like he was his kid brother's favorite person in the world.

Though he hated the nickname Andy, he only let Ant get away with it.

"Hey, Ant. I missed you." Andrew reluctantly let go of Mona's hand and hugged him tight.

"Where's my hug?" Aaron asked, fake mad.

"Me, or the kid?" Andrew couldn't help asking as he let Anthony go.

Aaron rolled his eyes. "As if you're the one sitting in the bed." Aaron leaned over the bed and hugged his little brother, who seemed thrilled despite everything.

Mona smiled but kept her distance in the back, not wanting to intrude on their moment. Linda rushed to his side and kissed her little boy on the head while caressing the hair out of his face.

"I'm so glad to see you, honey! Don't scare me like that again!"

Anthony looked down, avoiding eye contact with his mom. "I'm sorry, Mommy."

Linda hugged him again, shushing him. "It's not your

fault. We're just glad you're okay."

"Am I dying?" Anthony asked. His eyes held so many questions with a hint of fear, it broke Andrew's heart.

He sat on the bed, forcing his mother to step aside. "No, you're not dying. You are going to be fine. As long as we do what the doctor says, you'll be back to normal in no time."

Anthony nodded his head slowly. "Can we go home?"

Linda interjected, "Soon, honey. They just have to make sure you're completely okay, and then you'll get to come home, I promise."

Aaron stepped closer, squeezing Anthony's shoulder gently. "And when you come home, we'll all be there."

Anthony brightened up. "Really?"

Aaron and Linda looked at Andrew in question. He nodded, offering Anthony a warm smile. "Really."

Andrew dug into his pocket as he stood to let his mother and Aaron have a talk with Anthony. Looking at his phone, he saw a text from Cassidy, Adam, and Nina. He ignored Cassidy's and went straight for the other two. He could almost guess what hers would be about.

ADAM: *U can't just disappear and not tell anybody anything. That's just RUDE! SMH*

NINA: *Where have you stolen my best friend? Where the hell are you guys?!*

Andrew rolled his eyes. Instead of replying, he headed out the door but stopped halfway when he noticed Mona was no longer in the room. Where had she gone? Stepping outside, he looked up and down the hall, but she wasn't anywhere to be found.

He walked to the waiting room, but she wasn't there either. He almost panicked but he knew she could handle herself. Instead, he dialed her number. It rang twice before she answered.

"Hello?"

"Where are you?" Andrew asked, skipping the greeting.

"I went to the gift shop downstairs. I'm sorry, I know I should've said something, but you guys were in your moment, and I didn't want to intrude."

Andrew sat in one of the waiting room chairs. "You're not intruding. You're like family to them."

"And to you?" Andrew could hear the *ding* of the store entrance in the background.

He wasn't sure how to answer that question. It was weird for him to think of her as a sister because she felt like more than that to him. She always felt like home.

He cleared his throat cautiously. "You're my sidekick."

She laughed on the other end, and he breathed a sigh of relief. "A sidekick? I'm more of a Batman than a Robin."

"True." He laughed.

The *ding* he heard in the background sounded again. "I'm coming back up. I just wanted to get Anthony something."

"You didn't have to do that." Just her being there was enough.

He imagined she was shrugging on the other end. "It's no biggie. It's the least I can do."

Mona hung up soon after, leaving Andrew to linger in the

waiting room. When the elevator doors finally opened, a massive load of balloons tumbled out before Mona. Andrew got up to help her with the bag she was struggling to hold in her other hand.

"What the hell? Did you buy all the balloons in the gift shop? And where did you get money from? I thought you left all your stuff at the cabin?"

"Just half and I found a $100 bill in your truck, so technically you bought this stuff," she said cheekily. He couldn't be mad at her even if he tried.

Andrew opened the bag and pulled out a pack of cards. He held it up in question.

"It was the only thing I could find," she explained. "If he doesn't want to play, you and I can play if we're staying the night."

"I don't know?" Andrew looked down at his outfit. "I might leave and get some clothes from the cabin. I can drop you off if you don't want to stay."

Mona shook her head. "I'm not going anywhere. I can buy something from the gift shop if I need it with the change I got back. And these chairs are pull-out, so I can sleep on this." She fiddled with the recliner chair to make sure it pulls outs.

Andrew watched her closely. "Are you sure, Moe?"

She looked back at him. "Positive."

Andrew helped her get up and bring the items back to Anthony's room. Aaron opened the door before they could enter.

He looked between the two questionably. "Where've you two been?" He scanned the bag in Andrew's hand and the balloons and shook his head. "Never mind."

"Are you leaving?" Andrew asked, spying his keys in his hand.

"Yeah, I'm coming back later, but I have to finish some stuff before I come over to the house. Are you guys staying?"

Andrew nodded. "Yeah. I might leave later for some clothes, but I'll be here."

"Cool. I'll see you later, then. Bye, beautiful." He winked to Mona before maneuvering past them.

"I swear he gets on my nerves," Andrew said, pushing the door open. Mona giggled and followed close behind.

Linda was sitting on a chair while a nurse flushed the IV attached to Anthony's hand. Linda stood up wide-eyed when she saw the balloons. Anthony's face brightened.

"That's a lot of balloons," Linda commented.

The room wasn't anything special but thankfully wasn't shared with another patient, so they were able to find a spot for the balloons. Andrew moved around the nurse, who was preoccupied at Anthony's bedside.

Andrew stuck them in the corner by Anthony's bed and smiled at him. "All for you, buddy."

"What do you say, Anthony?" Linda said sternly.

"Thank you, Andy!"

Pointing to Mona, Andrew responded, "Not me. This is all, Mona. She wanted to do something nice for you. You remember her, don't you?"

Mona never really had a chance to interact with him before they lost contact two years ago. Around that time, Anthony was seven, and Andrew had already moved out of the house by then. At the time, they mostly hung out at his apartment though she would occasionally eat dinner with his family.

Anthony nodded and thanked her for her the balloons. She approached him and put the bag on the bed by his foot. "I got you a pack of cards just in case you get bored. I don't know if you know any games, but I'm willing to teach you if you want."

"Yes, please!" Anthony said eagerly.

The nurse finished up and excused herself out of the room. Andrew moved to an empty seat.

"We can play a little later," Mona offered.

Andrew checked the time, his eyes widening. It was going to get dark in a couple hours, and he wanted to get their stuff before night fell.

"What time is Dad supposed to be here?" he asked his mother.

Linda frowned and checked her phone. "He should've been here by now, to be honest. I'll call him and find out."

Stepping outside, she left the three of them back in the room. "I should probably go now for our stuff at the cabin. I want to get back before it gets too dark. Plus, I'm sure everyone is wondering where the hell we are."

Mona frowned. "You haven't told anyone yet?"

Andrew shook his head. "I know Cassidy is pissed, but I'll explain when I get there. I need to clear my head anyway. Do you mind staying and checking on my mom and Anthony?"

"Of course," she said gently.

"You're leaving?" Anthony asked, looking forlorn.

Andrew turned to him, gently saying, "Just for a little while. Mom and Mona are going to stay here until I come back. I'm spending the night with you, so don't feel alone."

Anthony gazed at him as if he were looking to see if he were lying. Finally, he nodded. "Okay."

Andrew ruffled his hair endearingly. Turning to Mona, he said, "Is there anything else you want me to bring back?"

"Hmm..." she tapped her chin in thought. "Just bring a suitcase of clothes. I'm not sure when I'll be back at the cabin. Wherever you go, I'll go. I'll call you if I need anything else."

"Gotcha."

Andrew took one last look at Mona, who was pulling out the game. Anthony's pleading eyes were no longer directed toward him. Instead, he smiled at Mona, who looked at Anthony as if he were the most important kid in the world.

Andrew left the room and bumped into his mother outside the door, who was still on the phone. He kissed her on the cheek and extended his farewell before heading out of the hospital.

Drawing his phone out of his pocket, he finally looked at the text Cassidy had sent.

CASSIDY: *Wow*

CASSIDY: *Not even a heads up*

CASSIDY: *I guess I made the right call*

Andrew stopped short of his truck to reread the message. The right call? She already made up her mind before he left. There was no point in being mad now. He checked his phone to see if he had any more messages or phone calls from her but there were none.

Running a hand over his face, he contemplated deeply. The conversation waiting for him was sure was not going to end well.

CHAPTER NINETEEN

Mona

"I WON!" ANTHONY yelled with his hands in the air. Linda gave him a stern look to tune it down, which he quickly obliged.

Mona giggled at his enthusiasm. "See? Wasn't so bad after all."

"Can we play again?"

Mona looked at Linda. They had already played Spades four times and she was getting hungry and tired. Linda nodded to her, understanding the look in her eyes.

"Maybe later, honey. Right now, you need to rest. It's getting late," Linda chimed in.

It had been about two hours since Andrew had left. Since then, she had spent most of her time playing with Anthony and scrolling through her phone. Her phone was on the brink of dying. She had texted Andrew to bring her charger an hour ago but hadn't gotten a response.

Getting up from the edge of the bed, she watched Linda

talk softly to Anthony. The amount of love she shared with her children was admirable considering how much her attention had to be divided between all of them. Since she's known Linda, she has always been a fair and caring mother. It wasn't something Mona was used to seeing with her own mom, and it made her yearn for a connection like that.

The closest she had gotten to feeling adored was from her father. He made sure she never felt left out as a child and made her feel special. Her eyes began to well up, but she blinked them back just as quickly.

A knock sounded at the door before it was pushed open to reveal Andrew's dad, Will "Ace" Sumpter. He was reasonably tall, towering over Mona and Linda by at least five inches. He was still as handsome as the pictures that littered their house the last time Mona had been there.

His brown hair was cut very short, but not military style. He still appeared to work out very often, not a beer belly in sight. His green orbs eyes were kind and inviting, much like Linda's. His dimpled smile was always present. He and Andrew favored, though, Andrew always looked more like his mom due to the curls. She couldn't remember the last time she had ever seen Ace anything but gentle, which was surprising considering his military background.

Growing up, he was like a second father to her. He and Linda were always open to having her at their home, even with an already full house. It was tough trying to maneuver in a house with eleven people.

Ace held up two bags of foods from Bristo's Restaurant.

"Sorry, I took so long. I got held up in a bad accident on the freeway, and then I was trying to order food for pickup only for them to get the order completely wrong. I hope this makes up for it."

He kissed Linda on the cheeks before setting the bags down and turning to Mona. "Hey, baby girl! It's been a while. You look lovely, as always. How are you?"

Ace engulfed her in a bear hug. "I'm doing well, Mr. Sumpter, thank you. It's great seeing you."

"What did I tell you about the name?" He asked playfully. He and Linda always had the rule of calling them by their first names. Mona always forgot the rule.

Mona blushed. "Ace."

"Now that's better!" he smiled at her. He turned his attention back to Anthony, who was watching the exchange.

"My boy! You almost gave us scare," he said, his tone sad but his face not giving anything away.

"I'm sorry, dad."

Ruffling his hair, he sat at the edge of the bed where Mona once was. "It's not your fault. I'm just glad we get to take you home soon. We have a lot to talk about."

Linda pulled out a few of the containers from the two bags and placed them on the food cart. "For now, let's eat."

Ace got off the bed and started to make a plate. "I bought enough food, I hope. Where's Andrew?" he directed to Mona. "I know if you're here, he's not too far behind."

Mona blushed. "He went back to the cabin for a few of our things. He wanted to stay the night here, and I was going to keep him company."

"Hmm," he said, amused. Mona frowned, not sure what that was supposed to mean. "Come get a plate. I'll leave some for him."

Since the nurse had squeezed in two more chairs an hour ago, Mona was able to sit and watch the television while she ate. Linda and Ace struck up a conversation while Anthony played on his dad's phone with a plate on his lap.

Because of his condition, his meal was light and offered more greens and iron-based food than the rest of them, much to Anthony's chagrin. If his face was any indication of how he felt, he wasn't too happy about the choice.

Mona quickly finished up and decided to take a walk around the hospital to give the family some privacy. Pulling out her phone, she checked to see if Andrew had texted back.

Not a peep.

She frowned but left it alone. Maybe he was on his way back and couldn't text a response. She wondered if she'd be better off calling, but since he wasn't answering his texts, he likely wouldn't answer calls either.

The evening was getting chilly and Mona huddled deeper into the borrowed coat, though she wasn't sure what good it did, since her legs were still exposed to the outside air. Cars zipped along the street to the emergency entrance and surrounding buildings.

Mona inhaled the fresh scent of carnations that were just planted near the main walkway. The layout reminded her of the hospital where her father died. At that time, she had felt blind, deaf, and numb when she walked through the entrance of the hospital to be escorted to his room.

She had never felt so alone like she felt that day. Her parent, her caregiver, her favorite person in the entire world, was gone. Her mother was at the hospital, her nurse standing beside her wheelchair as tears fell out of her eyes.

For the first time in her life, she wanted to embrace her mother and tell her everything was going to be okay. But it wasn't, and she knew that. They both did. The hardest part wouldn't come until after his funeral, though; as she found herself in a position, she wasn't ready for: being on her own.

No more crutches.

No more training wheels.

Being as he was her mother's primary caretaker since she was diagnosed with Lupus shortly after giving birth to her, Mona found herself having to take his shoes. Her mother, whom she's never gotten close to, refused her help, however, making it difficult. Eventually, she left her mother in the care of the nurse she had bonded with during the absence of her husband.

Mona shook the thoughts from her head and headed to the lake out front. She smiled at a family that passed by and watched the water ripple with the light breeze in a trance.

The vibration of her phone made her pull it out of her pocket. The phone warned her it was on five percent. Mona sighed and put it away.

The sound of crunching leaves caused her to look behind her. She gasped when she came face-to-face with Calvin.

Her eyes grew large with alarm. How did he know where she was? She wanted to ask, but her mouth couldn't form words. He stood there with an innocent smile on his face as if seeing her there was normal.

It wasn't.

If she hadn't known firsthand who Calvin was deep inside, her danger meter wouldn't be going off. Seeing him at the corner store was one thing. Having him show up at the hospital meant a whole lot of trouble.

Had he been following her this whole time?

"Fancy seeing you here," Calvin said, his blue eyes piercing her with an indecipherable stare.

"W-What are you doing here? How did you find me?" Mona asked, concerned.

Calvin automatically held up his hands in surrender. "I'm not following you if that's what you're asking. I'm visiting a friend who's recovering here. I promise."

It sounded logical, but he was known to be a damn good liar in their relationship. Plus, he had no friends that lived in the anywhere near the hospital to her knowledge. She knew to take everything he said with a grain of salt. Now, thinking back on their encounter in the corner store, she began to regret letting the situation be.

Had she inadvertently drawn him back?

He moved a little closer to her, causing her to step back. "I'm not trying to scare you, Mona. I just really miss you..."

Calvin looked her up and down with an intense gaze, causing her to shiver. "You look beautiful. You always do."

"Is there something you want, Calvin?" Mona found the courage to say. Without turning her head, she scanned the area to see where she could escape in case she needed to. The only solace she had was the several people walking along the sidewalk on the opposite side of the hospital.

The sense of fear was so much more overwhelming than the last encounter. What had changed?

The fact that he happened to know where she was, that was not a coincidence and she knew it. His tone was different. Less aggressive and combative than it was the last time he happened upon her. That usually meant it was the calm before the storm when it came to Calvin.

He chuckled lightly, but it caused a knot to form in her stomach. "I always want something. I want you out of my head if I'm being honest."

Calvin took another step forward, and Mona took two back. "It might help if you didn't look for me. Maybe if you leave, you'd forget all about me," Mona reasoned. Her voice was steady, but her fight or flight meter was going off.

Calvin shook his head. "Yeah... I don't think so. After seeing you at that store, I just realized how much I missed you. I wanted to call you, but I didn't know what to say. Then, I was going to drop in at the cabin—"

"The cabin?" Mona's blood ran cold. He had been following her.

He smirked. "Yeah, the cabin. Speaking of which, it's really dangerous for a pretty girl like you to walk in a forest alone. You could've gotten hurt. Good thing James is such a good

Samaritan. Almost gave your poor lover boy a heart attack. It's a shame Andrew is too much of an idiot to stake his claim."

"Calvin, stay the fuck away from me!"

Mona pulled out her phone, but it was dead. She cursed and jammed it back in her pocket. Wanting to keep an eye on him, she began to walk backward even further. He followed her every step.

"Mona, just stop. I'm not going to hurt you in such a public area. I just wanted to know if we could talk sometime, maybe over coffee at your place?" His smirk was gone, a dark undertone etched in his voice.

Not paying attention, Mona had backed into a wall. Calvin stopped right in front of her, but with enough space between them. His hands were jammed into his light jacket, and his eyes never left hers. She wondered if he ever blinked.

"There's nothing to talk about. We've been over for a long time. And you're not supposed to be near me. Seeing me here or at the store didn't change that."

"Are you fucking anyone? Are you fucking Andrew?" He said Andrew's name with a sneer.

The last time he and Andrew came face-to-face, Calvin had ended up getting his ass handed to him and arrested. It's no wonder that Andrew's name passed through his lips like acid.

"That's none of your business, Calvin. Even if it was true."

Calvin worked his jaw and looked away for a moment before swinging his gaze back to her. "Look, I'm sorry. I just wanted to see you again. I couldn't help myself. I can never resist when it comes to you." He whispered the last part long-ingly.

"Well, resist it because nothing will ever come of this—" she pointed to him, then herself for emphasis, "—again. *Ever*! Don't follow me anymore! Leave me alone!"

Calvin dared to laugh. "I'll never leave you alone, Mona. Don't you get that? If I can't have you, no one else will. You'll always be mine," he whispered.

His words chilled Mona to her core. But that didn't stop her from trying to get away.

"I'll never be yours. I never want to see you again."

Calvin stood in shock, his jaw tightening, his veins popping on his forehead. Nodding, he gazed at her with a look that she'd seen before. A shiver ran down her spine, but she continued to stand her ground.

Backing away, Calvin said, "Okay. We'll play it your way. I hope you have a lovely stay at your cabin, 'Moe' or wherever you tend to be these days. But you best keep an eye out. It's such a dangerous world out there. I wouldn't want anything to happen to you or your friends. Or better yet, Andrew."

He winked at her before turning around and walking away without so much as a backward glance. Mona hadn't realized she had been holding her breath until now. Shaken up, she hurried back into the hospital and didn't stop until she was back in the room with Anthony and Linda. Ace was nowhere in the room.

"Where'd you go?" Linda asked when Mona stepped through the threshold.

"Uh," Mona couldn't dare tell her what had happened, "I went for a walk. I needed some fresh air."

Linda looked at her strangely. "Are you okay, sweetie? You look a little pale."

Absentmindedly, Mona touched her face. "Y-Yeah, I guess it might be the change in temperature or something."

Linda didn't look convinced, but she didn't push any further, for which Mona was grateful for.

Mona knew that she couldn't tell Andrew about the encounter with Calvin. Either of them. It would set him off, and she couldn't risk things getting weird between them again. Calvin was a significant factor in their fallout. With her being so blinded by Calvin's lies, going against her family and friends, the dynamic of the group had never fully recovered from it.

Andrew had struggled to understand her mindset by sticking by her abuser but at the time, so did she. Calvin had manipulated her almost to the brink of total worship. By the time Calvin was finally gone, the damage was done, and Mona struggled to get herself back together, something her friends couldn't quite understand but to no fault of their own. She hadn't been a walk in the park.

Mona and Andrew had their own separate debacle after Calvin was no longer in the picture. The exchanges between the two had become so nasty, things were said that neither one of them could take back. Gradually, they fell out and stopped talking altogether.

Calvin coming back to ruin things would only distance

them, and Mona couldn't handle losing Andrew again. They had finally come to an understanding and she was determined to build and repair the shredded pieces of their friendship.

Mona kept quiet in the chair while Anthony slept, and Linda read a book next to him. Ace had returned and struck up a long conversation with one of the doctors in the hallway.

Patiently, Mona waited for Andrew's return. She dozed off at some point, Calvin plaguing every corner of her nightmares.

Chapter Twenty

Andrew

ANDREW RAN A hand through his hair in frustration. He was supposed to have been back at the hospital hours ago. As soon as he reached the cabin, he was bombarded with questions. To top it off, Cassidy had packed her stuff and left. Quickly getting everything he and Mona needed, he decided to go after her, not in an attempt to reconcile but to finally put an end to things.

He knew exactly where she was headed, and he wanted to catch her while he still had time.

Andrew tried calling Mona for the third time, but the call went straight to voicemail. It was only then that he realized her phone was probably dead since she was still waiting for him to bring her charger.

Throughout the drive, Andrew pondered what he would say to Cassidy. She was done with him as far as he knew, but he felt they needed proper closure. They had been together for two years while he struggled to open his restaurant. The least he could do was offer an explanation, he owed her that much.

It was now or never.

Rounding the corner, he parked his car in his usual spot at the front of his apartment entrance. Within no time, he was face-to-face with his apartment door. He could hear shuffling from the other side as he unlocked it.

Two suitcases littered the sofa, clothes thrown in haphazardly. With a handful of clothes from the closet, Cassidy brought them out with the hangers still attached and laid them in one of the suitcases. Startled, she jumped when she spied Andrew in the doorway.

With an eye roll, she continued to pack back and forth from the bedroom. "You're not stopping me, Andrew. I mean it."

"I wasn't planning to."

Cassidy stopped and looked at him in surprise, hurt flashing through her eyes briefly before she covered it up. "Then, what? We have nothing to talk about. Let me be on my way, and you can get back to the love of your life."

He already knew the answer before he asked, "Who's the love of my life?"

"You're precious *Mona* that you couldn't wait to run off into the sunset with."

"Cass—"

She held up her hand to stop him. "Just save it, Andrew. I know where I stand. I should've picked up on it a long time ago when I caught you lurking through her Facebook pages when we first started dating. You never stopped. I never stopped you because I believed that one day, you would look at me the way you look at her but seeing it in person is completely different."

Andrew approached her. "Cassidy, Mona, and I have nothing going on. We missed each other, sure, but nothing romantic. We never crossed that line."

Cassidy looked deeply into his eyes. "But you've wanted to."

The hurt in her eyes made him stand quiet. Admittedly, it had crossed his mind briefly when they were younger, but he never let his mind wander. Mona was always going to be a best friend to him first and he wasn't going to ruin that.

Cassidy scoffed, turning back to her task. "Thought so."

Andrew took a seat next to her suitcase, not sure how to respond. Cassidy had been building a case since the beginning.

How much had he really been caught up on Mona, then and now? Thinking back to when he left, he always found a way to incorporate Mona into his routine. Checking her social media, calling their friends to make sure she was doing well. Going to the funeral. Going to the cabin.

All of that for Mona.

He spent so much time thinking about her; he never dared ask himself why. But Cassidy didn't have to ask; she could see right through it. Maybe it was time to stop acting blind, for his sake and theirs.

When she walked back out to the sofa to place something else in the suitcase, Andrew knew what he had to say. "I'm sorry, Cassidy. I really am. You didn't deserve to only have half of me.”

"It's a little too late for sorry, Andrew.”

"I know,” he replied. "Doesn't mean I don't mean it.”

"I'm not sorry about it. I'm just sorry we wasted two years.”

Cassidy picked up her fully packed bags and opened the door. With one last look at him, she walked out of his life as fast as she had come. It took Andrew's phone ringing for him to finally move.

Looking at the screen, he debated if he should answer, but he couldn't ignore his mother's call. Not with Anthony in the hospital.

He cleared his throat before answering, "Hello?”

"Andrew! Where have you been?”

It took him a moment to answer. Closing his eyes and leaning back in the chair, he said, "I'm on my way back. I just ran into some... issues.”

"Well, you need to come back. I'm going to leaving with your father soon, and poor Mona will be here all by herself. She fell asleep waiting for you.”

Andrew groaned. Checking the time, it had been a couple hours since he had left. Mona was going to be pissed.

"Well, I'm on a roll today,” he muttered to himself.

"What was that, honey?” his mother asked.

"Nothing. I'm on my way, I promise. You can go home.”

"If you say so. Please don't leave sweet Mona here too long by herself. She looked a little frazzled when she came back in from her walk, I wonder if she's scared to be here all alone.”

Andrew frowned. "What do you mean? Did something happen to her?"

His mother sighed on the other end. "Honestly, I don't know. For all we know, the hospital could be reminding her of her father. I feel it for the poor girl. Just get here and keep her company."

She didn't wait for a response before she hung up. Andrew couldn't find the ability to move for several seconds. He instantly had a headache, and he couldn't think.

Two years down the drain.

He decided to wash his face with cold water to clear his head. He needed to get to Mona as soon as possible. He wondered if the idea of her staying at the hospital with him was such a great idea after all.

Was the memory of her father at the hospital too much for her? Or was it something else?

He didn't want to think about anything bad happening to her.

Taking one last look around the apartment, he strangely felt there was a lifted weight and he could finally breathe. Maybe it was baggage he should've gotten rid of long ago.

***

FINALLY ABLE TO find parking, Andrew made his way through the hospital to Anthony's room. Most of the buzz from earlier had died down significantly. The nightshift nurses barely acknowledged his presence.

Anthony's door was closed, but he could hear the television playing inside. Slowly, he pushed it open and stepped in.

Anthony was curled up on the bed, his back to the door. A known heavy sleeper, Anthony didn't even stir. Mona had taken the chair by the bed to curl up with a light blanket. Her hair sprung behind the chair, and her head was angled awkwardly on the armrest.

He decided to wake her up to take her to the waiting room. It would be too crowded for the both of them to sleep in the room.

Crouching in front of her, the bag in his hand falling to the floor, he waited for a beat before stirring her awake. Though uncomfortable, she looked peaceful sleeping. Her mouth was slightly ajar, a light snore escaping.

Her eyelashes fluttered her cheeks so angelically; he almost didn't wake her. Instead, he shook her shoulders gently to arouse her from her slumber.

"Mona," he whispered.

With her eyes still closed, she murmured, "Hmm."

"It's Andrew. I'm going to take you to the waiting room, so you can sleep."

"I am sleeping," she replied groggily.

Andrew chuckled lightly. "Yes, but not comfortably. Come on."

He stood and waited for her to sit up. Her eyes were barely open. She looked as if she'd fall over if she tried to stand. Nonetheless, she cricked her neck and stood lazily with a light stretch.

"Need any help?" Andrew offered.

Mona shook her head and started to walk out the door without another word. He picked up the blanket that covered her and followed her to the waiting room where she collapsed on the recliner near the window.

"Did you bring my charger?" she muttered.

He hadn't, but he did buy one from the store on the way. "Yeah, I'll put the phone on the charger for you."

He draped the blanket on her, and then took the recliner next to hers. As he got comfortable, she shifted to him, her eyes more alert than they were earlier. "What took you so long? I thought you weren't coming back for a second."

Andrew pondered if it was the time to relay what happened between him and Cassidy but decided against it. "I just ran into some issues, it's fine now. Why? Did you miss me?" he joked.

Mona rolled her eyes. "It would've been nice to have my stuff a few hours earlier or at least a text back."

"I'm sorry. By the time I tried calling you back, your phone must've already died." She handed him her phone from the jacket pocket. He laid it right beside him to charge.

"A little too late," she mumbled. Shifting toward the window, he could tell she was preparing to fall back asleep.

"Mona?"

Either she ignored him, or she had fallen asleep that fast. He was going with the latter. With a sigh, he got comfortable and pulled out his phone to look through his social media.

Mona's phone buzzed, the light of the phone catching his attention. The phone had turned on automatically after reaching ten percent. He ignored it, but the phone buzzed again.

And again.

And again.

Mona was sound asleep by then, and he wasn't going to bother her. However, he wondered if it was right for him to see why her phone kept buzzing. It technically wasn't his business and she'd be mad if she found out.

The phone buzzed again, and Andrew couldn't help but look at the lit screen. Her notifications indicated several missed calls and multiple messages. The phone sounded again, and at that point, Andrew's curiosity got the best of him.

Her phone had a passcode, but if she hadn't changed it over the years, then it would've been easy to get in. He typed in four digits and was greeted with her home page.

She hadn't changed it.

Taking a quick look at her to make sure she was still sleeping, he opened her messages. She had multiple unread messages from Nina and Adam, but he wasn't interested in that.

The unsaved number resting at the top of messages were what caught his eyes. There were eight new messages from the number, all within the last couple of hours. The previous six were within the last few minutes.

Andrew ran a hand through his hair, tempted to click on the messages. At the last minute, he decided to put the phone back down. He picked his phone back up for distraction, and for a few minutes, it was peaceful.

It didn't last long because her phone buzzed one final time. Without resolve, Andrew picked it up and opened the messages. With each passing message, his eyes grew wider.

UNKNOWN: *I miss you*

UNKNOWN: *Don't ignore me*

UNKNOWN: *Can't get you out of my head*

UNKNOWN: *I'm not going to hurt you*

UNKNOWN: *You looked beautiful in those sexy shorts*

UNKNOWN: *I don't like it when you ignore me, Mona*

UNKNOWN: *I miss seeing you naked on my bed*

UNKNOWN: *Andrew can't do what I can do*

"What the hell?" Andrew said a little too loud. Mona stirred but didn't awake thankfully.

Who the hell was this? How did they know who he was? What did the last message mean?

He tap-danced with the idea of replying, knowing he had no business even looking at the messages. The messages rubbed him the wrong way, however, and if he truly knew Mona, he knew this was somebody she likely wasn't interested in; hence the name not being saved.

Was this the reason why she had been shaken up earlier? Perhaps she'd seen the first messages and decided to ignore them. Or maybe she had deleted previous messages. Was it Calvin? No, she would've said something.

Whatever it was, this wasn't normal, that much he was sure. Although his gut told him otherwise, he deleted the messages and blocked the number. He put the phone down as if it had burned his hands and tried his best to ignore the uneasy feeling in his stomach.

It took a while, but Andrew finally was able to fall asleep.

By the time he woke up, a stream of light from the window was blinding him. What was likely hours of sleep felt like minutes.

A hustle of people passed, none even noticing their presence in the recliners. Andrew rubbed the sleepiness from his eyes and looked beside him to find the spot absent of Mona and her belongings.

Resting his head back, he closed his eyes briefly to gather some strength when he heard his name being called.

"Andrew! Sweetie, it's time to get up." It was his mom who was walking toward him.

Andrew groaned. He felt like he was in high school again, with his mom having to come into his room five times just to wake him up.

"I'm up," he said groggily. "Where's Mona?"

"She's saying bye to Anthony."

Andrew frowned. "Why?"

"Because I asked her to come home with me. She's been here since yesterday. She can't stay here forever in those clothes. Besides, I need to get a few things ready before the whole clan comes over and I need a girl's touch. I suggest you come and get cleaned up unless you plan on going back to the cabin?"

Home. He hadn't had much presence there in the last two years. He was actually looking forward to going back home. After yesterday's events, the rest of the crew could do without them for another day.

"What about Anthony?"

She pointed behind her. "Your father and Amir will stay

with him until he's released, so he doesn't feel lonely. Come on, let's go home."

It didn't take long for him to clean up the area and make his way to Anthony's room to tell him he would see him soon. Mona was walking out as he made his way inside.

"You left me out there by myself," he commented.

"I didn't want to wake you. You looked beat."

"You should've."

"Are you going back to the cabin?" she asked.

Andrew shook his head. "I'm heading back to the house with you. The cabin can wait. Do you want to ride with me?"

Mona smiled. "Of course."

He returned it and stepped into the room as she left. Amir was tickling Anthony on the bed while his dad was on the phone talking by the window. He greeted them with a nod.

Amir smirked when he spied Andrew. "Big bro! I see you're still uglier than ever."

Andrew mocked him and responded, "If by ugly, you mean the best looking in the family, then I'll take it."

His little brother was very much of a tyrant at the age of fourteen. Being that most of the siblings were away from home, he turned to his friends for companionship, ultimately leading him astray. In the past year, Andrew had heard that Amir had been more active and focusing his attention on family and sports to be a better role model for Anthony.

Anthony chimed in, "Mom says I'm cuter than everyone."

Amir pinched his cheeks playfully. "You keep believing that. That's like her motto to all of us behind closed doors."

Anthony pouted and crossed his arms.

Andrew chuckled at their banter. "As much as I'd love to stay and have meaningless conversation, I'm heading out."

With a quick farewell to the boys and his father, he hurried outside to find Mona and his mother laughing while they waited for him.

"What's so funny?"

Linda and Mona shared a teasing look. "Nothing you should worry about. Let's get a move on."

He pouted but it was good to see them both laughing.

The ride home was uneventful. Mona sang along to the songs on the radio. Andrew couldn't help but let his mind wander to the messages that were on her phone last night.

Should he tell her about it? Would she understand his reasoning for intervening?

He knew he overstepped boundaries, and karma was sure to bite him in the ass later for it. But he kept his mouth shut in hopes that he did the right thing.

"It's been a while since I've been to your parents' house," Mona said, turning to him.

Andrew rubbed his chin in contemplation. "Since a little before we stopped talking to each other, right?"

Mona nodded. "Just about. Have you been home since moving?"

He had visited a few times, though it was more impulsive than planned. He had spent most of the time trying not to contact his friends due to guilt.

"A few times," he answered instead.

"Wow, I didn't know you came back in town." Her tone held a whiff of melancholy.

"I didn't stay long. I missed them and my mom wanted to see me. And I can't say no to Mom."

"I would imagine she would with you being gone for so long."

Andrew scuffed, "Yeah, right. I'm probably not the only one that's been gone that long. I don't think Alex has been home since he got married."

"Oh, I forgot about Alex," Mona said dreamily.

Andrew rolled his eyes and chuckled. Alex, his oldest brother, had gotten married about three years prior. Back when they first entered high school, Mona had developed the biggest crush on Alex. It had annoyed him to high heavens when she forced him to invite her over just see him. Thankfully, it didn't last long.

Or so he hoped.

"Don't start," Andrew warned her jokingly.

Mona pouted. "What? He's the best-looking brother."

Andrew threw her a glare.

"Besides you, of course," she teased.

They both laughed. Mona opened her window, letting the breeze hit her face, her hair whipping with the force of the wind.

"I got a confession," Mona began. Andrew turned to her briefly, preparing for what she was about to say. She didn't wait for an inquiry before she continued. "I'm happy that we're not going back to the cabin."

Surprised, Andrew couldn't help but wonder why. "Change in scenery?"

"Change in friends."

Andrew gave her a questioning look. "That's not vague at all."

She took a moment to watch him before clarifying. "I'm happy that I'm here with you."

A small smile graced his face. Taking her hand without thinking and lacing his fingers through hers, he replied, "Confession: I'm glad you decided to come."

They stayed like that for a while before Mona slowly took her hands from his, a frown forming on her features. The loss of contact had him aching to reclaim her hand.

With a heavy sigh, Mona turned to the window. "What about Cassidy?"

"What about her?"

"Is she okay with you leaving her at the cabin?"

There was an underlying question somewhere in there he was sure. Andrew shrugged, not wanting to get into that conversation. Mona didn't look at him for the rest of the ride to the house. The air had shifted with the switch in conversation. Her silence carried her well. He could always tell when the wheels were turning in her head.

It wasn't that he didn't want to tell her, but the absence of Cassidy made him want to solely focus on Mona. Ultimately, the real reason she was gone was because of his inability to separate his longing for Mona. That was a topic he didn't want to breach at the moment.

Despite his little brother being in the hospital and what happened with Cassidy, Andrew felt the best he's felt in a long time, and he wanted to hold onto that feeling for as long as he could.

They arrived at the house a short time later with his mom pulling into the driveway first. Andrew hopped out of the truck to open Mona's door. She thanked him while still avoiding eye contact.

Andrew grabbed her arm before she could walk away so he could draw her into a hug. She stiffened, not sure what to do with her arms as he tightened his grip around her.

Mona pulled away with a quizzical look. "What was that for?"

Andrew shrugged and offered a small smile. "For being a friend."

He tucked a loose hair behind her ear and walked ahead of her into the house, leaving her dazed in his wake.

Chapter Twenty-One

Mona

"MAKE SURE TO put the timer on. When you're done, if you don't mind starting the ham…" Linda ordered to Mona.

Mona wiped the sweat from her face and completed her tasks as Linda disappeared in and out of the kitchen.

Mona was happy to help, anything to keep her mind from Andrew and the butterfly feelings she kept getting around Andrew. It wasn't as if they had been on eggshells, but since the ride home, the air around them had changed. Mona wasn't sure if it was a good thing or not.

Thankfully, with Linda handing out tasks to both of them, they were able to keep their distance, giving Mona a chance to clear her head.

Linda had learned shortly after entering her home that Anthony would be able to come home later since he was responding very well to the medications and had improved his condition in just a short amount of time. She had also learned the family was going to surprise him. The whole Sumpter gang would finally reunite.

Mona welcomed the change of faces and scenery. She had always felt welcomed into their home. Linda always made a point to include her in all the festivities.

Cooking was something that she had never done with Linda and frankly, barely by herself. In the past, Andrew had always taken a keen interest in being in the kitchen and trying new things. Growing up, he was her personal chef. In the last two years, she'd had more dates with fast-food restaurants than she liked to admit. For what it was worth, she wasn't a terrible cook, it was just something she never quite cared for.

Finishing the ham, Mona set the timer and walked to the cabinets to set the table just as her phone rang. Nina's name flashed on the screen.

Mona answered swiftly.

"Where have you been?!" Nina exclaimed before Mona could utter a word.

Oh yeah, she forgot to call Nina and Adam back.

Holding the phone slightly away from her ear, she replied, "I'm at the Sumpters' house."

"You just abandon us as soon as your *bestie* called for you? What are we, chopped liver?"

Mona snorted. "I did not abandon you guys. Anthony had an incident, and I wanted to support him. It's the least I could do. Andrew was distressed at the time."

Nina sighed defeatedly. "I'm not mad. It's just boring without you here."

"What about James? The two of you seemed to be hitting it off."

"We are. Actually, he asked me out. I finally got a date!" She sounded genuinely happy.

Mona couldn't help but smile. "That's awesome. See, you don't need me there."

"Yes! Yes, I do! I can't stay here if you're not going to be here. Remarkably, Adam is more annoying with a girlfriend— excuse me, *fiancée*— than he is without. Symoné is cool, but we don't relate as much, and Dixie is just a pain in my ass," Nina whined.

Mona hesitated. "What about Cassidy?"

"She left last night. I highly doubt she's coming back. She took all her things and left without so much as a goodbye. Andrew sure knows how to pick 'em."

Mona couldn't help but wonder if that's why he was delayed coming back to the hospital. If so, why didn't he trust her to tell her? Was he embarrassed?

Shaking the thoughts from her head, she turned her attention back to Nina. "No wonder you're bored."

Nina laughed. "You need to get your ass back here, or I'm coming over there. I don't care how Andrew feels about it."

"Andrew wouldn't care."

"Oh, trust me, he would. He likes to hog you."

Mona's eyebrows furrowed. "No, he doesn't."

"Yes, he does. Look, Adam and I know not to get in between... whatever it is you two got. Let's not act like you and Andrew didn't spend any unusual amount of time together before your fight."

"I really don't see the point you're trying to make, Nina.

We're not doing anything wrong, and we've always included you guys in our activities."

Nina stayed quiet over the line; Mona could just picture her lips pursed with an unconvinced look. "Okay, so, maybe not all."

"Whatever. I don't want to keep you, I just wanted to make sure you were okay. Send Anthony well wishes for me."

Mona smiled. "I sure will."

Mona hung up and jumped when she turned around. Andrew had been standing not too far away with a lazy grin on his face.

Suspiciously, she eyed him with question. "How long have you been standing there?"

"Long enough."

Mona rolled her eyes and pretended like he hadn't just scared the life out of her. "Aren't you supposed to be out back?"

Linda had asked him to clean off the patio earlier when she had begun cooking. Andrew shrugged and looked around the counters to see what was cooking.

"I finished and wanted to see if you needed any help."

"You don't always have to be the chef. I can handle the kitchen." Mona checked on the ham and began to cut up carrots Linda had taken out earlier.

"I know. Doesn't mean I can't observe. Maybe I like watching you."

Mona turned to him, catching the glint of mischievousness in his green orbs. "Well, that wasn't creepy at all."

Andrew chuckled. "You know what I mean. You do everything with such pride. It admirable."

A small smile spread on her face from the compliment. "I'd like people to think that I am dedicated if you will."

"You are," he agreed.

Mona briefly turned her head. "So, what really brings you over here? Can't be the meal."

He sat quietly as if he were mulling over his next words carefully. "I thought we could go somewhere when you're finished."

Mona started to shake her head, and she turned fully to him. "I don't know. What about your mom? Isn't she going to need more help? Where are we going?"

"Mom will be fine. There's not much to do. Besides, it's probably best if we beat the Sumpter traffic," he joked. "And I can't tell you where we're going. It's a surprise."

She understood that completely. All the boys especially were going to be a handful. Even though she already made up her mind, she pretended to think about it. His dough eyes were all she needed to make up her mind.

"Okay, we'll leave after I'm done."

"Good. I'll wait for you in the den."

He left her to finish the meal prep after that. Mona was eager to finish and apprehensive to know what he had planned. At some point, Linda had decided to take over and shooed her out of the kitchen, much to Mona's relief.

Making her way to the living room, she frowned when she didn't see him. "Andrew?" she called out but there was no answer.

Scaling the stairs, she headed to his old room to see if he was there. She paused as she watched him wander in the room he used to share with Aaron as a kid like he was unfamiliar.

"Find what you were looking for?"

Andrew whipped his head around, surprised. "It's been a while since I've been in here. I haven't technically been in my room since I moved out to stay on campus."

"You didn't come in here when you visited?"

"It was always brief. I never wanted to linger."

Mona remembered because they had moved out around the same time. They had gone to the same college and stayed there together in their own dorms.

"It looks the same," she commented. Nothing had changed in the room besides tidiness.

He didn't answer, instead, taking note of a photograph of them both from their first day of grade six. He picked it up and held it out to her with a chuckle. "I looked so nerdy in this photo."

Mona laughed, taking in his plaid shirt and the glasses that were too big for his face. "At least you can look back at this and realize what a glow-up you had."

"True." He took the photo back from her and started out the door. "Ready?"

She nodded and heading out of the house in tow. She walked toward the truck but paused when he went the opposite direction.

"Are we not taking the truck?"

Andrew shook his head. "Don't need it."

Mona hesitated but nonetheless, walked alongside him. "You're really not going to tell me where we're going?"

"I'm not taking you to the woods if that's what you're asking," he joked.

Mona punched his arm playfully. "I'm serious."

"So am I." He chuckled. "Just enjoy the walk. Maybe I wanted you to come because I like your presence."

"You'd like it more if I knew where I was going."

Andrew shot her an amused look but still hadn't offered an explanation. The sun was blazing by now, and the jeans she had on were starting to feel hot, but manageable. Her white t-shirt stuck to her skin like a glove and she began to regret choosing it over her second option that morning.

Andrew accessed her made-up face. "What's wrong?"

"I'm a little hot. I should've changed into shorts at least if I knew it was going to be this hot."

Andrew's eyes scanned the length of her. "We can turn back if you want. I'm in no rush."

Mona waved him off. "It's fine. Let's just see what you got in store for me."

Andrew smiled. "You make it sound like I'm leading you to doom. This is me we're talking about."

Mona trusted him wholeheartedly, but it was fun getting into his head. "I don't know. They do say it's always the people you trusted most."

"So, you trust me, then?"

"Well..." She pretended to think.

He winked at her. "That's all I need to know."

They bantered with each other the entire time, effectively distracting her from her whereabouts. She stopped right behind Andrew, who was staring across the street to the elementary school they attended kids.

It looked the same as it had over the last decade. The playground had a few updated placements, and the bricks on the building looked a little refreshed.

Mona turned to him in question. "This is where you wanted to take me?"

Andrew nodded. "Figured it'd be fun to step back in time for a bit."

He started walking toward the open gate to the playground. Mona could only trail behind, the memories flooding her mind.

Back then, life was so simple. Often, she and Andrew would spend their entire recess under one of the trees, sharing lunches. She was fearless to his bullies. Then, it was only the two of them.

Mona smiled as her fingers trailed the bench where she first ran his bullies off. "Are we allowed back here?"

Andrew shrugged. "I saw it open a few times when I visited. Figured I'd stop by."

"This is trespassing, you know?"

"Not if we don't touch anything inside. This is the closest thing we have to a park in the area. I'm sure they wouldn't care."

Mona shook her head. He was always so nonchalant about things she'd usually worry about. She sat on the swings and began to push herself. "You're so dangerous."

Andrew positioned behind her on the swing to push her further.

"Only for you, babe."

Mona clasped her hand over her mouth when she giggled like a schoolgirl. Where had that come from? She was not sure. She got a giddy feeling with his hands pressed against her back to push her swing. As simple as it was, it felt intimate.

She closed her eyes and let the wind wisp past her face. It didn't matter that the sun was on the verge of melting her skin, or the increasing height of the swing left a free-falling feeling in the pit of her stomach. All that mattered was the hand against her back and the freedom she felt.

That was until she tilted her head back without thinking and crashed right into Andrew by accident, shattering whatever euphoric feeling she had.

"Shit!"

"Ow!" She grabbed her head as pain seared through her head as she stopped the swing with her foot.

Jumping off, she rushed to Andrew's side to see him holding his lip, a silent curse escaping his lips. "I am so sorry! I got caught up in the moment."

"You think?" he said, his voice dripping with sarcasm.

"Let me see."

Removing his hands, Mona winced at the thin trail of blood, sliding down the side of his mouth. Her head must've connected with his lip. It wasn't gushing, but it was noticeable. She used her thumb to wipe it away.

"It's not as bad, it probably hurts more than it actually looks, though."

"If your head wasn't so big, I wouldn't be in pain." He looked at her pointedly.

"Aww," Mona teased with a smile. "Do you want me to make it better, you big baby?"

Andrew stood silent, his eyes far away as he pretended to think. "You can kiss it and make it better," he proposed.

Mona rolled her eyes, not taking him seriously. "You're such a baby."

"Kiss it and make it better, or I'm telling my mom you hit me. That means no dinner for you."

"She has to feed me," Mona challenged.

Andrew shook his head. "I don't think so. I'm the favorite."

"I thought Anthony was the favorite?" Mona grinned.

Andrew frowned. "She can have two favorites. Now, kiss it before I change my mind."

Mona opened her mouth to argue but closed and shook her head. Andrew was going to pester her until she did it, and if his grin was any indication, he was going to get his way, regardless.

Taking a deep breath, Mona approached him. Cheekily, he pointed to the spot above where his gash was by the corner of his mouth.

"I can't believe you're making me do this."

"Less talking, more kissing," he replied.

Quickly, she hovered over his gash, closing her eyes and

pressing her lips to his skin before stepping back. "Happy?"

Andrew tapped his chin. "I don't know. It still hurts. Maybe one more for the road?"

"Andrew!" Mona exclaimed.

Andrew threw his hands up in surrender. "Okay! Last one, I promise. I won't bother you anymore."

With a frustrated, but playful, sigh, Mona reproached him and looked him right in the eyes. "Last one."

Andrew grinned as he looked down on her. Holding up three fingers, he said, "Scout's honor."

"You weren't a boy scout, and that's not even the correct sign," Mona pointed out.

"Whatever! You're not getting out of this, so keep talking, and I might just have to steal it."

"Steal it? You cannot steal something I—"

Mona was cut off by his lips brushing hers. It happened so fast; she did not have time to think. Immediately, she responded, her hands going through his curls. Without thinking, she opened her mouth to give him more access, deepening the kiss.

His hands ran the length of her sides, gripping her waist. Without notice, she pushed him back, catching him off guard.

Mona unconsciously touched her lips that felt seared after having his soft lips on hers. Up until that point, she hadn't noticed how fast her heart was pounding. Not able to look at him, not out of disgust, but out of nervousness, she turned her back to him with the hopes of gathering her nerves.

"What was that?"

It took him so long to answer; Mona had to turn around to make sure he was still there. He stood silent with a frown etched on his face.

"I don't know. I'm sorry."

Mona dared to look him in the eyes, feeling trapped once his stormy green orbs touched hers. She couldn't decipher that look he had, but it was like he was trying to figure something out.

Mona wanted to dwell on the encounter. How her insides felt like butter. The butterflies that made her feel like a schoolgirl. Her sides still tingled from his fingers, sliding down the fabric of her shirt. Instead, she clammed up and retreated into herself with more questions than she had answers.

"We should get back," Andrew forced out.

She didn't wait for his response, instead, opting to rush out of the park and out of his presence before she found herself doing something she'd regret.

***

THEY WALKED HOME in silence, Mona stretching more feet between them both. He hadn't said a word, something that irked her nerves but at the same time, she was thankful for.

How did an innocent day at the park turn into an afternoon she would never forget?

It the first and only time Andrew had tried something like that.

However, as much as she wanted to be mad, she couldn't ignore the lingering feeling that ran through her at the mere thought of their encounter.

Moreover, there was the simple fact that Mona kissed him back. She was angrier with herself for giving in to the moment than the moment itself. How could she be so reckless? Andrew was her friend and whether or not this was a joke, that was not a friendly gesture.

So why did she kiss him back?

So many questions circled in her brain, but her mouth stuck together. Her eyes focused on the sidewalk in front of her because she felt if she dared to look back, she would lose sight.

Andrew was her friend, and regardless if she liked the kiss, he couldn't ever be more. He had a life outside of her and he had someone on his frontier.

Her heart tugged at that thought but retracted the thoughts from her head as they were entering dangerous territory. Maybe she was overthinking.

Not maybe.

She was overthinking.

Her thoughts ran so deep, she didn't pay attention to where she was walking until she was snatched to the side.

"Jesus! You almost walked into the pole," Andrew said, his hands still around her forearm.

Mona looked up at the light pole that was suddenly in front of her. Walking into it would have likely put her in a daze.

On the other hand, it may have cleared her mind.

"Thank you," Mona mumbled, sliding her arm from his

and continuing on her way.

Andrew trailed behind like before, but closer this time. She could feel him behind her, which unnerved her.

"Moe," he called out. She looked up to make sure she wasn't anywhere near a pole but otherwise continued to ignore him.

"Mona," he drew out. He gently grabbed the same arm he had before to twist her around.

"What?" She said harsher than she had anticipated.

"Will you look at me, please? Stop avoiding me."

Mona dared to look up at him. He looked frustrated, but her eyes couldn't focus on his eyes as much as they did his lips.

They were on hers not too long ago.

Andrew let her go but stood in front of her until he was the only thing she could see. With a heavy sigh, his shoulders sagged, and a look of regret passed his features. "I'm sorry."

Mona let his apology sink in but still offered no words.

Did she even want him to be sorry?

That thought scared her.

She nodded and turned, but he stopped her from walking away again.

"I mean it," he urged. "I was out of line, and I took a joke too far. I don't know what I was thinking."

A joke. Was that all it was because it sure didn't feel like it. Nonetheless, her heart sank a little.

His eyes were guarded, though, so she couldn't tell if he was sincere.

"Okay, apology accepted." The words felt hollow flowing

through her lips, and she couldn't help feeling like she had to swallow a hard pill.

She wanted more, but she couldn't admit it out loud.

"So, that's it?" Andrew looked at her as if he was expecting more of a fight.

"What else do you want me to say, Andrew? What happened was a mistake. We shouldn't let it happen again." Mona shrugged and continued her walk, this time, with a small chip on her shoulder.

"Are you mad at me?"

Yes? No? She wasn't sure herself.

Regardless, she put up her front. "No, there's nothing to be mad about. What's done is done. It meant nothing, right?"

His apology bothered her, and the notion it meant nothing—her heart was feeling something.

Andrew didn't bother trying to engage with her further, instead he took the hint from her tone. Thankfully, they reached the house much faster than she had anticipated. Mona, not wanting to make things even more awkward, decided to make a beeline for the guest room she would be staying for the night and did her best to forget Andrew and that stupid kiss.

First Dance

Conner Middle School Dance

ANDREW FILLED HIS cup with punch as he stood by the food table and watched his classmates dance to a cheesy slow song the DJ put on. He rolled his eyes as he watched a few of them holding hands and getting a little too close for school policy. Where the chaperon had disappeared to escaped him. He headed back to his table where Adam sat with his date flirting.

"You couldn't get us a drink?" Adam whined.

Andrew gave him a funny look before taking his seat to people-watch. "You got legs."

Adam's date huffed and got up to get a drink, allowing Adam to move to the chair beside him. "Come on! Liven up! Your sitting here like your cat just died."

"I can't believe I let you drag me to this stupid dance."

Adam looked offended. "Well, excuse me for trying to get you out of the house for our last middle school dance. You would've been bored at home babysitting while the rest of us have fun."

Andrew was glad he didn't have to babysit, although that idea wasn't looking too bad as the night wore on. "I think I would've managed. Don't you have a date to entertain?"

Adam shook his head in defeat. "You'll thank me later."

Andrew watched him walk over to his date and head in a different direction, leaving Andrew at the table all by himself. After two songs, he got up for another drink, but stopped short and stared at the double doors to the entrance of the gymnasium.

The blue sparkle on the dress danced in the spotlight against her small curves. The dress had a split on the side, so her right leg could peek out as she walked. Her hair swept to the side in soft waves, the light catching the red tint. She was far enough away that he couldn't see her face entirely, but knowing her, she could come natural and still be the most beautiful girl on the floor. His eyes traveled the length of her until she spotted him and waved.

Andrew's palms suddenly felt sweaty as he waved back and watched her approach. He felt stuck as he hadn't moved since he first spotted her. It wasn't until she was right in front of him that he put down his empty cup, forgetting all about his punch.

"What are you doing here? I thought you weren't coming?" Mona asked once she stood in front of him.

It took a moment for him to gather his thoughts. "I wasn't, but Adam practically begged me to come. I don't have a date or anything." He wasn't sure why he felt the need to include that last part.

"Me, either."

Andrew frowned. "I thought you were coming with Emmitt?"

Mona shook her head. "Yeah, I was until I got stood up. But he's not going to ruin my fun." She touched the bowtie around his neck and smiled. "You clean up nicely."

"And you look... beautiful," he replied nervously.

She blushed and looked down at her dress. "Thanks. This is actually my backup choice. I'm glad I bought it, though. It's really comfy."

Another slow song began to play, and suddenly, Andrew wanted to be on the dancefloor with her. He felt the urge to hold her hand and show her a good time. She shouldn't have been dateless, but at the moment, he was glad she was. He wasn't sure if he wanted to share her with anyone else.

Clearing his throat, he gathered his wits and asked, "D-Do you want to dance?"

Mona stared at him in surprise. "I thought you don't like to dance?"

"For you, I'd do anything," he said without thinking. He mentally kicked himself for how it sounded, but he meant it. He would do anything for her. "I mean, since we're both dateless, it would seem like a waste and all."

For a split second, her eyes seemed to dim, but he could've just imagined it.

With a smile, she took his outstretched hand. "I would love to dance with you."

Andrew bit his lip for the smile that threatened to appear

as he guided her to the dancefloor and pulled her close, his hands planted on her waist. She wrapped her arms around his neck and they started to sway lightly to the music.

"You could've had any date, you know. You seem to be a hit," Mona gestured to the group of girls standing idle at the edge of the dancefloor, glaring in their direction.

He chuckled. "I'm not interested."

"Why not?"

"Because they're not... my type," he caught himself as he looked away nervously.

Leaning her head on his shoulder, she muttered, "I'm glad."

He wasn't sure what she meant by that, though at the moment, he couldn't dwell on it. He was too busy, hoping she wouldn't hear how fast his heart was racing. He didn't want to think about how nicely she fit in his arms or how good she smelled. He didn't want to think about how sweaty his hands were around her waist.

He couldn't.

He wouldn't.

The only thing he cared about was being the happiest he was that whole night in her embrace on that dancefloor.

He couldn't have thanked Adam enough.

Chapter Twenty-Two

Andrew

SITTING AT THE table with his whole family was like stepping back in time. The clanging of dishes, the loud talking and laughter, and the constant arguing between the twins was something he hadn't missed since he'd been gone.

Not. One. Bit.

Then, there was Mona, who was engaged in conversation with Aaron and his older sister Audree, laughing and pretending he wasn't sitting across the table from her.

He ruined it, or so it felt. They were just getting their dynamic back, and he had to kiss her. It was supposed to be a joke. The impulse to pull her closer and crash her lips with his was so strong in the moment, he couldn't think straight.

Then, there was the fact that she kissed him back. He hadn't anticipated that either. Was that impulse, too?

He had to make this right. He needed to restructure the balance before it fell apart again. He couldn't afford to go back to the dynamic they had before the cabin.

Andrew caught her eye from across the table, but she

swiftly turned away to talk with Aaron again.

A ploy. She needed a distraction, that was clear. Was she affected by that moment as he was?

He eyed her carefully, noting her stiffness and her obvious avoidance. As if sensing his stare, she snuck a glance but turned away again. The look was there. The body language was there. Though it was never directed toward him in the past, he recognized her shy act.

She was trying to hide it. Maybe deny it, but it wasn't translating to her body language.

Watching her laugh with his siblings and seeing how well she fit into his mold, he began to question what he's been doing all this time with her. He was always her friend first, but he couldn't deny she shook something deep within his core.

This is where she belonged. He couldn't imagine her being anywhere else or with anyone else.

It was more than just being comfortable around her. It was more than just having her presence. His mind ran to her constantly. It was just her. Cassidy never garnered those feelings within him.

Suddenly, the term friendship didn't sit right with him anymore. Watching her, mesmerized by her presence, he realized he wanted more. More than the shy glances. More than the thought.

He wanted her.

He was in love with her.

The rush of feelings paralyzed him at his core, and he instantly felt knots in his stomach. Pushing his chair back, he caught the attention of the table, Mona included.

"You okay, honey? You don't look so good," his mother asked, concern written on her features.

"Yeah, I..." He tried to think of a quick lie. "I just remembered I have to check on something at the restaurant. I have to take a call. I'll clean up."

"Okay..." she said, not all that convinced.

Picking up his plate, he avoided their confused stares and disappeared from their sight into the kitchen.

Immediately, he felt like he could breathe again. Grabbing the counter, he hung his head, mixed emotions swirling through his chest.

"Are you sure you're okay?"

Andrew whipped around at the sound of her voice. She stood there, innocent, with a concerned look etched on her pretty face. He took her in for a moment before breaking eye contact.

"I'm fine," he tried to reassure her. "I just need to get some things done."

Mona frowned but made no move toward him. "Why do I feel like that's an excuse?"

Because it is, he thought. Andrew shook his head and started for the stairs to his room. "I'm fine. I just have something to do."

He left her standing in the kitchen with a perplexed look. He couldn't face her. Not yet.

Despite using the restaurant as an excuse, Andrew found himself calling Dave anyway, if only for a little reprieve.

Dave answered on the second ring, "Nice of you to remember your temporary replacement. When will you be back to grace the restaurant with your presence?"

"I'm not sure yet. Sooner, rather than later, perhaps."

The sound of dishes clattering could be heard in the background. "I'm starting to think you've abandoned us."

Andrew chuckled. "The restaurant is my life. I wouldn't abandon it. You, on the other hand..."

"Oh, hush. By the way, I need the code for your office door. You forgot to give me the budget list to order supplies."

"It's one-one-two-eight, and I gave you the code before I left."

Andrew could almost see him shrugging. "Oh, well, I forgot."

Andrew rolled his eyes. "Of course, you did. Just make sure my restaurant is still intact when I get back, or you're fired," he joked.

Dave snorted. "You need me more than I probably need you. But seriously, don't fire me."

Technically, he was right. Dave ran the operations Andrew knew he couldn't handle on his own. Since meeting two years ago, when Andrew first got the city approval to build the restaurant, they'd become great friends. Andrew knew he could count on Dave to run things smoothly in his absence.

"You know I can't."

"Speaking of fire, how's everything going with the old flame?"

"What old flame?" Andrew asked, genuinely confused.

"The one that's drawn on the back of your notepad that you keep on you 24/7?"

Andrew groaned. And here he thought he could escape her.

Playing coy, he said, "I don't know what you're talking about."

Dave caught on quickly. "Ah, I see. Well, don't lose the spark then. A wildfire comes few and far in between."

Andrew quirked an eyebrow. "Did you just spit wisdom? That's shocking coming from you."

"Fuck off. I'm trying to get your head out of your ass. Someone is going to swoop in and take her from you one of these days, and you're going to be too late. Not saying you should jump headfirst into anything but take a leap of faith, why don't you. Don't let a relationship ruin a potential long-lasting love."

"You mean Cassidy?"

"Yeah," Dave agreed.

Andrew hadn't told him that the ship had long sailed. As much as he wanted to take Dave's words to heart, he knew it wasn't going to happen, at least not now.

"As much as I enjoy having you counsel my love life, I think it's time for you to get back to work."

"In other words, 'Let me avoid the conversation because it's hitting too close to home.'" Dave laughed.

"Whatever," Andrew said as he hung up, Dave's laugh still ringing in his ear.

Andrew rubbed his forehead in frustration. Getting Mona out of his head would be the bane of his existence. If he didn't find something to do besides think of her and where his mind wanted to venture, he knew he would go insane.

Taking out his notes for the new menu he planned to unveil in several months for the restaurant, he decided to stay cooped up in his room until his heart would stop beating with anxiety with the mere thought of her.

***

JUMPING UP AT the sound of a knock at his door, Andrew looked around, trying to adjust his eyes to the darkness that engulfed his room. Looking at his phone, he frowned at the time. It was a little past midnight. He had no idea he had even fallen asleep.

The knock sounded again before the door opened slowly. Mona peaked in shyly, noting the open blinds and his haphazard look.

"Were you sleeping?" Mona waved it off. "Don't answer that. Dumb question."

Rubbing his eyes clear, he got up to turn on the light and close the blinds. Clearing his throat, he said, "Yeah. What are you still doing up?"

He opened the door wider for her to enter before closing it behind her. "Couldn't sleep," she responded, flopping down on his bed.

Andrew took a seat beside her on the bed, making sure not to touch her. His carefulness caught her attention, and she frowned but didn't say anything.

"You disappeared from the dinner table and never came

back out. Have you been in here the whole time?"

Andrew nodded and chose his next words carefully. "Yeah, I had some work for the restaurant that needed my attention immediately."

Mona eyed him suspiciously, cocking her head to the side. "I don't know if I believe you."

Instead of avoiding her gaze, he matched her energy. "Then don't. I've been working hard while you flirted your way through the family."

He almost punched himself for how that sounded. He had meant it as a joke, but it came off like jealously. Maybe it was jealousy.

Before she could even retort, he stopped her. "I'm sorry. That's not how I meant it. I just—"

"I can take your jabs, Andrew. I'm not a child. What I won't take are your implications."

Mona got up to leave, but he grabbed her hand to stop her. "I'm sorry. I swear I didn't mean it..."

He thought about how he should explain it to her. He couldn't tell her that he was jealous. He couldn't tell her that seeing her talk and laugh with his harmless brothers irritated him because they had a real shot with her if it was reciprocated.

She looked at him, expectantly waiting for an answer. "I didn't mean it that way. It was supposed to be a joke and it came out wrong. I wasn't trying to call you names. I promise."

She deflated almost immediately. Sighing with relief, he sat back down and patted the seat next to him, which she eventually took.

"Do you think we would ever be able to go back to where we were? I mean, I know we've kind of fallen back to our old ways, but it's different, you know?"

Andrew really wanted to ask about the kiss and how she felt about it, but if it made her uneasy before, he was scared to see her reaction. Yeah, things had changed. He realized how much time he wasted not taking a chance with her.

Mona shook her head. "No, but I don't think we need to go back to who we were or what we were."

"What do you mean?"

Mona turned to him, scooting further onto the bed beside him. "I mean, despite where our friendship was, we weren't complete. We learned how to stand on our own, and while we still have our differences, we've grown into better people and hopefully better friends by learning from our mistakes."

Better friends. He wasn't sure that part was entirely true, not after his revelation. How could he look at her the same again? She meant more now. Maybe always have.

Not sure how to reply, Andrew changed the subject, "Do you remember our sleepovers?"

Mona scoffed, "How could I forget? You always kept me up with your snoring."

"Stop lying. I never snored. You always snored."

"I've never snored in my life, and I'm sticking to that story." Mona crossed her arms.

Andrew laughed. "You do that. That pout isn't helping you none."

Chapter Twenty-Two

Mona stuck her tongue out.

"You get on nerves."

"But you wouldn't change it," she said.

"Not for the world," he muttered as he caught her eye.

Mona tried to hide her smile by looking away.

"Good times," Andrew reminisced. "If only we could go back in time and..."

"And what?"

Andrew shrugged. "And relive our greatest moments."

"Was it, though? Was it our greatest moment?"

"Yeah, it was. It was mine."

Mona turned to him, her eyes glistening. "Maybe we can make new moments. Better moments."

"How?"

"Well," Mona began, stripping of her shirt to reveal her undershirt, "we start by taking a trip to the pool."

Andrew could only watch with his jaw wide open as Mona slipped out of his door. Quickly taking off his shirt and slipping on swim trunks, he could only follow the quiet trail she left behind.

Chapter Twenty-Three

Mona

WHAT WAS SHE thinking? Taking off her shirt in his room and having him follow her to the pool in the middle of the night? It was a bold move. But then again, she didn't feel quite herself since the kiss. Thankfully, the awkwardness had vanished once they got to the pool.

With her feet in the pool and Andrew resting against the edge, she never felt as comfortable in the last couple weeks as she had been next to him in that moment.

"I've been thinking... maybe I should open a new restaurant location here," Andrew said.

"Here? As in, you're staying here?" Mona couldn't help but feel elated at the idea of him moving back home. The idea of him leaving again stung.

"Yeah, maybe. I don't know. I just—I don't want to leave here. I don't want to leave you."

Mona glanced at him, and her breathing hitched. "What about the other restaurant? What about Cassidy?"

Andrew sighed. "Cassidy is no longer a part of my life,

for good. I have someone in mind to run the other restaurant. He's loyal, and he really helped me during the startup. It's only right I give him a better role."

Mona was stuck on the Cassidy part. A little flair of delight bubbled in her stomach, but she eased past it. That explained her sudden departure from the cabin and Andrew's absence from the hospital.

"Does he know about us?" Mona decided to stay clear of the topic of Cassidy.

Andrew gave her a questioning look. "Us?"

Mona blushed. "'Us' as in your friends back home."

Andrew smirked, catching her blush. "Yeah, I guess you can say that."

Swimming away from the edge, Andrew called out to her, "You should get in. The water feels amazing."

"So, you can chase me in the water like you used to? No, thank you. I like the sidelines."

Andrew laughed. "When have I ever chased you in the pool? I don't even swim that fast."

Mona looked at him incredulously. "Like, all the time minus the trip to the cabin. I don't think you've ever been able to behave in a pool, ever."

"I beg to differ," Andrew began. "If I recall correctly, you started this whole mess junior year of high school when you were trying to show off with your asshat of a boyfriend, Mikey."

Mona splashed some water at him. "Mikey was a great boyfriend! He just had a hard time filtering his words sometimes."

"So, a blunt asshole."

Mona flicked him off. "Fuck you, Andrew. You couldn't stand him because he wasn't intimated by you."

"That's not true, and you know it."

"Isn't it, though? Think about it. You literally scared off anyone who I brought around you." Mona watched Andrew carefully as he swam back to her.

"I've never scared off any of your boyfriends in high school. If they left, it was because they wanted to."

Mona rolled her eyes and leaned back on her elbows, her eyes never leaving his. "Andrew, you intimidated them."

Andrew shrugged nonchalantly. "It's not my fault they're easily intimidated. Find stronger guys."

Mona laughed. "You say it like it's that easy considering you run them off."

Andrew took a hard look at her. "You're beautiful, smart, and damn stubborn. How could you not find someone?"

The intense stare he was giving her was enough for her to take her feet out of the pool and sit on the pool chair to try and hide the heat rising in her face. Besides her pajama shirt being off, she hadn't taken off any other article of clothing. Her bold move in his room was the only moment of courage she had gotten that close to him. If she knew any better, she'd go back to her room for some sleep.

Much to her slight annoyance, he followed her out the pool and took a seat in the pool chair next to hers.

So much for running away.

Realizing he was still waiting for an answer, she answered

quietly, "I find it hard to open up again, sometimes. Not since Calvin." Not since Andrew left, is really what she had in mind but kept that thought to herself.

Andrew seemed to mull that over, running his hand through his wet locks. "So, you haven't been with anyone since..."

Mona shook her head. She thought she heard a small sigh of relief but chalked it up to imagination.

"Maybe it's for the best, then. With everything that's been going on—"

"I needed this break. Time for myself."

Andrew tugged at the side of her pajama shorts, a contemplative look on his face that she couldn't quite decipher. "You know if ever need me, for anything, I'll be there."

Mona gave him a meager smile. "I know. Always."

He returned it and got up, his hand leaving the seam of her shorts. He pulled her up by grabbing her wrists lightly.

"Come inside the pool."

She quickly took off the rest of her pajamas, leaving her in her blue bra and panties. The night air gave her a slight chill. She looked up at Andrew to find him watching her heavily before a smirk crossed his lips, and she regretted ever coming to the pool.

"Andrew, no!"

With complete disregard, he threw her over his shoulders and threw her into the pool, Andrew jumping in after her. His laughter echoed throughout the pool area.

Mona hit his shoulder. "You jerk! I knew I shouldn't trust

you!"

Andrew, still laughing, tried to wipe her hair from her face, but she moved away in anger. "I'm sorry! I couldn't resist."

Splashing water in his face, she swam to the edge and hopped on the edge as she had before. Swimming toward her, Andrew crossed his arms on her knees and rested his chin.

"You're not mad, are you? Andrew asked innocently.

"What do you think?" Mona asked with a frown.

"I'm leaning towards a no." Andrew chuckled. "Seriously, I'm sorry. Come back in, please?"

"Why do you want me to be in the pool so bad?"

"Maybe I want you close to me?"

Mona's heart picked up speed, but she wondered if it was from being thrown in the pool or from the undertone of desire in Andrew's voice. Either way, she could feel the heat from his arms on her legs creep further up.

Finally giving in, she said, "Fine."

Andrew didn't move completely. Instead, he caged her in as she slowly slid back into the pool, practically meeting him face-to-face. She hadn't expected him to be so close.

"Close enough?" Mona couldn't help asking.

"Not nearly," Andrew murmured, his eyes never leaving hers. A moment of silence fell between them as they seemed to be lost in each other's eyes. She could feel the electricity between them, his stare so intense she felt naked.

Suddenly, he disappeared underwater, then he grabbed her legs and wrapped them around his torso, his back to her.

Coming back up, he grabbed her arms and wrapped around his neck. He did it so fast she hadn't realized he was trying to give her a piggyback ride until he started to tread to the deeper part of the pool.

They swam for a while, laughing, reminiscing, and ignoring the growing feeling of intimacy between them. It was enough to help her forget everything that had clogged her mind besides him.

"You promised to teach me how to make that meal you made after prom, and you left me hanging," Mona said as Andrew trod the water with her on his back.

"I promised a lot of things I didn't get a chance to accomplish."

Mona scoffed, "Tell me about it."

Andrew craned his neck to look at her. "Hey! I came through enough."

"Says the guy that said he'd never leave." Mona fell quiet when she realized what she had said. "I'm sorry."

Andrew turned to her with a sad smile. "It's okay. I deserve that."

Mona released herself from his back and swam in front of him. "No, it's not okay. I shouldn't have said it. We both played a part in that. I'm sorry."

Andrew touched her face gently, wiping some of her wet hair from her forehead. Mona couldn't help but lean into it. "No more apologies, Mona. We need to move on. Officially. Starting now. Promise?"

Mona searched his eyes before smiling and nodding.

Chapter Twenty-Three

"Promise."

A roll of thunder sounded from a distance, causing both to look up at the dark sky.

"Well, that was unexpected," Mona said.

"We should probably head inside now."

Andrew hopped out of the pool and helped her out. Drying off, Andrew followed Mona to the guest room she was staying in a few doors from his room. Stopping in front of her door, Mona turned to him.

"Thank you for coming to the pool with me. It was fun."

Andrew smiled. "Anytime. I couldn't have asked for a better night."

"You're not just saying that, are you?" Mona joked.

"No, I'd rather spend time with you than anyone else, to be honest."

Mona blushed. "So, I guess this is goodnight?"

Andrew thought for a moment. "More like 'good morning.'"

Mona nodded. "Right."

They stood in silence as if either one was waiting on the other to do or say something. She watched as droplets of water fell from the tips of his curls to the wooden floor. Her eyes fell on his lips briefly, the memory of them touching hers seared into her brain. After a pregnant pause, Mona opened her door but didn't step in, though she wasn't sure why.

"Andrew?"

"Yeah?" he responded.

"I'm really happy you're back in my life."

"Me, too," he whispered.

Pushing her way in, Mona closed the door swiftly before she did something stupid. With her hormones raging, there was no telling what her body had in mind. The whole night had been so tense, it was palpable. With a flutter of breath, she leaned against the door and closed her eyes.

What a night, she thought.

Before she could peel her clothes off, a knock sounded at her door. Eyebrows furrowed, she opened it to see Andrew standing there with a dark look in his eyes.

"Andrew? What—"

Mona was interrupted by Andrew's lips crushing hers. Without thinking, she wrapped her arms around his neck, ultimately drawing him closer and returning the kiss. Her mind went blank, her only consumption being his warm lips upon her own.

Gripping the back of her neck, Andrew deepened the kiss, their tongue gradually fighting for dominance. Mona allowed it with some exploration of her own as she tangled her fingers through his hair. Backing her to a wall, Andrew lifted her by the waist. Mona wrapped her legs around him as their movements became hasty.

With their lips stilled attached, Andrew's warm hands began to inch up her torso until they found her breasts. Still a little wet from the pool, her shirt felt like a glove with his hands over her.

Finally, he slid his lips to her neck, eliciting a moan from the back of her throat. With his hands prodding over her nipples, she felt the heat between her legs began to grow exponentially.

Grinding against him, she whispered his name as he pushed off her shirt and bra to gain better access to her breasts. The cold air caused her to shiver with pleasure as he continued to hastily undress her.

They couldn't get to the bed fast enough. By the time the back of her head hit the pillow, her bottoms were already off. Wrestling to take his shirt off, Mona moved his head from her neck and attacked his lips.

The heat between her legs grew as she rubbed herself against his growing bulge. A deep-throated groan escaped his lips as they continued to assault each other. Unable to wait, Mona pushed him off to pull his trunks down, exposing his member.

Taking a hard look at it, she couldn't help but bite her lips in anticipation. It was almost perfect. Without a thought, she grabbed him and slowly began to stroke.

"Don't start something you can't finish," Andrew struggled to get out through his teeth.

"Who said I couldn't finish it?" Mona whispered as she pushed him onto his back, still gripping him. Now it was her time to dominate. With his hands gripping her waist, she let go of him and focused on trailing her lips down his chest. Stopping just above his navel, she made eye contact with him.

He looked ready to pounce at any moment. Taking advantage of his attention, she continued to lower herself, grabbing and stroking him with her hands slowly but stop short of his readiness.

He groaned with pleasure and grabbed her hair to raise her back to his face. Unable to take the pressure anymore, he flipped them over with her legs automatically wrapped around him.

She was ready to explode at that point, and she knew Andrew could feel it with him pressed against her.

"I need you now," she whimpered.

Andrew obliged, taking in a deep kiss before positioning himself in front of her entrance. Before his tip could touch her, he drew away, muttering under his breath.

"Shit."

"What's wrong?" Mona asked, slightly annoyed at the absence.

"I forgot I don't have a condom."

"I'm on the pill, and I'm clean," Mona said quickly.

"Me, too."

"Okay, then it's settled," she said impatiently.

"You sure?"

"I've never been surer of anything."

He looked at her long and hard before nodding and repositioning himself. Before he entered, he lowered his forehead onto hers, staring intensely into her eyes.

Mona hissed with pleasure as he entered her fully, stretching her beyond her limit. It had been months since she last had sex, she wasn't ready for the slight pain that came with Andrew being inside her and stretching her more than anyone had.

Taking in her lips, he began to rock slowly at first. In and out, he continued his rhythm until pressure began to build between them. Mona squeezed her legs against him, moaning deeply as he plunged harder into her and hitting all her spots.

Their breaths mingled together as they continued to soar with each other.

No words were spoken, only the rhythm of their flow singing tunes between the sheets.

Not when he allowed her to get on top and ride him until he couldn't take it anymore.

Not when they came together.

And certainly not when they fell asleep in each other's arms.

CHAPTER TWENTY-FOUR

Andrew

ANDREW AWOKE TO the sound of shuffling. The sudden cold spot on his arm wasn't lost on him. Opening his eyes—or rather, squinting—he watched as Mona tried but failed to quietly step into her clothes that blanketed the floor from their night together.

Was she trying to sneak away?

He could tell it was still early as they hadn't fallen asleep until well after four. The lack of sunlight streaming through the curtains was a dead giveaway.

He stirred as she hopped into her pajama shorts hastily. He could watch her all morning, and she wouldn't even know it. Instead, he propped himself on his elbow with a lazy grin displayed on his face.

"Was I that bad?"

Mona jumped and whipped her head in his direction, covering her breast with the shirt she picked off the floor as if he hadn't been playing with them for most of the morning.

"You scared me."

"You didn't answer the question." He quirked a brow at her.

A faint blush crept onto her cheeks. "No."

She said it almost like a whisper. If the house wasn't so still, he might not have heard her.

"I never you took for the 'walk of shame' type." He was toying with her. The blush was full-fledged at this point, and he couldn't help but feel turned on. Her innocence was so damn cute.

"I—I wasn't trying to flee..." He gave her a pointed look. "Okay, I was trying to flee."

"Why? Did I do something wrong? If I did, I'm sorry." The grin slowly slipped from his face. What if he had done something he wasn't aware of? He would never forgive himself.

Mona shook her head quickly. "No! It's just—" He could tell she was struggling to find the right words. "It's just that this is awkward?"

Andrew scooted to the edge of the bed and leaned to grab her and drag her in front of him. The thin sheet they were previously laying under wrapped around his torso to obscure his nudity.

He allowed her to step between his legs as one hand grabbed her waist, and the other found her cheek. "Do you trust me?"

"Yes," she said without hesitation.

"Then you know that you can always be yourself around me. I don't regret last night. Do you?"

"No," she breathed out. "but what if this changes everything?"

The worry in her voice was understandable. Before he almost lost his nerve, he stood outside her door after their night wishes, wondering why he didn't go for it. Would it change them for the worse? What if she didn't feel the same? And then, he stopped overthinking it. It only served as a setback if he didn't go for it or at least try.

The nervous feeling went away and getting the chance to sit on the edge of the bed and hold her at that moment was all worth it.

"Everything's already changed, Moe, and I don't want to go back to what we were. I like what we are right here, right now."

Andrew stared into her eyes, mesmerized by the intense color of gray. Sliding his hand to the back of her neck, he leaned into her and paused before their lips could touch.

"You're so beautiful," he whispered to her before claiming her lips. She loosened up immediately, taking him in as she wrapped her arms around his neck.

They stayed like that for what felt like hours before Mona broke apart first to Andrew's displeasure. "I need to shower. It's best you do too or at least get dressed before your parents or brothers find out you're in here."

"Hiding me like your own dirty secret, huh?" A slow grin spread across his cheeks.

Mona winked at him. "I don't like to share. Now. Get dressed before anyone gets up. The sun will be up soon and you know your family wakes at the crack of dawn."

Andrew sighed in defeat, knowing she was right. His brothers would antagonize his soul if they found him sneaking out of her room. "You're right. Are you sure you don't want any company?"

Mona turned to him after grabbing a towel and putting on her shirt, shaking her head with a smile. "Tempting but we'd really be in trouble, then."

Andrew watched her saunter out of the room with a silly grin on his face. With a groan, he laid back exasperated.

It felt like a dream. From the moment she kissed him back, it felt like he had entered heaven for a while. Would it always feel like this if they were together?

He berated himself for sounding corny with the questions floating in his head. But the idea of never getting to touch her again made him feel crazy. He missed her already, and she hasn't left his sight since midnight.

A door closing down the hall jolted him from the bed. It was too soon for Mona to be out of the shower. Someone was up.

"Shit," Andrew muttered as he tried to find his swimming trunks that were thrown carelessly on the ground.

Listening by the door, he heard another door close before a pair of feet began walking past the door and out of range. Waiting a beat, Andrew carefully retreated from the room, making sure the hall was clear of potential run-ins. He could've stayed in her room but considering he had nothing with him, including clothes, he needed to get back to his room.

He was able to make it to his room without a hiccup. Sighing with relief, he spread against his bed, relaying the better part of his morning with Mona. His thoughts were short-lived, however, by the knock at his door.

"Andrew?" It was Aaron. He pushed open the door without any further preamble. Spying Andrew's shorts, he quirked an eyebrow. "You went swimming? That's a little early, don't you think?"

Choosing to ignore his inquiry, Andrew asked, "What do you want? What happened to knocking and waiting for an answer?"

Aaron shrugged. "As long as I don't see you naked, it's not a lesson learned. To answer your other question, have you gotten in touch with Dave? He left a weird voicemail on my phone. I didn't even know he had my number."

Andrew frowned. He had given Dave Aaron's number when the restaurant first opened as an emergency contact since he was the only one who knew about the plans at the time. Dave and Aaron had never met but were well acquainted.

Andrew wouldn't have gotten the message as he had left his phone in his room the entire night.

Looking around the nightstand for his phone, he finally spotted it on the charger and turned on the screen. There were six missed calls from Dave spanning from an hour ago.

Andrew cursed as he tried to redial the number, but it went straight to voicemail.

"What did the voicemail say?" Andrew asked as he typed out a quick text message to Dave.

"I don't know. There was a lot of shuffling in the background. I could make out him or someone saying, 'Call Andrew' and then nothing. It just didn't sit right with me by the tone."

Andrew hoped everything was okay with the restaurant. Dave wasn't one to call early in the morning, much less several times. But he didn't want to panic—at least not yet.

Checking the local news in the area of the restaurant from his app, he didn't find anything unusual going on.

What could possibly be so urgent for him to call?

"Where were you last night, anyway?" Aaron eyed him suspiciously. "You disappeared from the dinner table and never came back."

The question threw Andrew off course. He really didn't have time for an interrogation. "What?"

Aaron came in and crossed his arms, a gleeful look on his face. "I've been up since five this morning, and I checked the whole house looking for you. There was only one place I didn't check."

"Maybe you didn't look hard enough," Andrew deterred.

"Or maybe you were having an early morning rendezvous." The glint in Aaron's eyes was all Andrew needed to know that he was not getting out of this conversation without a distraction.

He reverted the conversation back to Dave and the restaurant. "I should probably call the restaurant line; if not, I have to drive down there. I really don't like that Dave isn't picking up. He would've by now."

Aaron thankfully got the hint and backed out of the room. "I'd say you get a move on it then. But our conversation is not over, little bro."

Aaron disappeared, leaving Andrew with a mess to sort out in his own head. Dialing the restaurant line, he waited until he heard the voicemail before hanging up.

"I guess early morning trip it is," Andrew muttered to himself as he closed his door to quickly get changed and head out.

He decided to tell Mona about leaving after grabbing a quick bite to eat but met up with her in the kitchen anyway. He planted a tender kiss on her lips, effectively interrupting her buttering toast. Thankfully no one else was in the kitchen.

He could get used to this.

She eyed his attire and the keys in his hands. "You're leaving?"

"I'm going to the restaurant. Dave, my step-in, isn't answering the phone. I'm a little worried."

"Let me come with you," Mona said quickly.

Andrew shook his head. "No, stay here. It's probably not that serious. I won't be gone long."

"Please. I haven't seen the restaurant yet. I want to see what you've accomplished without..."

"Without what?"

Mona turned away. "Without me. I've never gone to your restaurant, and I'm sure it's beautiful. Please, just let me come with you. Plus, I can be your backup in case something goes wrong."

Andrew thought about it before letting out a defeated sigh. "Okay, but I'm leaving now. You should probably scarf down the toast."

"What about you?"

"Grab me an apple."

Mona obliged before following him out the door after gathering her things. It didn't take long for them to reach the interstate, a comfortable silence fulfilling the ride.

Andrew watched her out the corner of his eye, fiddling with her phone and looking at ease. Amazingly, he feared things would be awkward, much like she had been earlier after last night's events, but everything felt natural and *right*. He had the urge to reach over the console to intertwine their fingers.

It was tempting. Even after using most of his energy with her, he still had a hard-on for her. What he wouldn't give to stop the truck and hit repeat.

But it wasn't the time nor the place to fantasize.

Turning his attention back to the road, he steered his mind to the restaurant. He had tried calling Dave several more times since leaving the house but was not successful. At this point, panic began to flutter in his stomach. The restaurant would've been open by now, and the phone would've been answered.

It would take another two hours before they reached town. The unease Andrew was feeling would settle into the pits of his stomach.

"You okay? You look a little pale."

Mona seemed concerned as any reasonable person would seeing him in this state.

"I'm okay. I just hope everything is okay with Dave and the restaurant."

"It will be. I'm sure it's nothing," Mona tried to stay positive. He didn't want to tell her he was beyond past that point.

"God, I hope so," he muttered.

"So, tell me about this Dave guy."

She was trying to keep his mind off the negative thoughts circling his brain. He was thankful for the break, though he knew the topic was bound to end with the same feeling.

"When I moved, he was one of the first people I befriended at the time. He was looking for a job, and I promised him a spot at my restaurant when I got it open. He's an excellent worker and a great friend."

Mona didn't say anything, just nodded as if she was deep in thought. He could probably guess what she was thinking.

Despite his better judgment, he grabbed her hand and interlaced their fingers. Thankfully, she didn't pull away. "Nobody will be as great as you, though."

Mona turned to him with a small smile. "I wasn't fishing for compliments. I'm glad you were able to find someone to be there for you."

"I know, but I meant it. I'm grateful I have you. You're irreplaceable."

"So are you," Mona replied.

Silence found its way between them as they listened to the soft melody of the music playing through the car speakers. Andrew couldn't help but feel delighted at the notion that they really found each other again. He welcomed the bubbly feeling in his chest.

He massaged her the top of it with his thumb, thinking about all the time wasted between them. They could've been doing this years ago.

There was so much he wanted to say to her, but it would have to wait.

"Are you nervous?" Mona asked as she turned to him.

Andrew was on a cliff. "About the restaurant? Yes, I am. I trust Dave, but I'm worried for him, too."

Dave gave no indication of any troubles when they spoke last night. His unusual silence and the voice message tugged at his nerves.

Mona nodded as if she understood. "If this were the store, I would've been driving like Speedy Gonzalez."

Andrew took note of his speedometer. He was going the speed limit. Overreacting only to get there and nothing be wrong would haunt him. Not to mention, he had Mona in the car. Her safety was his biggest concern while on the road.

"I won't make a big fuss until I get there. I'll check the restaurant first since it should be open and then go to Dave's apartment if I need to."

It didn't take too long before they were pulling into the parking lot of the restaurant.

Eyebrows furrowed, Andrew stopped the truck short of the front. The parking lot was empty. The restaurant should've been opened an hour ago.

Seeing the worried look on his face, Mona asked, "What's wrong?"

"The restaurant should've been open..." he answered more to himself. Looking closer, he spied a 'CLOSED' sign on the door.

Absentmindedly, he got out of the truck and approached the door to look inside. Mona followed close behind and peered in as well.

"Now, I'm worried."

Heading back for his key in the ignition, he opened the door and stepped inside. The lights automatically turned on as they both entered. Mona canvased the restaurant, amazement twinkling in her eyes.

"Wow, Andrew! This is beautiful!"

Mona's eyes scanned the light beige walls to the chandelier above the waiting station, to the waterfall trapped between glass in the opening. The chairs were black and gold, the table clothes red and clean. The colors, which wouldn't normally mix well on anything else, did so in the room. There was an elegant feel to it.

The leap of happiness with her approval of the restaurant was swallowed by the fear that started to creep up the back of his neck. Looking around, nothing seemed out of place.

Andrew slowly made his way to the kitchen. "Dave?" he called out. The sound of his voice echoed against the room.

No one was there. Next, he went to his office in the back to search as he continued to call out for Dave. Mona stayed close behind him, looking around in nervousness and fascination.

Opening his office door, Andrew froze. There lying on the floor was Dave.

Rushing to his side, Andrew called out, "Dave?! Mona, call an ambulance."

As Mona struggled to pull out her phone in shock, Andrew went to check for a pulse.

He was still breathing.

"I can't get any signal in here."

A slow clap sounded from the one stall bathroom in the office. Both whipped their heads in the direction as someone came out of the shadows.

Mona dropped her phone by accident as she backed away.

It was Calvin.

"Aww, look at you. Andrew to the rescue as always, except when it counts." Calvin turned to Mona. "And Mona, forever the damsel in distress without direction. Pathetic."

"What the fuck did you do? I swear to God..." Andrew said through clenched teeth as he stood in an instant ready to charge until Calvin reached in his back pocket and pulled out a silver pistol.

"I wouldn't do that if I were you."

Stepping out from the bathroom, he raised the gun higher to Andrew's chest. He smiled at him before pointing it at Mona instead as he cocked it.

"I can't leave you alone, Mona. I can't. You broke me, baby. For this—" Calvin pointed at Andrew. "—like he wasn't the first one to leave your side when you were begging for mercy."

Andrew turned to Mona, confused before turning his anger towards Calvin. "Leave her alone. I mean it!"

Calvin threw a glare at him, his gun still pointed at a frightened Mona. "Or what? You couldn't save her last time. What makes you think you can now? After all, you are at a disadvantage."

"What do you want?" Mona asked shakily.

"What I always deserved—*you*."

A tear ran down her face. "Why can't you just leave me alone, Calvin? You never loved me."

Calvin approached her, the gun placed against her neck. Leaning over to her ear, he whispered, "That's where you're wrong, Mona." Sweeping a look at Andrew and his angry face, Calvin smirked. "I mean, Moe."

Andrew was nearly on the verge of tackling him but refrained from doing something stupid. The gun in Calvin's hand was enough to rethink any sudden movements.

"Get away from her!"

Calvin swung the gun to his face. "Or what? You want to end up like your precious friend on the floor? Why don't you mind your business, like you should have the first time?"

"Calvin, I promise you won't get out of here, unscathed," Andrew warned him.

Out of the corner of his eye, he could see Dave's fingers jolt. Mona looked at him, tears streaming down her face. The fear in her eyes was enough to push him forward. If anything happened to her—

He couldn't even finish that thought. Trying to keep Calvin's attention on him, he began to inch forward.

"Andrew!" Mona cried out.

Calvin cocked his gun. "I suggest you listen to her, Andrew. I would hate to see a hole in your face."

"You don't scare me, Calvin. You didn't then, you don't now. You think because you have a gun in your hand, it makes you invincible?"

"Andrew, stop!"

Ignoring Mona, he stepped closer to Calvin, prepared for him to do his worse. "You come to my restaurant and think you're going to just walk out of here after doing your worse?"

"Choose your next words wisely," Calvin seethed.

Despite Calvin's increasing anger and heavy finger on the trigger, Andrew continued to bait him. "Why? If you were going to shoot me, you would've already."

Calvin smirked and slowly put the gun down. "You know what? You're absolutely right."

Before Andrew could blink, Calvin raised the gun at Mona and fired a shot. She let out a shriek before she dropped to the ground. Thankfully, the bullet had missed her. Andrew threw himself into action, throwing Calvin to the ground without thinking.

The gun dropped from Calvin's hand, giving Andrew the opportunity to punch him. Struggling for control, Calvin head-butted Andrew, knocking him to the ground and grabbing the gun as he got back up.

"I hope all of you burn in hell!" Calvin yelled as he swung the gun wildly at Andrew and Mona.

Before Andrew could get up, Calvin ran out of the room, shutting the door after him. Andrew got up quickly to run after him but realized the door was barred from the outside.

"Fuck!"

Pushing against the door with his shoulders, he twisted the knob to no success.

He turned to Mona who was still paralyzed on the floor. "Are you okay?"

She could only nod. "What is he doing out there?"

Mona got her answer when they both could hear what sounded like matches and a blaze starting. The light smell of smoke made them look at each other in distress.

"Fuck! We need to get out of here. I think he started a fire outside the door."

Looking around frantically, he tried to find a vent they could possibly get through, but his office was completely boxed in. There were no windows or vents big enough on either wall. Their best bet was the bathroom. It would buy a little time.

Of all the times he could've left his phone in the truck, he had to pick this day. Now he regretted not putting a restaurant line in his office sooner.

Black smoke began to filter from under the door, causing them to cough heavily.

From the ground, Dave began to groan and move. Andrew rushed to his aid as he tried to get up.

"Dave! Be careful!"

"W-What's going on? What happened? What's that smell?"

"There's no time to explain. We should go into the bathroom until we come up with a plan or help comes hopefully."

Andrew tried to help him up with Mona also offering assistance. "Who are you?" he turned to Mona. She ignored him as they hoisted him into the bathroom and shut the door behind them.

Recognition filled his eyes, but he remained quiet as he tried to nurse his head wound.

Through coughs, he exclaimed, "This smoke is hell! We need to find a way out before we die here."

"At this point, the smoke might do us in way before the actual fire," Mona pointed out.

"Maybe we should turn on the water from the sink?" Dave offered.

Andrew tried the sink, but no water escaped.

"Shit."

As a last-ditch effort, he checked the toilet to see if there was any clean water in the bowl, but that too was empty.

The bathroom grew increasingly hot, they could all feel the intensity of the fire and smoke through the door. They all used the tail end of their shirts to cover their mouths from the smoke as it grew thicker in the bathroom.

Coughing was inevitable as they all doubled over in an effort to keep their throats clear but were unsuccessful. Andrew could only squint with his eyes watered and fatigue overtaking his body.

Andrew watched Dave drop to the ground beside him, Andrew too weak to call out. Slowly, he turned to find Mona, only to see her stretched out next to him.

"Mona," he could only manage a whisper as tried to shield her face but turning her into his chest.

The last thing he could hear was the faint sound of sirens as his vision faded to black, blinded by the highlights of his life descending with him.

EPILOGUE

Mona

HER HEAD POUNDED heavily as she struggled to open her eyes. Waking up nearly a day later in the hospital was relieving not only for her but for her friends as well. With all of them surrounding her bed—James, Symoné and Dixie included, Mona truly felt how loved she really was. According to Nina, she was rushed to the hospital minutes within passing out.

It all started coming back to her after that. Calvin confronting them in the restaurant.

Andrew.

Mona shot up. "Where's Andrew?"

Nina could only take her hands, a solemn expression on her face. "He's in the ICU. Because of his asthma, smoke inhalation caused respiratory failure. He's doing better but he hasn't woken up yet."

Mona took a moment to process, her body stiff with shock.

This was all her fault. If only she had told him before about Calvin visiting her or threatening her, none of this would be happening—

"Mona, don't do that. This is not your fault. This was never your fault. Okay? You have to believe that. Andrew would do anything for you, no matter what. He saved you."

Nina embraced her in a tight hug. Mona could only cry silently as she prayed, he would be okay. "I have to see him. Please, take me to him."

Adam pushed his way to her bedside. "You're not leaving this room, Mona. You need to recover. Andrew is a strong man. He will pull through; you know it and so do I. But you have to have to get better, for him and yourself."

He was right, but that didn't mean she didn't want to see him. Nonetheless, that night she could only cry herself to sleep as the events played over and over again in her dreams; only this time, Andrew never makes it through.

It would be another two days before she was officially cleared to leave the hospital. Mona decided to head to ICU instead. With Nina and Adam by her side, she met Linda and Aaron in the hall for a briefing.

Both, including the rest of the Sumpter family, had visited her a few days prior. Neither blamed her for the condition Andrew was in, much to her relief, but it didn't ease the pain of knowing he was in the hospital due to her mistakes.

"He's doing a lot better. He's breathing on his own at this point. The only thing left is for him to wake up," Linda said, a weak smile present on her face.

"Can I see him?" Mona asked.

"Of course. Maybe it's you he's been waiting on all along."

Mona left Nina and Adam in the waiting room with Aaron

as Linda showed her to Andrew's room.

"I'll let you have the room," Linda said as she closed the door behind her.

Mona turned to the man in bed she called a best friend as far as she could remember. The last week, however, she didn't know what to label him.

Watching his chest rising and falling softly, she let a tear escape as she inched closer.

He looked normal, laying in the hospital bed in his gown. Thankfully, Nina told her firefighters had doused the flames before it reached them so there was no physical damage to either of them. But seeing him stuck in the bed with wires attached to his arm and chest was heartbreaking.

Taking a seat in the chair next to his bed, she ran a hand through his curls and cupped his cheek, noting how frail he looked.

"I'm so sorry. I'm sorry for not telling you about Calvin showing up and harassing me. I'm sorry for putting you through all this. I'm sorry for pushing you away for so long. I'm sorry for everything. You've always been my rock, and no matter what, you've always put me first and I never did the same for you. I hope you can forgive me because I don't know what I would do without you. I love you," she whispered the last part as she moved to kiss him on the lips.

Mona's heart filled with butterflies as she uttered those words knowing she absolutely meant it. She loved Andrew. Maybe she always had.

Reaching for his hand, she squeezed it as she intertwined

her fingers with his. She felt a pressure on her hands and looked down, noticing he was also trying to squeeze her hand.

She gasped and glanced back at him, but his eyes were still closed. "I hear you loud and clear."

Andrew woke up the next day to Mona at his side as soon as visitor hours had begun. The look of relief on his face when he saw her was something that tugged at her heart.

"I'm so glad you're okay. I don't remember much about what happened after passing out. I didn't know what to expect when I woke up. I'm so glad you're here," he managed to get out as he caressed her cheeks when she got near him.

"I would never leave you, Andrew. Never. Especially since this is my fault."

Andrew shook his head. "This is not your fault, Moe."

"But it is. He's been following me for weeks, and I never said anything to you. I'm sorry."

Andrew took a moment to process that. "Did he hurt you?"

Mona shook her head. "No, not physically. But he threatened to hurt everyone else, and I brushed it away. I could've gotten help, but I thought it would go away. I'm so sorry."

"Shhh. Moe, I don't care about that. This is not your fault. Calvin is a psycho, and whether you knew he was there watching you or not, he was going to find a way to get to you. You can't control that. I'm not mad at you. I can never be mad at you. I'd die for you if it meant keeping you safe because I love you, and nothing is going to change that."

Mona let out a shaky breath. Hearing him confirm her feelings toward him made her feel like her world was no complete.

"I love you, too."

Mona bent to give him a longing kiss. His lips were slightly chapped, and a mild shadow had begun to frame his chin, but she welcomed it as it sent a heat throughout her entire body.

"I wish I can wake up like this every day—well, minus the hospital bed," Andrew suggested.

Mona could only giggle as she pressed another kiss to his lips.

***

BY THE TIME Andrew made it out of the hospital, it had already been a week since the incident. After waking up, he had been moved from the ICU to a regular room where everyone, including a recovering Dave, had come to visit and wish him well. He moved into his parent's house temporarily while he recovered further, where Mona nursed him back to health every chance she could.

Mona finally felt like she could breathe. The days of looking over her shoulder were over. After a massive manhunt in the city, police were able to find Calvin hiding out at a motel where he surrendered and eventually plead guilty to multiple charges including arson and attempted murder.

Calvin was facing life in prison to Mona's relief.

Andrew officially decided to move back into town and have Dave manage the old restaurant after repairs were finished. He also decided to follow through with his plans to build a new one close by.

"I need to look for an apartment," Andrew said as they lay under the covers on Mona's bed. Andrew had intertwined his fingers with hers as he played with a strand of her hair that lay on her bare shoulder.

"You can move in with me," Mona offered. She had been thinking about asking him since he decided to move back. She had extra space in her apartment, and she honestly didn't want it to go to waste. Plus, she liked having him in her apartment. He'd been there almost every night since recovering.

Andrew frowned. "Are you sure? Don't get me wrong, I'd love to, but I don't want to invade your space."

"Andrew, you'd never invade my space. I love having you here with me. I don't want to be anywhere but by your side."

Andrew grinned and push her back against the bed as his lips met hers. "You can have all of me. In fact, you always did," he whispered against her lips.

"Good, because I don't like to share," she replied.

"Oh, don't I know it. Like the way you ran Cassidy off when she tried contacting me after hearing about the fire?"

Mona blushed. "In all seriousness, she had her chance. That ship sailed long before she got on board. And I've been nice enough."

Andrew growled. "I like this fierceness I'm hearing, Ms. Bridesmaid."

"I'm not a bridesmaid for another six months. As for me, I'm going after what's mine. And you, sir, are all mine," Mona said as she placed a lingering kiss on his lips, tracing her finger on his infinity symbol.

"I wouldn't have it any other way, Moe."

Acknowledgments

Publishing a book has been a dream of mine since I was in elementary school, and this was one of the first stories I ever wrote. After sitting on over 15 versions of this story for more than 10 years, I finally garnished the nerve to publish.

I gained a lot of confidence throughout that time in my writing and I now embrace the freedom writing gives me. I've learned a lot and I still have much more learning to do. As my first story, I am thrilled to have accomplished this feat, and I cannot wait to publish many more books very soon.

I want to thank my mom, Elizabeth, for always telling me not to give up on my passion for writing. She has had the most significant impact on my journey and saw the potential I had, engraining in my mind that I should never give up on what I am passionate about even when it feels impossible. I truly appreciate you, Mom.

I would also like to thank my sister, Tameika, for also pushing me to finish this book and thank her for allowing me to explore book publishing by letting my company publish her first book: **Expressions: A Poetry Book**. My nephews, Tyriq and Tabari, were incredibly supportive as well, and thank you for reading my early drafts when I needed an extra pair of eyes.

For those out there that want to write a book and don't feel confident enough to do it, please don't hold yourself back. Someone out there will absolutely love your book. But don't wait for someone to tell you. Write it for yourself. Write the book you would like to read and see on bookshelves. There's a guarantee that someone else has been waiting for a story like yours.

About the Author

Nandra Hoffman is a Canadian-born, 20-year Florida resident. Since her quiet days of elementary, she has found solace in fine print and the exploration of literature. When she is not running her publishing company, Nandra Publishing, LLC, Nandra spends her days playing with her adorable Siberian Husky, Dakota, and googling random questions. For more about Nandra, you can read her full bio on her website at https://www.nandrapublishing.com/nandra-hoffman.

OTHER WORKS

Be on the lookout for others works from Nandra Hoffman coming 2020-2021.

The Artisan Way (2020)
When All Fails (2020)
When Skies Were Gray (2021)

PUBLISHING NOTES

Visit Nandra Publishing for books and publishing services at
https://nandrapublishing.com